OF BLOOD AND CROWNS

BROKEN BONDS
BOOK ONE

RAVEN MORE

RAVEN
MORE

Of Blood and Crowns
Book I
Broken Bonds Series
Copyright ©2023 by Raven More
All rights reserved.

❀ Created with Vellum

CHAPTER ONE

"Destiny or Death."

I repeated my mother's words aloud to convince myself that what I was doing this day was for the greater good. The ritual was not only a symbol but a necessity to earn my place on the ruling council. If I failed, the Cursed would rise up again and murder us all. We only survived the Great War of 2185 thanks to mother discovering a way to control their powers before they burned or froze or electrocuted us all.

The airship jolted, but my eyes remained on the scene outside the porthole. Blood-orange streaks shot across the lifeless sky and the land below remained barren. Nothing survived in this desolate, sand-covered region since the war.

Wrapping my arms around my middle, I dreamed of returning to an earlier life. One filled with the childish pleasures of swimming in a crystal-blue lake, sunning on the beach, running over soft dirt and climbing tall trees.

Of freedom.

Clank.

"Mother?"

A sting of warning flashed through me, but the sound of her natural foot hitting the ground didn't echo through the corridors the way her metal appendage did. I hiked up the yards of crimson and black fabric and ran, but I stumbled and slid on the slick metal floor. Even after four years, I couldn't manage to walk properly in fashionable royal clothes despite Mother's constant corrections to my behavior.

I peered out my chamber door and scanned the hall. No sign of her. Only endless, sterile hallways twisting and turning with no end in sight.

Stubby fingers jutted through an air vent halfway down the wall and curled over metal slats. The large vent plate thrust out and short arms pulled the silver cover sideways into the opening. A moment later, two small feet dangled, followed by a pudgy man who dropped to the floor on his rear with a thud. He pulled his legs beneath him and stood.

My heart soared at the sight of his friendly face, especially today. "Boaz. I'd hoped to see you."

"Princess Valencia Sade." He bent, retrieved the screws, and replaced the vent. "You ready for the day of glory?"

The familiar sting of tears begged for release, but I turned my head and steadied my nerves. *No crying, not today, not for myself.* "I'd love some company."

"Face sad today. Fate not what you think."

I flashed a warm smile and nodded as if I understood his ramblings. Many of the workers' brains had been scrambled by the uranium-filled engine room. "Thanks, my friend."

Friend.

A word I hadn't said since I'd carried out the death warrant on Emery Valant four years ago. She'd been so brave, never breaking under interrogation. Even in the end, she

2

didn't confess what powers she possessed that threatened Mother.

If only I had been that brave.

I'd never be able to forget how I'd betrayed her. Boaz studied me with his morose brown eyes. How could he still bear to look at me? Did he worry that I would turn against him, too?

I tugged at the constricting corset and yanked down the ties hiking up the overcoat.

If only we could've done more to save her.

Clank...thump...clank...thump.

My heart raced faster than a power burst during takeoff.

He spun on his heels. "Boaz go, or Queen toss me out as waste."

His tiny feet pattered down a different hall, away from Mother's approaching steps. Hearing the clang of the air vent closing, I knew Boaz was safely in his world—the belly of the ship.

I'd heard the servants speak of how the little people's size was a curse, but I envied him.

If only I could hide, too.

I took a deep breath. At least Boaz and our secret were both safely sealed away.

Clank...thump...clank...thump.

Mother rounded the corner and marched into my room. Hair the color of flames danced above her sheet-white face.

A tremor raced from my shoulders to my fingertips; fear threatened to consume my body, paralyzing me into mute stillness.

The smell of bleaching serum and the tangy scent of metal

fought for dominance as Mother's one eyebrow rose. "Daughter!"

Her mechanically enhanced, muted gold eye with its glass iris reflected my hideous upswept hair wrapped in a cornucopia of flowers. I hated the thick face paint Mother forced me to wear, along with the flowers adorning each twist and turn of the golden-dyed curls piled high on top of my head.

As servants scurried into the room close behind Mother, I relaxed a fraction. With a witness present, even a servant, Mother's corporal punishment *might* be held in check.

She grabbed my arm with her clinically bleached white hand while the copper-plated mechanical one tugged my corset down. "Your destiny awaits."

I struggled to control my desire to flee and steadied my nerves. Running would do no good. After the fourth beating since my arrival on her ship, I learned there were no good places to hide.

"Today, you become a ruling member of the council and sit by my side." Mother stood even straighter, towering over me, pushing my shoulders back before she placed the tamer device on the table—the black opal of death I'd use to subdue a Cursed Mualite in the upcoming ceremony.

I sucked in a quick breath and averted my gaze.

A servant shuffled around me, fluffing my skirt and spraying my hair until Mother shooed her to the corner of the room. "When we land, you'll choose your parasite for sacrifice. The guards will take it to the holding area until the ritual can be performed. Once it's over, you'll officially be a ruling member of the council."

It. Emery hadn't been an *it*. I choked down the rising lump in my throat. My stomach constricted even tighter than the corset cinched around it. "Mother, I—I don't know if I'm ready for—"

Her palm slapped my right cheek with a radiation-hot sting.

I stumbled backward, my feet catching in the tangle of fabric. Gravity tugged me toward the floor. My head hit the table, sending the black opal of death skidding across the floor as lights flickered in my vision.

I licked at the trickle of blood on my lip. *Everything around me tasted like this blasted ship.* Scraping my tongue through my teeth, I attempted to rid myself of the horrid taste.

Bright red locks of hair arched over Mother's lineless forehead. "You dare question me?"

I rubbed my face, forcing back the tears. Crying would only prompt another smack.

"You're heir to the throne. Act like it." Mother's perfect features never changed. Only the dark pupils expanded and contracted with each heated word, even the right eye, which stuttered with its mechanical movement, half a beat off the natural one.

I pushed off the floor and concentrated on steadying my nerves. If I showed weakness, it would only fuel Mother's fire. "I did not mean—"

"Of course you didn't, dear." Mother pivoted and marched to the doorway, then paused and looked to the servant in the corner of the room. "Clean her up." Her nose crinkled, the only thing on her face still able to twitch. "Don't treat her wounds, just cover up the outside bruising. She needs to remember her place."

"Yes, my queen." The servant scurried over to clean the

blood from the floor. Swirls of red gave color to the dull white surface for a moment, only to be wiped away.

Mother paused in the hall and gave me a creaseless smile. "I've chosen your enhancement for tonight." She placed her hands on her hips. "You won't have to worry about your pathetic sympathy for those unworthy of a princess's attention anymore."

My chest tightened.

"You're getting an improved heart."

As if the ship had hit turbulence that sent it into a spiral, my world spun, the white walls, floor, and ceiling no longer distinguishable.

Mother's cackles echoed then faded down the hall.

There would be no escape. I'd have to use the tamer or face more beatings and torture. I wanted to crumple to the floor and dream of the days when I lived with Father.

I would have to take the life of a Cursed or die myself—or worse, be transformed into a completely new enhanced being. I shuddered at the thought of steel mounted as a permanent organ—a heart as cold and hard as Mother's.

The gruesome ritual of implanting a device to be a member of the ruling council was not something I understood, nor did I want to.

I retrieved the tamer. My fingers clutched the bronze outer ring of the black opal. Its intricate gold-lace patterns wrapping around the dark, shiny sphere appeared harmless. I knew better. Its unassuming beauty masked its ability to electrocute a person into submission.

The ceremony was pointless. I didn't need an implant to prove I was worthy to rule the people. Mother was an original Tertian; it was obvious I possessed the gift of a supreme mind with no cursed powers. No human peasant or Cursed Mualite could handle an implant, which was why Emery had been so ill after the interrogator experimented on her. Of course, Mother gave the order. She always looked to improve technology at any cost, and Mualites were usually her test subjects.

A zing of electricity shot from my center, through my shoulder, and down my arm to my fingertips. The outer shell of the tamer shook and cracked.

Shocked, my fingers unfurled and the tamer clanged against the floor. The solid surface rippled like waves on the lake back home in the Resort Territory.

Behind me, the human servant gasped.

"Speak of this to no one or I'll sacrifice you to the innards of the ship." The harsh tone of my voice resembled the queen's. *Maybe I'm a princess after all.*

The servant fled from the room, sealing the door behind her. I lifted the device. Black oozed over the melted latticework of the ring. Should Mother notice its altered state, she'd be suspicious. How would I explain it had just changed in my hand?

That was something a Cursed did, and I didn't want to face being accused of committing a Mualite crime. Not to mention the torture that went with such an accusation.

I crossed the room and dropped it down the waste containment chute.

Gnawing my lower lip, I paced the floor, one word beating like a drum in my head.

Escape. Escape. Escape.

The door swished and Mother's general stood before me in all his self-proclaimed glory. Medals marched down his long, blood-red sash. Disgust radiated through me as I fought the desire to rip out the small sprouts of implanted hair dotting his false widow's peak.

He gave a mock bow and licked his lips. "Good morning, Princess Valencia."

My morning meal churned in my stomach. Acid inched up my throat. The memory of the last time his rancid breath and slobber had covered my mouth assailed me.

"One more year and you're mine." His meaty hands grasped my shoulders and he pushed me against the wall. "I told you…I always get what I want."

"But not now, for now it's forbidden." I pushed hard against the metal chest plate hidden under his adorned coat, ignoring the throbbing pain in my head. "I must remain pure until my wedding night. It's the queen's orders."

I prayed my words were enough to keep him at a distance.

He pulled away, wiping his sweaty brow with his sash. "Yes, I'm aware of the queen's command."

The door slid open. He glanced back at the vacant door-way. Then, with a smile, he grabbed the back of my neck. His nails pierced my skin. "Someday you'll know your place. No one speaks to me like that."

"I just did."

His face turned crimson and his jaw clenched tight.

"Go ahead, hit me." I knew he wouldn't leave evidence. But somehow, some way, I'd convince Mother not to force me to marry him. I'd never let him touch me.

Once again, the doors swished open and shut, and I knew Boaz was watching out for me.

This time the general backed away. "I'll do a lot more than hit you on our wedding night." He marched from the room.

My legs shook beneath me. I palmed the wall, fighting to stay upright. I took a deep breath and straightened. In less than an hour, I'd be forced to murder an innocent person, just because he or she was a Mualite.

No. I couldn't think that way. They weren't innocent—just because Emery had seemed nice. Mualites had killed millions of humans and Tertians. They had taken Mother's arm, leg and eye during the war. If it hadn't been for her, humans and council alike would be extinct.

I stalked from the room, head held high, and nodded at the guard. Memories of Emery strapped to a table invaded my mind. Saw grinding, tears, screams. I grasped the wall to steady myself. A zap of heat pricked in the center of my chest as it did a few hours ago when I melted my hairbrush and again with the tamer.

No, no. Not again!

This time it shot through my entire body, exploding every nerve ending. Sweat pooled at the back of my neck. I yanked my hand away before the wall could melt under my touch.

Shaking my head, I prayed no one noticed the less than smooth wall and followed the guard until we reached the infirmary.

Maybe I was going mad, like the Cursed I'd seen carried from the holding cells after interrogations.

What was happening had to be a trick. Perhaps it was the general's newest attempt to drive me insane—or worse, make Mother believe I possessed the powers of a Mualite. Maybe a Mualite stowaway on the ship found a way to bypass the warning alarm or hadn't been collared, allowing him or her to play with my mind. Mother always said they were life-sucking monsters that shouldn't be trusted. Not knowing what power each Mualite possessed made them all dangerous. They were only safe as long as the collars kept them under control.

Yes, that had to be it. I was a princess of the queen's empire, sole heir to the throne. No way could I possess a Mualite ability. Besides, unlike the Mualites, I had no desire to murder someone or crave war over peace.

"Are you well, Princess Valencia?" asked the sleek-skinned man standing in the infirmary doorway.

"Yes, of course." I lifted my chin and stepped inside.

At the smell of oil and the sound of gears grinding, my body froze.

The machines on the far wall buzzed and hissed. Two assistants dressed in white coats hustled about the room, pushing green buttons and pulling levers on various computers. Steam rose in plumes from the main unit in the back. The medic spun a box on a long arm and pointed it downward at the table in the center of the room.

The same table on which Emery's leg had been amputated.

"Please." The medic gestured for me to lie on the table.

My legs wouldn't move.

One of the medics guided me onto the table. Lying back, I struggled to remain still and wait for a beam to shoot at my face while it altered my appearance, just to cover a few bruises. Images of interrogations I'd witnessed when the machines severed limbs from bodies and eyes from sockets plagued me.

"She's not ready yet?" demanded the voice of Esmada, Mother's assistant. Her bony hands grasped my arms from behind and pushed me flat onto the table. "Child, your mother will have you whipped if you don't make haste."

Cuffs clamped over my wrists, pinching my skin. I fought against them in vain, but they secured my arms tight.

"Only to ensure you don't move, Princess. You don't want an eye where your mouth should be, do you?" Esmada's chuckle ripped through me as if the laser had slipped and sliced my core to ribbons.

The sting deep inside my ribcage returned. It grew and spread until thousands of pinpricks radiated from my head and shoulders. Fire surged up my spine, searing each vertebra. My insides vibrated and twitched. I bit down on my lower lip and concentrated. If it didn't stop soon, I feared I'd melt the machine.

It's only a skin-alterer. It won't harm me. Everything will be fine.

The box overhead shuddered and a scarlet light radiated across my cheek, erasing Mother's mark. When the exterior doors slid shut, the hum of the laser echoed in the small room. I closed my eyes tightly and dreamed of open land and walking barefoot on soft dirt instead of metal floors. Heat seared my skin. Sharp pain shot up to my temple.

Tears slipped from my eyes.

"Child, you'd best not smear your makeup," Esmada snapped.

Yet more tears fell as the laser traveled to my forehead. The smell of melted flesh made me gag, but I swallowed the cry as the pain increased.

My chin pulled and stretched as though it would touch my hairline. The thin silver bed rattled beneath me. My teeth ground and my jaw popped. I twisted and pulled against the restraints, trying to escape my body.

"Hold her head. Her hair must be perfect when we land," Esmada screeched.

The doors slid open and the laser faded. Good thing, too. Another moment and I thought the energy inside me would have escaped and turned the entire room into bubbling orange goo.

Inhaling, air swooshed into my lungs and I relaxed against the table. My eye throbbed in pace with my heart.

"It's time," a deep voice sounded from the hall.

The ship swayed like my insides. *It couldn't be time already.*

Esmada pulled me upright and a soft cloth blotted at my eyes and cheeks. "Makeup!"

The room spun, not just from the pulse of heat still surging through my face, but from the thought of the murder I was about to commit.

I slid to the edge of the table. One foot hit the floor. Two hands grabbed my arms and ushered me out the door while Esmada still pressed stiff brushes to my face.

"Get control of yourself, Princess. The skin-alterer isn't that bad. Your mother utilizes it daily."

Daily? No wonder her skin had the appearance and mobility of a sheet of glass.

Finding my balance, we passed through the outer corridors to the ship's hangar. Scout ships lined both sides of the main walkway.

Spotting red whiskers poking through a vent, my tension lessened. The knowledge that Boaz followed me provided comfort. He was the only ray of light in a sea of straight-faced, highbrow, altered beings.

The engines fired energy pulses, slowing our descent, and landing gear dropped from the belly of the ship. I wanted to scream at the captain not to land. To keep flying until we reached Acadia East and the safety of the council.

"We've entered the Mining Territory. All guards report to the bay door," a deep voice boomed from the speakers.

The echo took me back to my last hours at Emery's side, when I hid her down in the engine room with Boaz.

What would I find when we landed in the Mining Territory and the bay door opened? Had any green trees grown like in the Horticulture Territory, or was the landscape still limited to dark sand and rubble? I'd studied the history books and seen pictures of buildings and trees in the region. I imagined what the places called states, like Arizona and Utah, were like in the late twenty-first century. Before the war.

The humans back then had done jobs on computers and everyone lived like royalty. Now, according to Mother, everyone needed to work if we were to survive. War destroyed most of the resources. If Mother hadn't stepped in, they all would have perished—humans, Tertians, and Mualites.

"Look alert, Princess," Esmada scolded.

I shook the memories away. My destiny waited on the other side of the large bronze bay door. The scent of burning oil filled the air, and hisses of steam sounded from below deck.

No more time. As always, I would follow orders.

I shifted, struggling to control the cacophony of emotions beating me apart inside.

One last thud and we'd reached the ground.

Thump...tap...thump...tap.

My stomach constricted at the rhythmic beat.

"Daughter, you have forgotten something." Mother's stern

voice indicated her displeasure, so I braced myself for another attack.

I turned to see a glittering tamer resting in Esmada's milky white palm. "Sorry, Mother," I choked out, unable to hear my own words over the thundering beat of my blood.

"No worries, dear, sweet daughter of mine. Soon you will not have to concern yourself with such devices to control the parasites."

"Really?"

"Of course. You'll have an implant soon. No need to carry things around. You're not a mere human like your father. You're my daughter, a Tertian, soon to be ruling member of the council. Your brain will handle the devices. Well, it should."

My heart thrashed at my ribs. If only my father still lived.

I curled my toes in my boots and clenched my fists. The walls vibrated, but I didn't care. "What will happen if my brain doesn't—"

Mother waved her hand as if batting away annoying sand fleas. "Why is the door still shut?"

Boaz scurried out from the hall. "My queen must know sand is dangerous. Flush the engines or we will disintegrate." He glanced at me and winked before hobbling off to a stairwell on the other side of the compartment. His smile always consoled me. It was the closest thing to the way I felt when my father held me in his arms.

"Annoying gnat." Mother grumbled. "Hurry up!"

Gears in the wall ground and the door squealed open. Light shot into the dark bay through the partially opened gangway, momentarily blinding me. I winced and shielded my eyes. Pain radiated from my cheek. As Mother had ordered, only the surface was treated.

"The people await, Daughter. It is time for you to choose your sacrifice."

I shivered. My skin crawled like the time Meroder bugs got into my quarters and nested in my bed. Then, as now, only one of us would survive.

A great plain of orange sand extended to the horizon. This was nothing like the Resort Territory where I'd spent most of my life. My breath halted behind my ribs, unable to escape.

This was the land where I'd left Emery to die. I fought back tears. Now wasn't the time to lose control.

Council members and witnesses exited from a different part of the ship and sauntered to benches lining the right side of the street. The ship rested on the landing field at the edge of town, the bay door opened to a platform at the dead center of the main street. All eyes rested on the Queen, and by extension, me.

Heads bowed low, people hustled by us. A row of buildings lined each side of a wide path. Guards corralled Mualites into lines in front of the ship.

I clutched the tamer tightly in my hand and stepped onto the platform. None of them looked like monsters or murderers. How would I choose? A plump man waddled out through green swinging doors and plopped down on a barrel. Two girls dressed in ratted old skirts and tops that barely covered their breasts sauntered down the street. No black control collar lined their necks. They had to be humans. Only Mualites wore collars.

Speakers crackled down the street. "To commemorate the auspicious occasion of Princess Valencia's sixteenth birthday, the gracious queen provides ale and food for all humans in the Mining Territory," the captain announced.

Dread crept up the back of my neck. My lungs seized and I drew a painful breath.

Men standing along the boardwalk outside the storefronts hooted and clapped.

"Hurry up, girl. This awful sand will have to be blasted from my joints. Which parasite do you choose?"

I scanned the streets, looking for my prey. How could I choose someone to die just so I could take my seat on the council? I swallowed hard.

What would Father do?

Mother grasped my arm in a death grip and pointed at the line of Mualites below, then released me.

A guard shoved a young girl toward the front of the line. She stumbled in front of me. Her basket tumbled, its contents spilling across the compacted pathway. My heart twisted as the young woman scurried about trying to retrieve the fruit.

Then she lifted her head, revealing the collar around her neck. Her dark eyes and hair were familiar.

"Now," Esmada spat.

A cold claw trapped my neck in its grasp. "Do it now, child, or you will be sent below deck and whipped again," Mother warned.

A young man in his late teens or early twenties burst through the swinging doors and stopped cold on the porch. His chiseled face pinched tight and eyes that matched those of the girl narrowed; his fists clenched tight by his side. His deep, guttural cries echoed through the town. If not for an older man restraining him, he would have bolted to the girl's side.

The girl stood, her skirt catching on something. The orange light from the sun reflected off her artificial leg.

My heart soared. "Emery?" Had my friend survived all these years despite her infected body being left in the Wasteland?

Mother's iron grip squeezed the back of my neck. "You betrayed me."

My hands shook. I had lied about burning Emery's body in the incinerator. Not that she should have survived being dumped in the desert half-dead, yet somehow she had. And now mother knew. The evidence stood in front of us.

Lava slid down my windpipe, snaked around my ribs, and traveled through my intestines. My insides vibrated and my eyes stung. Before I could stop, the tamer melted in my hands.

The platform started to spin beneath my boots...girls screamed...men shouted...cold, sharp nails pierced my hand.

One glance at Mother told me I'd just signed my own death warrant.

Or worse, my marriage certificate.

CHAPTER TWO

Pain hammered deep in my brain.

Implant

"No!" I shot upright. Blurs of bronze and steel swirled. Gravity pulled me back down. As the back of my head smacked the wall, a twang resounded through the cell. Fingering my matted hair, I searched for the cold foreign object. Thick liquid and a metallic smell drew the air from my lungs, but there was no implant. Relief flooded me.

Panting, I pulled my hand free through the knots of over-sprayed curls.

Blood.

I sighed and tears spilled down my cheeks. I narrowed my eyes trying to focus on the blurred door.

Tick...Tock.

Emery. *This was her cell.* I choked.

Tick...Tock.

That blasted clock. It had ticked through one nightmare after another, as I'd stood by and watched my friend's torture.

I longed for something to bust the mechanisms in that over-sized torture device.

Images of Emery's infected leg flashed through my mind.

Emery's alive?

With all the strength I could manage, I tried to stand.

Bang.

My knees slammed against the floor, sending painful vibrations up my body into my cracked skull. Sand gritted between my teeth, leaving my parched tongue begging for moisture. I swallowed hard, but something blocked my throat.

A control collar. I didn't have to look or touch it to know. It was tight, leaving me with no doubt of Mother's plans. Only one question remained. Would she give me to the general as a wife or a Cursed to serve him?

I clutched the collar and yanked, but I knew there would be no way to rip it off. The collar's thoroughly researched design made removal impossible. Only the queen herself could disengage it, and that had never happened.

Fate was cruel. I'd learned that long ago when my father was murdered. But until this moment, I'd always believed things would work out. Somehow.

"It was a dream. She can't be alive."

"Emery alive, it true." A hushed whisper came from the far wall. I didn't need to see the rust-colored beard to know it was Boaz. Even in my darkest moments, he was always there.

"Boaz?"

"Yes, yes. I here. You need get out."

I rubbed my hands, trying to remove the dry blood. "Even if I manage to escape this cell, I'll never get off this ship."

Boaz didn't respond.

We both knew my fate, but what of Emery's?

"Do you speak the truth? Is Emery alive? Where is she?" I managed to drag my body to the wall as a guard stomped past the door.

Boaz threaded his fingers through the slats above my head. "Princess Valencia not worry. First you escape."

I bit my lower lip, desperate to feel something other than numbing pins and needles. "No. Save Emery. I will face my punishment, but she deserves better."

My lids grew heavy.

Boaz rattled the ventilation cover. "No. You good girl, saved Emery. Guards ushered council on ship." A retreating thump sounded from the airshaft.

Good. I was ready to die. Death didn't scare me, but what if... My stomach churned. Mother would make good on her threats now. I'd be fitted with metal, forced to marry and produce Tertian heirs. "No, Mother. You can't," I whimpered.

A clang ricocheted through the walls as stale air poured into the room. I stretched out and smacked my palm on the floor, pulling myself toward the door. Perhaps there was time to hide somewhere in the innards of the ship. I'd gladly take uranium exposure over bedding the general.

My head began to clear by the time I reached the impenetrable door. The mocking clock overhead tormented the moments I pressed my head against the cool metal, trying to figure a way out.

I beat my fist against the door. "Why?"

Because you have a gift, a little voice in my head answered.

Gift? *That's right.* I'd nearly melted a wall on the way to the infirmary.

I pulled my legs under me, then, kneeling, I placed my

hands near the opening of the door and concentrated. Warmth surrounded my heart and the beat echoed in my head. My ribs vibrated. My arms shook. Pulses reached my fingertips and energy passed out of me into the door.

Alarms blared and the intercom crackled. "Mualite alert! Containment area. Cell—"

The door swooshed open and I fell onto the general's spit-shined boots. He connected one with my sternum, sending me rolling back into the room. Waves of fabric twisted around my arms and over my head.

"Such a waste to bruise tender flesh," his husky voice sneered.

My head throbbed. I yanked the material back down and forced myself to stand, leaning against the end of the bed.

The general took one long stride and cornered me in the cell. His rough knuckles raked down my cheek. "Smooth to the touch. Queen talks of making you into a servant. And you thought you were above being my wife. Now you'll be my—"

"Either way, I'll still slit your plastic throat in the middle of the night," I shouted.

His massive hands grabbed my upper arms and pinned me against the wall. "That's the last time you'll speak to me that way. I'm the general of the queen's army and soon to be your master. You will treat me with the respect I deserve," his voice boomed.

Fear zipped through my body, testing my resolve. But I refused to be indentured to him. I'd die first.

He clutched my chin and forced it to one side then the other. "It's a shame your natural beauty will be tainted by metal, but your mother will never stop until everyone suffers the price she did in the war."

"That's why I had to get implanted, to be on the council?"

"You don't have a clue, little girl, but I'll be happy to teach you all that I know."

I wrenched my chin from his grasp.

"Remember, I'm the only chance you have now. Your mother always gets her revenge, and you've embarrassed her. Only one other person ever achieved that before, and that person paid the ultimate price." The general backed away, taking with him the odor of garlic and lubricating oil. He summoned a guard in. "Take her."

The guard swept me over his shoulder, the ceiling and floor rotating around each other before I knew what happened. The general exited the cell and followed us down the corridor. "Let's see how fired up you are once the implant is in place."

Implant.

No. A sting rose up my throat. I jerked my head off the guard's back, "Implant or not, you'll never have me."

The general leaned in. "Oh, I'll have you all right."

I thrust my head out and smacked my forehead into the general's. He stumbled back and for a moment, looked as if unconsciousness threatened.

The guard stumbled, dropping me. I ignored the searing, bone-deep pain radiating from my forehead and thrashed, flailing my arms and legs, trying to land a few blows to his groin. It took two guards to subdue me, one grabbing my arms and the other my legs before they could carry me out.

The general rubbed the red mark on his forehead. "So much for behaving like a princess. All those etiquette rules your mother spent years drilling into your head, not to mention the lessons from tutors and members of the council. You were never destined to lead our people."

The general reached into his red coat and retrieved a tamer.

My body went rigid in anticipation of the zap. The collar pricked my skin and shot electricity into my neck. I wanted to scream but couldn't. Air was trapped in my lungs. A charge electrified every nerve in my body leaving me helpless, unable to move.

The general leaned close to me and, resting his lips next to my ear, whispered, "But I was."

"Mother will kill you first," I hissed back, then concentrated on counting the flickering lights overhead, trying to keep from giving into the darkness. The fire inside my body lessened after a few moments. But I didn't have the energy left to fight now. Once we turned the corner and the doors swished open, resignation settled in. There was no reason to care. We had reached the infirmary and the end of my journey.

As the guard dropped me onto the metal table, medics started flicking switches. Boaz's familiar rust-colored beard poked between the vent slats near the open door. Or was it my imagination?

Then flaming red hair bounced into the room.

"M—Mother" I struggled.

"Is she ready?"

I tried to mumble and cry out, but no words formed.

Mother leaned over me with a disapproving eye and stroked my forehead. "Don't worry, dear child. All will be well once your pathetic heart is ripped from your body and replaced with this."

She held a burgundy-colored stone with a black ring.

I thrashed to no avail. The restraints denied my freedom.

"Sorry, no metal for you to melt. Only leather." Mother cackled before she spun around, her long red and black dress swooping. "General, with me."

"I thought—"

Though I couldn't see her, the swish of her skirt indicated she'd turned on him. "There is a situation."

"Yes, my queen." He managed to hide his disgust at her commands, but I knew the truth. Somehow, I had to show Mother he wasn't faithful to her. Then, maybe, she'd spare me from him.

"Get it done," she called from the outer corridor, her distinctive footsteps echoing until the door closed.

Heaving, I fought to catch my breath and scanned the room. Vent? Door? Hopeless. With the leather restraints, I didn't have a chance.

A dull hum sounded from above, followed by a clank from behind. The machines fired up and steam rose from the center of a large contraption. A long metallic arm swung around and a gray-coated medic pointed the silver box attached to the end of the arm directly at my heart. Unbuttoning my blouse and untying the corset, he nodded to someone beyond my field of vision.

My body trembled. Fire shot from my core.

The laser pierced my chest.

I cried out. Tears flooded my cheeks.

A blurred figure jumped from an air vent. Boaz?

The smell of burned flesh confirmed he was too late.

Sparks ignited and shot across the room. A commotion followed.

A tall, dark-haired figure stepped out from the shadows.

My chest burned. Excruciating pain radiated from the line between my breasts where the laser sliced me open. My racing heartbeat slowed. Choking, thrashing, I tried to get away from the heated light.

It intensified. My heart shivered. If I was lucky, they wouldn't be able to get the implant in before I died.

I blinked a few times, waiting, knowing the agony would cease with my death.

The sparks faded. Choking and gurgling sounds echoed around me. The figure made his way to me with his arms outstretched overhead. It was too big to be Boaz. The laser screeched and faded. The straps were ripped from my arms and I lifted into the air.

A pulse shot from the intruder into my chest. The pain in my chest lessened.

Sirens roared. Red lights flashed.

"Hurry or both dead—" Boaz's voice sounded faintly over the sirens.

My savior shuffled to the open vent and lowered me into the opening. "Pull her in."

Thunder sounded from the corridor. The guards were coming. The ship was now on alert. All he had done was prolong my suffering.

A second later, he dove into the air duct and closed the vent behind him. As he pushed me through the next opening, crimson swirls of blood covered his Mualite vest and the duct's silver walls.

My heart stuttered, its beat faint. My eyelids drifted closed.

Mother hadn't won, yet.

Knees and hands crawled over me. An ear rested on my chest.

Death roared closer, life draining with each drop of blood that fell from my body, and all I could think was *finally*.

He lifted his head from my body. "No heartbeat. All of this was for nothing."

CHAPTER THREE

My eyelids protested as if a blast door held them closed. Then, they fluttered open, revealing a blur of golden brown. Strong arms lowered me onto a solid, rough surface. Dark walls of dirt and stone surrounded me, while agonizing pain ravaged my chest.

"You'll be fine," a strange masculine voice whispered before his cool hands pushed my arms down to my side. "Don't touch the wound. Relax, we're below ground. No one'll find us here…not even the queen."

Beads of perspiration coated his forehead above his dark, arched eyebrows. Biceps bulged against bloodstained brown sleeves rolled above his elbows.

I groaned, my mouth dry as the Wasteland. Odors of dust and damp earth mixed with my blood. Moving my hand, I touched my chest. Liquid saturated my clothing. Not just any liquid. My blood. My head spun and my muscles seized at the memory of the hot laser carving me open.

He leaned over me, jet black hair brushing his defined cheekbone. Slowly, he lifted his gaze to mine. His compassionate golden eyes met mine and a smile curved his lips. "Relax, I've got you. You need to be calm." His eyes darkened with amber swirls and the outer edge ebbed into metallic gray until the whites looked like ice. Cool serenity eased my fear, draping it with a blanket of calm.

He examined my wound. His shirt opened revealing a strange tattoo of six dagger tips swirling off a central sphere. The dark center pulsed gray. Silver spun around the edge of the circle, snaked out from one of the knife points, and down his veins to his fingers. A light fixture overhead popped and the scent of ozone filled the air.

"You're a Mualite," I murmured, unafraid of his glowing hands. He'd saved me from becoming a servant to the general and being converted to a walking machine. I knew Mualites couldn't be the monsters Mother made them out to be.

He glanced back at the light fixture and gave a perplexed scowl.

I scanned the room but saw only the table I lay upon, a chair, and a door. No windows or air vents. For the first time in four years, no red beard or small fingers poked through, alerting me of Boaz's presence.

"Stay still. You've lost too much blood." His hands touched my shoulder and stomach, then flattened and pressed. Soothing waves penetrated my skin. Energy the color of diamonds flowed from his fingers into my veins. Ice shot into my chest and exposed belly.

Pulses of electricity snapped at every nerve ending and my body jolted. I bucked under his grip. Then light shone so brightly his hands looked like the winter sun.

The white hue faded and he pulled back.

He shoved what remained of the black corset out of the

way and unbuttoned my undershirt. "Inside's mended. Must seal your wound."

My pulse raced beneath his touch. He exposed enough skin to access the wound. A rough finger grazed my skin, running from sternum to collarbone, in a gentle sweep. A wake of trembling muscle remained behind.

Skin pulled taut and mended together; his gift worked more efficiently than a laser. With slow, determined strokes, he continued to brush his finger from my lower sternum to my neck, tracing the remaining red line.

He leaned over me, his mouth so close his cool breath caressed my skin when he blew against the fading scar. Then, even closer, his lips brushed my neck. My toes curled and a soothing cocoon wrapped around my body.

"You'll be fine now," his whispers danced in my ear. "Give it a minute and the anesthetic aftereffects will wear off."

Aftereffects? Who cared? I wanted to wrap my arms around him and never let go.

A long cool breath soothed my sore ribs. His hands grazed my skin again where his mouth had just been.

He backed away. "Um, think I'll give you a minute."

Everything shattered like an overheated luminary. I bolted upright, pulling my blouse tight, my chest barely contained under the sheer red fabric. "What was that?"

"Told you. It's aftereffects from my gift. Person receiving life force feels pleasure instead of pain. They envision their greatest joy in life for a few moments. I'm guessin' you were thinking of a lover."

"Lover?" I huffed and jumped down from the table, swaying for a moment. I grabbed the gritty edge of the dusty table to keep myself upright. "I am a princess! No man has ever touched me."

He laughed, soul deep. "Uptight, huh? Well, *Princess*. No worries. You're not my type." He rubbed his cheek while he sauntered to the other side of the room and tossed some clothes from a nearby bench at me.

"What's this?" I asked.

"Clothes. Might want to rethink that frock, unless you aim to be conspicuous and hauled back aboard the ship."

I looked down at the brown pants, chocolate top, black boots, hat with goggles, and vest. "Where do I change?"

"Here—it's not safe to leave the room."

My pulse quickened. "I can't change, not with you here."

He waved at my torn and blood-soaked clothing. "Then stay in those."

I scanned the empty room. Four bare walls taunted me. "Turn around." Even as the words left my mouth, I felt like a fool. He'd seen most everything when he'd healed me.

He folded his arms across his chest. His smirk as he pivoted and faced the wall told me he knew it, too. The material of his shirt pulled, revealing a strong, muscular back and shoulders. Warmth spread over the skin on my chest where he had touched me moments ago. A trick or side effect from his healing, I didn't care.

I frowned and turned my back to him. Mother had warned me about such tricks and told me that was how parasites dominated us. That was why they needed the collars to control them.

For the first time, I questioned what she had told me.

Mother.

What would happen to all the people in this town when

she discovered I'd escaped? A shiver rippled over my exposed skin.

I'd deal with the repercussions later. Now I needed to change. I tossed my ripped shirt to the side, yanked my skirts off, and grabbed the pants. The soft animal skin glided up my leg to my waist—a perfect fit. Although tight, the shirt and vest, unlike the corset, left room to breathe. Only the boots, heavy on my feet, and the hat felt foreign.

The strange attire hugged my skin as if it had always been a part of me. No long, cumbersome skirt or ties to lace. While not the simplistic dresses of my childhood, this outfit wasn't far removed from them.

"You can turn around." I faced the room and discovered him already gawking at me with a mischievous grin. "You have no respect, do you?"

He sauntered over, stopping in front of me, and scanned the length of me with a hungry expression. "None whatsoever."

His massive shoulders were wider than any I'd seen among the council members and royal subjects. The scent of leather and earth, so unlike the metallic and oil odor of the ship, drew me, but I remained in place, refusing to indulge in the temptation. I was still a princess.

No man, other than the general, had been that close to me. The corners of his mouth curled up and he leaned forward, his lips brushing my ear. Warm breath caressed my lobe. My breath hitched.

"Bleached curls would be a dead giveaway." He tucked my hair up under my hat. Then his hand cupped my face and he leaned in. "As I said, not my type."

Fury bubbled up. He had no right to play these games with me. So, I swung.

He captured my wrist, and, holding it loosely, he bowed mockingly. "Not behavior I'd expect from a princess."

My insides tightened and my hands fisted. I wanted to pummel him. But I wasn't sure why.

The solid brown door swung open.

"Ryker, all is w-well upstairs." A young girl with long dark hair, and golden-brown eyes, limped into the room. A familiar *thump...tap* echoed from under her petite dress and I flinched at the sound. "I'm R-Emery."

I narrowed my eyes on the girl. "Emery?" I whispered. No! It couldn't be her. She was almost dead when Boaz and I left her in the Wasteland. Yet earlier, I'd seen her stumble and Mother had called me a traitor because the girl lived.

"Uncle d-dropped off food so I th-thought I'd bring it to you. I'm just across th-the hall if you n-need anything."

The door clicked shut behind her.

My head spun as the memory of shoving the half-dead twelve-year-old out the bay door filled me. Boaz and I had hoped we'd succeeded, prayed she'd be found. Yet in our hearts, we'd known Emery couldn't survive the Wasteland. Maybe it wasn't her.

"How can she be collared? Is she a Tertian?" I asked.

His temple twitched. "No, she's no Slag."

That derogatory word for my people showed how much he despised us. "What happened to her?" I asked.

"Your people did that to her."

Yes, they had. "I always thought a Mualite couldn't handle an implant. Their brains won't—"

"You ain't believin' Slags've got higher brain capacity now, do you? That's a lie they tell everyone to maintain power."

"No, that's not true. They've tried to help regular humans who've lost their limbs, but their brains short-circuited from the implants."

"Zamolci zugur!" He smashed his fist down on the table I once laid on, spraying blood that still dripped down the side. "Lies!"

"You speak in strange tongues. I've heard that some still speak an ancient language."

He stopped and faced me. "It is the language of my people. We used it during the war."

"Why speak it if no one else—"

"You'd never understand. You're one of them." Contempt dripped from his words.

The door flew open. "The s-soldiers have been called back to th-the ship. Uncle w-wants to see us. I th-think he's got a plan."

Plan? What sort of plan?

Emery smiled and nodded for me to follow. My mind still reeled at the thought of Emery being alive. She would be sixteen now, yet this girl remained thin and small. I analyzed her from head to toe. Same brown hair and dark eyes, but her face was no longer that of a little girl. Even the way she twirled the loose fabric of the thin dress with her fingers was familiar. Perhaps all the torture had stunted her growth. It had to be her. I stepped closer, but she backed away and shook her head.

I froze.

Did she hate me? Of course she did. I left her for dead.

If I hadn't been looking, I would have missed her canting her head toward Ryker before she walked out of the room.

Ryker nudged me in the back. "You goin' to move or do I have to carry you again?"

I shuffled out the door, not too sure I wanted to know what fate waited for me above ground. "I've got it. You saved me. Now what?"

"No need to thank me or anything.'Course me being a Cursed and all, I guess it's beneath you."

I opened my mouth in protest, but he shrugged past me and headed up some stone steps that soon turned to wooden planks as we ascended. Emery glanced back before she opened the door, flashing a reassuring smile.

Sunshine blinded me as we emerged out of the side of a building through a cellar entrance. Ryker bent down and closed the door with care, then moved a barrel over it.

Like the innards of the ship, these people had found a place to hide. Was I the only one who never discovered a safe place away from Mother?

Ryker smacked his palm against the old, green, dusty doors and we entered a smoky saloon. At least, that was what I assumed it was. The general had spoken about it often enough, as did the guards.

I stood in the doorway, my gaze held by an old lady with a painted face who sat in the corner. She waved her mug around merrily. The loose skin under her arms bellowed like sails. Her joy, age, and flaws were real, unlike those on Mother's ship who wore smooth, expressionless masks.

A tall, distinguished man rose from his chair and opened his arms to Emery. She raced into his welcoming embrace and buried herself in his hug.

There was no collar secured around his neck, so I assumed he was human, but how did he have a niece and nephew that were Mualite? He seemed familiar, someone I had known for years, yet I couldn't place him. While watching them together, a twinge of jealousy snapped in my deepest thoughts for a moment.

If only Father were still alive.

"Uncle. Th-thank you," Emery murmured into his chest.

Ryker snarled. "Should've stayed out of it. Why's she worth our lives?"

Their uncle scanned the room and stepped closer to Ryker, keeping his voice low. "Anything for my niece." He nodded at the barmaid and shouted, "Greta, get him a drink. He needs to cool off."

His voice drew me. Where had I heard that deep tone before? It carried well and reminded me of my father. Flashes of memory assailed me and I saw Father and a man like Emery's uncle hovering over a map, discussing the queen's location and their agent's safety.

"Hi, I'm Fallon. Nice to meet you."

He dipped his head in respect. *Now that's the first familiar sight I'd seen all day.* I shook off the odd feeling and started to curtsy, but the pants made the movement strange.

"Don't mind him, he's hot-headed and all this business with the queen is stirring up old memories."

"What memories?" I asked, hoping to learn more about why he rescued and brought me here.

Emery rapped her knuckles against her leg. "He t-took life force from friends w-when he t-tried to s-save me from dying from infection."

My hands shook, and I wanted to run. But where would I go? Instead, I followed behind her, pulling my cap low. "You mean he murdered his own friends?"

Emery shook her head. "N-no. He blames himself, th-though. Lost control, people died."

I sat on the edge of a bar stool next to Emery and opened my mouth to ask another question, but she shook her head and darted her eyes at her brother. Why did she want to keep it a secret that we knew one another? Did he blame me for all those people dying? I'd have to get her alone to find out, but now wasn't the time.

Silently, I watched men drink and paw at women. The musicians played their tunes and the barkeep poured drinks. Life continued despite my inevitable demise. None of these people would get involved to help me or Emery or the person seated next to them. If there was one thing I understood from Mother's long-winded explanations of why it was so important she rule over all, it was that humans didn't want the job. They were lazy and ineffective in keeping things safe.

An icy chill slid from the back of my skull to my toes. Humans didn't care and Mualites would gladly turn me back over to the queen. There was nowhere for me to go. My head spun and I wobbled on the stool. I lifted the murky glass and took a sip of golden liquid. It scorched my throat. I choked, dropping the glass which shattered on the floor.

The music stopped. Drinks stilled. I glanced in the mirror and met the humans' reflected fear-filled gazes. Did they recognize me? Were they waiting to turn me over in hopes of saving themselves?

Fools. They blindly followed Mother with no questions asked.

"Nothing to see here." Fallon ordered the band to continue with a wave of his arm and scooped the chairs off the floor.

Why did they bring me here? Wouldn't they just turn all of us over to the queen?

Fallon motioned Ryker to the bar. "Don't worry about them. They don't want any business with the queen. Just want to drink and gamble. You're safe for now."

"Besides, any of them think about yapping, Uncle will take care of them." Ryker tapped his head. "Mualite gift of reading minds comes in handy around here."

A young woman placed her fiddle under her chin. Within minutes, her jig lightened the mood of the customers. Soon a stout man joined in on his keyboard and the long brass pipe that shot straight above him vibrated.

Did Fallon read my mind? I watched him make his way from the crowd to behind the bar, but he gave no indication he had read my thoughts.

"Done waiting around. What's the plan?" A short glass slid across the bar. Ryker halted it with his open palm, sloshing the pale green contents onto the aged, scarred wood.

Fallon grabbed a towel from the bar, wiped down a glass and poured some drinks.

"Need to get her out of here. What's the plan?" Ryker whispered.

Fallon put the drinks on a round brown tray and handed it to a barmaid. "Turns out the Queen's angry with her daughter for refusing to use the tamer against your sister for the ceremony today."

Emery sat straight up with a bright smile. "T-told you. She s-saved me."

I tugged at my constricting control collar. Trapped, choking on my actions and inactions. Both would haunt me for the rest of what remained of my life.

"Follow me." Fallon maneuvered around the bar into a back room and shoved open a door to a dark stairwell. "Take the underground." Fallon stopped and faced Emery and Ryker. "Go to the hotel and stay hidden for now. The queen is going to do another sweep, but not until morning. Once that happens, you'll be leaving."

I fidgeted with the edge of my vest, waiting for them to cast me out into the street. "We're leaving?"

Ryker huffed. "Can't stay here. You've sealed our fate. We'll be dead within days once they discover I had something to do with your escape. Boaz is probably already being tortured for intel."

A lump rose in my throat. "No! It's not true."

"For a princess, you're a mite dense. What did you think would happen? Queen's going to give us free food and ale for rescuing her only daughter from being turned into a Slag?"

Emery shuffled between us. "Harsh. V-Valencia, don't listen to h-him. Not your f-fault."

Fallon stepped back and I glanced at Emery. "I'm afraid this time he's right. You'll need to go."

Emery stumbled forward, a little awkward on the wood planks. "Wh-what about you? Won't they know you helped us?"

Fallon tousled Emery's long brown hair. "You don't need to worry about me." He tapped his head. "I can always send them on a hunt in the wrong direction."

Ryker leaned against the wall folding his arms over his chest. "You know the queen won't think twice about blowing up this town. Your gift won't be able to stop that."

A wave of icy fear shot through my body. This entire town could be destroyed because of me?

CHAPTER FOUR

Greta stormed into the back room. "Fallon! They're sweepin' the area. Mandatory search of every building."

Fallon turned on his heels. "Go, I'll handle this."

"Neuki budala." Ryker stomped down the stairs.

Each step cracked under my heavy boots as we descended to the sandy bottom. The men tromping above our heads, only one level up, sent dirt raining around us in a white cloud.

"I told you, I didn't even know of this passageway. No one's down there," Greta's voice hollered from above.

"Th-there's no more t-time," Emery squealed. "If they f-find us here, they'll k-kill Uncle."

Ryker headed down a confining tunnel. "Need to find a place to hide. Uncle can handle himself."

We turned down a narrow hall, only lit by small luminaries every several meters. Dust and sand kicked up from Emery as she galloped like a lame horse in front of me. My heart ached at the sight.

We rounded another corner and before I could slow, I ran into the back of Emery.

"There they are!" Straight ahead, only fourteen or fifteen meters down the hall stood a dozen guards, thankfully out of range for their tamers to work.

Ryker yanked Emery down another passage, and I quickly followed. Thunderous footsteps and gunfire exploded around us.

Orange shots whizzed by our heads, and white clouds of dirt burst from the walls. Dust coated my tongue and I struggled to breathe. We made another turn and halted at a dead end.

I spun around to face the closing guards. Twelve meters, eleven, ten…

A guard pulled a tamer from his vest pocket and pointed it at Emery.

The walls shook, cracking the ceiling halfway between us and the guards. Ryker clutched Emery's shoulders to pull her behind him but she didn't budge.

Her golden eyes pulsed and hands clenched at her side.

"Emery?" I touched her arm, but she didn't respond.

Ryker's eyes shot wide as he turned and shielded us with his body.

Fissures formed over our heads like the webs spun from Spiderats I'd seen in pictures.

Is this Emery's power?

Massive chunks of rubble crumbled. The guards rushed forward. Jagged rocks plummeted to the floor forcing everyone back.

"Move!" I yelped.

I yanked Ryker back against the wall. Emery emitted an earsplitting high-frequency sound and pressed her hands against the wall behind us. The solid surface exploded into a million pieces revealing another room.

Ryker leapt into the room, landing in a fighting stance.

Ice dusted then thickened on his skin. He lifted his arms, his hands already silver, but no guards waited.

Dirt faded to the ground. I squinted and wiped particles from my eyes.

A cold chill ravaged my bones.

"Ryker," Emery murmured as she fell to her knees.

I collapsed beside her, my lungs pinched tight.

My face hardened and Emery's turned ashen. Life tugged from my body as if a needle punctured my core and was draining my soul.

The sounds of labored breaths broke through the pounding in my ears. I could hear something move in the distance, clawing at the rubble.

Dust sizzled against the luminaries, causing the light to flicker. I caught a glimpse of Ryker before my head sagged against the dirt. He stood, eyes shut as if meditating, but silver lines covered his hands. "Get control," he mumbled.

Epileptic coughing fits ravaged Emery and me. I clutched my throat, my hands almost translucent.

Ryker knelt beside Emery, his hands pressed to her shoulders. After a moment, she waved him to me. "H-help her."

He rested his hand on mine, offering comfort. "I didn't mean to lose control. I just wanted to stop them." His thumb brushed my knuckles. " Valencia, take deep breaths and imagine something calming."

He scooted close and tucked the fallen curls behind my ear. Leaning my head into his chest, he held me. He stroked my arms from shoulder to elbow and slowly they turned a fleshy white. I let out a soft cry.

"I'm sorry." He swallowed loudly.

Emery scooted closer. "It's fine. W-we're fine. D-don't blame—"

"Of course, I blame myself. I'm poison and shouldn't be around anyone." Ryker gently propped me up against the wall. A chill radiated down the back of my neck. He shoved away from me, ran his hands through his hair, and paced the small area.

I managed to sit up on my knees. "What're you talking about?"

"My b-brother—"

"No. Don't tell her anything. She's not to be trusted."

Warmth rose from my chest and heated my neck. The familiar tingling began. My gift churned inside like a dust storm. I glanced at the illuminator in time to see the metal casing droop like that old lady's arm skin from the saloon.

I steadied my breath and calmed my anger. "Why don't you trust me? I'm a fugitive like you and Emery ." *How many more things could go so wrong in one day?*

"Still a Slag. Don't matter the circumstance. You'd turn us over the minute you had the chance," Ryker accused.

"N-no," Emery protested.

Ryker kicked a loose pebble. "Talk about traitors later. Have plenty of time once they get through the cave-in."

I ignored him. "We need to get out of here. Emery, you think you can blow out another wall?"

"I th-think so, shouldn't be a p-problem. There is p-plenty of earth to p-pull energy f-from."

Ryker turned on us. "You'd best tell me how you got your gift back."

"I've been p-practicing. Never b-been successful until n-now, though."

"Where will we go? You forget so easily. We're collared dogs." He fingered the black choker around his neck.

"But they'll f-find us if we s-stay here."

"There has to be another place for us to hide." My knees knocked together with fear, but I did my best to hide it. Ryker would just see me as some scared little princess.

Not that I cared.

Ryker pointed at his neck. "They'll use this here tamer to incapacitate us."

I swallowed hard. "Then we take them off."

"Neuki budala."

"Stop with the Mualite talk."

His jaw twitched. "You think if we could remove them, we wouldn't?"

"Brother, w-we—"

My hands trembled. *Do I dare reveal my power to them? What choice did I have?*

Warm pulses shot through my body from heart to fingers. "I said we take them off." I reached up for his collar.

It had to work.

"W-what are you d-doing?" Emery asked.

"Removing the collar." I concentrated on the sensation that had plagued me right before I melted the tamer.

Ryker stepped back, his eyes wide. "It's impossible to remove."

Emery moved closer. "D-don't be ridiculous."

Men tromped above our heads, only one level up, sending dirt down in a white cloud around us.

"Th-there's no more t-time," Emery squealed.

I backed him into a corner and focused on the collar. My hands burned red when I fingered the smooth surface. I'd never tried to harness the power, only to keep it suppressed.

The collar bubbled and crackled under my touch.

"Sh-she's a—"

I ignored Emery's voice, the footsteps overhead, and the deranged look on Ryker's face, and concentrated on the swooshing energy pumping through to my fingers.

The collar sent a shock through my hand and I stumbled back as it fell to the floor.

Tired beyond anything I could remember, I leaned against the wall to remain upright.

Relief flooded me. It worked. "Hurry, now you." I repeated on Emery's collar what I'd done to Ryker's, but nothing happened. Not even a sputter of warm tingles. "I don't think I can do it again. I don't know how it works. Is it because I'm exhausted?"

Ryker pulled us both to a power box in the corner. "Touch this."

It was probably what provided energy for the humming lights above our heads. I had no idea why he thought it would help, but I reached out with my left hand and placed it on top, then touched Emery's collar with my right.

Current zinged from my left hand, through my heart, which thundered so fast it sounded like one continual beat, then out my right hand, and into the collar. As with Ryker's, Emery's collar snapped off and so did mine.

My heart slowed and I collapsed to the ground, the black

collar clutched in my palm. The metal box, now a melted ruin, fell to the floor.

Footsteps stomped down the stairs. I dug my knuckles into the ground and pushed myself upright onto shaky legs.

A wall burst to rubble. Ryker swept me into his arms and ran. My head thumped against his shoulder a few times until I managed to regain enough strength to keep myself steady.

We maneuvered through damp, musty halls. Dim lights hummed every three meters. I caught my breath and gradually energy returned to my limbs. As we reached a set of stairs, I felt stronger and pushed free of his arms. "We need to find a place to hide and as far from the ship as possible."

"I know a place right in front of them. A place they'll never look." Ryker's eyes gleaned with devious pride. "Then you're gonna explain how the Slag Princess has gifts."

CHAPTER FIVE

Ryker led us down a corridor several meters before turning.

"Do you think we could pose as humans? I mean, the only way I ever knew you were Mualites were by the collars."

He halted and turned with furrowed brows. "You sure there ain't trackers inside us?"

I clutched my forehead and massaged with two fingers back and forth. "I can't be sure. Mother only shared certain things with me. I'm not positive of anything anymore."

"How long you been able to alter metal?" he asked as he continued toward what I assumed was the way to the hotel.

"Since this morning. Well, a few days. I don't know. A day or so back, I started to feel strange," I sighed.

A wall crumbled and Emery stood with a broad smile on her face.

Ryker's eyes shined with obvious pride. "Wow, I believe your powers be a mite better than before."

Emery's smile grew wider. "It's n-nothing."

He stepped over the rocks and offered his hand to both of us. Emery struggled across the broken stone, then stopped and pulled a pebble from the foot joint of her altered leg. My heart ached, wanting to make it easier for her.

Guilt consumed me and I couldn't take his hand. Something deep inside me screamed to stay away. It was obvious he didn't know I'd dumped his sister in the Wasteland. If he had known, he probably wouldn't have saved me. He'd hate me, if not kill me, when he found out what I'd done, so I ignored his hand and stumbled over the opening on my own.

"Stubborn, just like a Slag," Ryker mumbled under his breath. I ignored him and continued to follow Emery.

Emery glanced back and rolled her eyes. "Do you th-think your birthday h-had s-something to do w-with it?"

"All I know is for the past four years I've been groomed to rule by my mother's side. It wasn't until I learned what I had to do for my birthday that I began to question things. You see, when my dad was alive I lived in the Resort Territory. I didn't even know my mother existed then. My life consisted of afternoon swims in our lake, and lessons in art, music, and reading at my father's side. That all stopped when a Mualite murdered him." My chest tightened.

"Why do you th-think a Mualite k-killed your f-father?" Emery asked.

"Because that's what happened. I was there," I snapped. But in truth, the memories were so clouded and obscure. Did I really see it, or did Mother tell me what happened? My head throbbed the more I tried to remember. "At least I think I saw it. I don't remember much. Mother says I blocked most of it from my mind. Of course, she won't talk about him."

"Sorry about your Pa," Ryker said before dropping a few paces behind us. I wanted to steal a quick glance, but I didn't dare. He'd probably say something rude and ruin the first nice thing he'd said to me. Heck, other than Boaz and Emery, he was the first person to be nice to me in years.

Emery strung her arm through mine. "W-why won't sh-she?"

"Don't be getting attached to her. Not your family, you know," Ryker barked at Emery from behind.

Emery didn't acknowledge him, so I continued. "For some reason, Mother and Father never viewed things the same way. Their relationship was always distant, and he never left the Resort Territory. He said there was nothing beyond it but waste."

"B-but you didn't have a clue th-then about your gift?" Emery asked.

"Gift, humph. I thought it was a curse until I released our collars. I didn't even know I could do it for sure. This morning when Mother gave me the tamer, I became so upset about the ritual I had to perform, the outer ring altered. I knew if anyone discovered what I could do, I'd be indentured or put to death." I froze.

"What's wrong?"

"I just realized something. Mother would silence me any way possible to save herself the embarrassment of having a Mualite for a daughter." I wrapped my free arm around my belly and fought back tears.

"You need to stay calm." Ryker cupped my face in his strong yet gentle hands. "Look at me now. Don't go letting those memories consume you. Can't use power without a source and there's no metal down here. It'll kill you, and us, too."

I bit my bottom lip, hoping to stop it from trembling.

He swiped the tears that escaped from my eyes with his

thumb. "Some reason your powers are a mite hypersensitive. Like a newborn's." A laugh escaped his lips. "I remember Emery bringing down the whole roof when she was no more than eight months old. She crawled across the floor and got bit by a desert beetle on her knee. Our folks were so proud, they didn't mind rebuilding the roof." His eyes glowed at the memory of his family.

I nodded but didn't pull away. His hands provided a comfort I hadn't felt since I lived in the Resort Territory with Father. "We need to go," I said, my voice weak, betraying me.

He released me. "Come on."

"N-not much further," Emery encouraged me.

I stared at my hand. "This morning, I altered my hairbrush when I woke up. Then the handle of a door. By the time I altered the tamer, I knew something was wrong. Although, I wouldn't admit it to myself, not with only hours until we celebrated my sixteenth birthday."

"Nothing right about sacrificing people. And they call us parasites?" Ryker cursed in Mualite tongue.

He was right. No one should have to suffer the way Emery had. "I grew up that way. Emery, I—"

"You m-may have woken th-this morning ready to s-sacrifice me, but instead you s-saved me, so we'll s-say it's even." Her voice was light and happy as if discussing the weather instead of her death sentence.

"Prokleto čudovišta! But they were going to sacrifice you!"

I jumped at his abrasive tone.

"Y-yes. But th-they didn't. So all is well."

How did she stay so optimistic? Beaten and thrown in a cell for hours, shot at, and running on a Slag leg.

Ryker stomped ahead, smashing his fist against something.

"S-sorry, brother has th-that manly self-brooding th-thing down. Most of th-the girls fall at his feet b-because of it, but I f-find it annoying."

"So do I," I muttered.

He spun toward us, his mouth hanging open. "I…"

I stood firm. If there was one thing I'd learned being a princess, it was to never back down.

"I…you… Ugh." He clutched his hair then swung his arms down to his side and stomped ahead.

I whispered to Emery, "Was it something I said?"

She giggled, and I hoped for some crazy reason she forgave me for not saving her the first time we met. Finally, I had another friend.

Music filtered down from overhead as we turned down a new tunnel. Sulfuric smoke greeted us at a wooden doorway.

Emery pressed it open and peered out. "It's the c-cellar. We're f-fine, come on."

I ran my hand down the rough, wooden wall trying to find an illuminator.

A door flew open at the top of the stairs. "Come on woman. Get yourself down here and work off that drink I just bought ya." A man's voice traveled down before his steps. The general's voice.

No, I'm just imagining it.

A woman giggled and we ducked behind several barrels. "It'll cost you fifteen mecha."

My head swarmed with the proximity of my demise. I slid and fell with a thud against the wooden floor.

"Who's there?" The general stopped at the last step and peered around the dark cellar.

The broad-shouldered, disheveled man stumbled toward

us. He drew his weapon in his right hand while still clutching a bottle in his other and walked straight toward us. My head swarmed with possibilities.

Could we overpower him? No, we'd never survive against the gun.

Emery sat beside Ryker covering her ears with her hands and squeezing her eyes shut, rocking back and forth.

What was wrong with her?

The general stumbled forward. The bottle dropped from his hand and clanked to the floor. It rolled to my side. The dirty label read Verillian Juice.

"Ten mecha, no more," The general yelled.

I wanted to scream and run. I'd rather take on a thousand guards than feel his touch against my skin again.

The woman of the night glanced around the room. "You sure it's safe? I hear Mualites run this joint."

"No parasite would dare show themselves around me. Get yourself down here and take care of business."

I peeked between the barrels. Each breath stung as it entered my tight lungs. The sight of the general churned my stomach.

The woman reached the bottom step. "Fifteen."

He lifted her onto a barrel only a couple meters away. "Twelve."

"Well, aren't you the strong one," she giggled. "Deal."

He ripped the ties from her corset and tossed his belt to the side. It thudded against the packed earth. "Now, we can have some fun."

I stared at the gun, only a few steps away. Could I reach it without being noticed?

Ryker shook his head. I leaned back into the darkness and

covered my ears. He ran his hand down my upper arm and stared straight into my eyes. A trail of frosty pleasure soothed my raw nerves.

The upstairs door creaked open. "General, sir, um, some guards found the princess. The queen has new orders."

"I'm busy."

"Sir, the queen is requesting you lead the search immediately. They have her below ground. Trapped with no way out. She doesn't know how long before the parasites murder her."

"Go on, get. We'll finish this later."

I heard the click of his belt and footsteps pounding up the stairs. I let out a long breath.

"You okay?" Ryker asked before he slouched over Emery and rubbed her shoulder. She lay on the floor curled into a ball.

"Yeah, fine." I shuddered at the general's lingering scent of oil and spirits.

Emery sat up but still rocked back and forth.

"What's wrong?"

"She's checked out again. Emery, come on. You need to get a grip on this. No time to be wasting 'round here."

"To think, if I'd stayed on board, he would have—" Every muscle in my body tightened with the image.

"Y-you w-won't have to now." Emery stood up with Ryker's help. She still shuffled back and forth with agitation, but she lifted her head with a faint grin.

"Have to what?" Ryker steadied her before checking the stairwell.

I opened my mouth to answer but couldn't say it out loud.

Emery shuffled over and locked her arm through mine.

"M-marry him. Q-queen p-promised the general on her n-next b-birthday."

"How did you know?"

"I hear th-things in the saloon."

We moved under the illuminator at the bottom of the stairs and listened to the ruckus above. A woman's soulful song meandered down with words about heartache and loss. Something everyone could relate to.

Ryker grabbed the handrail and eased up the stairs. The strong engine-fume-like scent became overpowering when we exited the cellar into a small back room. We maneuvered around to another stairwell.

"Move it."

We followed him up another set of stairs and walked along a railing that overlooked the main dining area of the hotel. People ate at the tables. Others sitting in a lounge smoked out of spherical glass bowls. The room began to spin. My stomach churned and threatened to spill its contents, if there were any. I couldn't remember the last time I ate.

My feet wobbled beneath me and Ryker caught my elbow. We went to a room at the end of the hall. I heard myself giggle uncontrollably.

He helped me onto a bed against the wall. "It's the Arvenati smoke. You've never been exposed, so you've got low tolerance."

"Low tolerance. Ha. She's s-snorked. H-how long do you th-think it'll last?"

Their voices sounded as if they were speaking through a long tube, their faces looking stretched and flattened. I blinked. Acid rose. I lunged forward and spewed into a round pot.

Strong hands grasped my arms and helped me sit back up. Ryker stroked my hair. "You'll be fine now."

The room moved like an accordion-machine waving in and out. But after a moment, the room only shimmied and blurred with a slight yellow hue. "This is because of Arvenati smoke?"

"Yeah. You'll be swaying and have a mite headache for a bit, but you'll be fine."

"I've never heard of it. Is this a Mualite thing?"

"Guards partake quite a bit. It's a chemical waste from the uranium mine. You'll be fine after a couple more exposures. Body needs to build up tolerance."

At two slow knocks, followed by one, then a pause and three more rapid ones, Emery opened the door. "Uncle."

I thought I saw Ryker glare at Emery, or maybe it was the smoke still playing with my head. I didn't care as long as he remained by my side on the thin mattress with his arm wrapped around me so I wouldn't topple over.

Fallon halted by the door. "Nevesen bog."

Great, more Mualite talk, as if my head wasn't spinning enough already.

The tall man clicked the door behind him. "Hi." He started toward me but glanced at Ryker and Emery . "Where's your collars?"

Emery smiled. "V-Valencia removed them. Sh-She's got Mualite gift to m-melt metal."

Fallon dropped his load of supplies on the small wooden desk. "Interesting."

I didn't know how I felt about Emery sharing my secret with her uncle, but there wasn't much I could say about it now.

Emery rummaged through the supplies, "Now we look human like you."

Ryker grunted. "Never told us how you managed to avoid being collared."

Fallon's lip curved up into a knowing grin. "You guys look awful. How'd you escape from below? The entire town shook and then dust came through the hall like a typhoon."

Emery stood tall with a proud smile.

"Whoa, you did that?" Fallon sat on the corner of the desk and rubbed his chin. "But how?" He glanced at her leg, then back at her face with brows furrowed.

"Don't know. Been p-practicing, but the bugger didn't get in the w-way this time. It felt like my mind routed the current down one side of my leg and b-back up the other. Kind of c-crazy, huh?"

"Yeah, but wow. If it worked for you, then—"

"Don't be jumping ahead there, Uncle." Ryker stood.

The bed rocked. I grasped the metal frame and blinked to stop the world from moving.

The vein on the side of Ryker's temple bulged slightly. "There ain't no way any of our people are going to agree. And even if they did, where'd we get the parts? You forget how much Emery was ostracized by our people because of that damn Slag appendage."

I stumbled across the room, but after a few steps found my footing. Most of the smoke's effects had faded, except my balance, which was still a little skewed. "What're you guys talking about?"

"There are many of us the Slags have tortured and maimed. Even now, to get information, they'll remove limbs," Fallon said in a solemn tone.

My head throbbed from not only the aftereffects of the smoke but the memory of Emery's torture. Tears welled in my eyes and I fought them back. It was obvious Emery hadn't mentioned what happened between us on the queen's ship. I needed to get her alone and learn the reason before I messed up.

"That's awful," was all I could manage without tears.

"Queen enacted a law after the war, The Mualite Indentured Act. It declared anyone believed to have an affiliation to a terrorist cell could be incarcerated for questioning without proof. No trial date has to be set. They can rot in confinement forever or be tortured for information they don't have." Ryker paced the floor, his voice deep and tormented.

"I had no idea." My heart twisted with the half-lie, but how could I tell the truth? Ryker's narrowed eyes spoke volumes. He'd never understand.

"No offense, Princess, but you seem to have lived in your own little world."

"Don't call me that. My name's Valencia."

Fallon scrubbed his face, his salt-and-pepper scruff moving up and down. "She's right. You guys need to think about new names and identities. No way you can get around here looking like that."

Ryker shoved his hands in his pocket and paced. "Even with a new face, we'd never manage to hide. Sure there's a mighty big price on our heads."

Fallon cleared his throat. "Boaz said there's a rumor of a resistance across the ocean."

"Boaz? You know, Boaz?"

"Yes, child."

I blinked rapidly. "He was my best friend, my protector.

Now…" How I missed his little tapping feet. If only I could've brought him with me.

As the sounds of horses snorting and ships revving permeated the room, I realized life continued whether I was Princess or Cursed, alive or dead.

Ryker paused at the window, turned, and glared at his uncle. "Across the ocean? Are you insane? That might as well be in a different world."

Fallon stood. "Listen for a second. I know there are obstacles—"

Emery rolled her eyes and rummaged through the supplies. "Obstacles? R-really, Uncle?"

"Yes, but there are ways to cross the sand," Fallon insisted.

Ryker glowered at Fallon. "Without a ship, we'd be sermechtapede food—"

"Okay, okay, I get the picture. So we'll appropriate a ship."

At Fallon's suggestion, my mind raced with possible options. "I know where we can get one. Before the queen's ship takes off, Scouters go out to check the area. We could steal one of those."

Ryker gave a crooked smile. "Great, the princess has gone scavenger on us."

"I told you not to call me that."

"L-let her finish."

"They're not well armed. With our powers, we could take one easily."

"What happens when the ship doesn't return?" Ryker asked, his voice dripping with sarcasm.

"It helps us."

Ryker opened his mouth, but Emery cut him off. "Wh-what do you m-mean?"

"We'll steal the scout ship that heads in the direction we want to go."

Ryker slapped his hands to his thighs. "Oh brilliant! Why don't you announce where we're going—"

"They won't follow." Fallon's face lit up. "They'll go the opposite direction."

"Right. You see, Mother doesn't take any chances. Scouts go out more to see if they come back. If not, they know something is out there they would prefer to avoid. We might capture two going in different directions."

"Let's stick to getting one. Also, the queen knows she's not immune to the animals of the Wasteland," Fallon added.

"Yes, and she also has more than Mualite enemies. Scavengers, foreign terrorists—"

"So we take the ship and go?" Ryker asked.

"Not that simple. These are short-range ships with little space. With our extra weight, the fuel won't last long enough for us to reach the coast. Even if we get there, I'm not sure how we would cross. The ship isn't meant to handle the wind over the ocean. We'd crash within a few hundred meters of shore."

"Don't worry about ocean transport. I've got that covered," Fallon reassured us. "Just capture that ship and get to the ocean."

"Right now we can't even make it down the stairs." Ryker turned back from the window. "There must be two dozen guards outside the hotel. Of course, half of them are drunk."

"N-no worries, brother. Uncle has b-brought gifts." Emery held up silver dye, scissors, and some robes.

"No way," Ryker protested.

Emery smiled, a real white-teeth-baring grin. "It's th-the only way to escape."

I glanced between them. "What?"

"Not going to be a human temple worshiper," Ryker growled.

"Why not?" I asked.

"Why? It's sacrilegious to our people. The queen's manmade religion is an abomination to Mualites."

"You mean there's another religion?"

"Yes-no, there's another way of life. But I'm not getting into it right now." He held up a robe and twisted his mouth in disgust. "As for wearing these—"

"You have no choice. If you can reach the rebellion and help build their forces, someday we could all be free again," Fallon said in a voice that brooked no argument.

"You speak of war." No matter how evil Mother was, the thought of betraying and murdering her seemed wrong. "Even if they weren't really—"

Ryker crossed the room in two steps. "War? Slags murder, steal, indenture my people. We only wish for freedom."

Fallon waved his hand at us. "Shh, a bunch of guards came in the building."

I raced to the door and peered out between Emery and Fallon. Ryker squeezed in above us, hand clutching the molding around the door.

Not just guards poured into the hotel, but three hunters entered as well. They sniffed the air and snarled, baring their canines. I'd only seen a hunter once, its white coat covered in blood after it caught an intruder on the ship.

"What are th-those things?" Emery whispered.

I grasped her hand. "You don't want to know."

CHAPTER SIX

"Sit still. The fume from the dye will only throw the hunters off for a short time." Raking my nail along Ryker's scalp, I yanked his hair a little harder than necessary to divide another section. His hair was soft despite the bits of sand which were to be expected in the Mining Territory.

"I saw them down in that ther' cellar," a woman yelled from the restaurant below.

Ryker squirmed. "Only a matter of time before they begin searching upstairs."

The last squirt of dye echoed as if blasters fired in the room. "At least they still believe we're wearing the collars. That should keep them below ground for a while."

"W-we need to hurry. Won't t-take long for them to check here. D-don't want Uncle p-punished."

"Punished?" No, I couldn't bring that upon their uncle.

Ryker bolted from the edge of the bed to pace the room before sitting on the edge of a chair and staring at the door. "Room we're in is for high-ranking officials. No guards will enter without cause. Not until they become suspicious. Which won't take long after the hunters catch our scent."

Emotions swirled inside me. This was all happening because Mother wanted me back. How far would she go to capture me and force me into servitude? I glanced at Ryker as he flopped onto the bed, his expression solemn. "Ryker? Why did you save me? What keeps you from turning me over to the hunters downstairs now?"

His forehead crinkled. "Don't paint me as a hero. The only thing that kept me from turning you over is my sister."

His words mimicked the laser, searing my skin to my heart. Swallowing the lump rising in my throat, I turned to look at the clock resting on the table. No way would I shed a tear in front of this heartless jerk.

Emery thumped toward me. " Valencia, he doesn't mean—"

I refused her excuses. The facts were clear. Her brother would happily turn me over or kill me himself if he discovered my part in Emery's torture. "Why did you save me?" The words blurted from my mouth before I could stop them.

Ryker huffed. "Emery threatened to save you herself if I didn't go. Had no choice. Uncle thinks you can help with the rebellion. I think you're just a spoiled princess."

"It's time." I yanked his head back over a bucket, took a water pitcher and dumped the liquid over his head. He could believe what he wanted to. I didn't care.

A blaster fired, followed by sounds of a struggle. Ryker bolted upright, spilling water all over the floor.

"Please, don't hurt me. I have—"

"Shut up, whore."

The woman continued to plea for her life until another blast sounded. Then nothing but deafening silence.

We needed to get out of there before more blood stained my hands. I snatched the towel from my head and rubbed the ends of my hair. It would be hours before the long strands would dry. Eyeing the scissors on the desk, a wicked thought crossed my mind. For the first time in four years, defiance took hold. I gathered my hair in one hand, snatched the scissors from the desk and leaned over the bucket. In two cuts, the heavy mane fell in a pile.

Ryker smiled and nodded his approval. He shook his head and towel-dried the ends before glancing in the mirror. "Black and silver streaks?"

I looked at him with apologetic eyes. "We didn't leave it on long enough and your hair is so dark."

"You'll still p-pass for a p-priest."

Ryker grimaced. "Best be putting our robes on and hurry."

I pulled the thick gray cloth over my arms and lifted the hood over my head. Glancing in the small mirror on the desk, I discovered my silver hair and gray robe made my eyes shine bright. In spite of Ryker's protests about his own hair, I preferred the silver over the bleached curls Mother forced me to wear.

Fallon opened the door and peeked through a crack at us then slipped inside. "This is your chance. The guards are still concentrating their search below ground. You best hurry. I'll stall them as long as I can."

"N-no, you'll be hurt or k-killed," Emery pleaded. "C-come with us."

"Can't and you know it. Anyone disappears, it's a lead to finding you. But I look forward to the day you return with an army on your back to fight the queen."

We all smiled yet knew the words he spoke were an

impossible task. If we did make it to the shore and across the ocean, would there even be a rebellion? If so, would three more make any difference? Still, it was the only chance to keep Emery and me from suffering further mutilation.

Emery and I gathered the dye and put it in a satchel. "Guess we can't cover the smell."

"Hold up." Ryker grabbed a bottle of liquor from the cabinet and dumped it over the bed and floor. Then he placed the bottle on its side against the head of the bed making it appear as if it had been dropped during an intoxicated blur.

Fallon rolled his eyes. "Great, I guess I have some cleaning up to do."

I opened the window and searched the dusty road below and spotted Boaz. My heart soared. "Look." I couldn't believe my eyes. He was safe and well.

A smile danced across Emery's face, the kind that made me think everything would be better. Boaz jumped up and down, then scurried down the road. The guards scattered after him.

"Now." Ryker crawled out of the window onto the angled roof. I followed close behind with Emery in tow.

Options for a clean escape were few with the guards below us. Ryker leaned back and whispered. "Don't fall or Queen's army will be on us faster than a spiderat on prey."

We slid down the shingles and crawled on our hands and knees to the edge of the building, all the time watching the guards. Ryker's robe caught on a nail and he tumbled down the shingles and off the ledge.

Snaps of heat jumped along my skin. I grabbed his arm, his cool skin soothing the fire. Concentrating on not allowing the fear to ravage my senses, I held tight to his forearm. His feet dangled a couple meters over a guard. A wind whipped down the street and the guards looked back. Just then, a red head popped out of a hole and scurried to the other side of the road.

I would have laughed if Ryker weren't about to kick the head of one of the queen's soldiers. The man raced after Boaz, his red coat a blur in my peripheral vision.

Ryker's hand slipped from mine and he jumped to the ground with a thud. He lifted his arms up and I jumped into them. The contact sent a soothing calm down my back and arms before I pulled away and Emery followed.

Without a word, we all ran to the back of the building. Even with the disguises, we couldn't afford to be near the hotel. Someone would recognize us. We made our way behind three more buildings, then exited to the street.

The queen's ship rested on three braces on the landing field, but the engines hummed indicating take-off time was near. Mother was due back in Acadia East for my birthday celebrations with the council, where she'd be forced to report my death or suffer my return.

Stopping, I bent over, palms on my thighs, to catch my breath.

Ryker stood over me. "Listen, Valencia. You need to alter the engine. That way it'll cut off when the scout leaves. But don't damage it."

My pulse quickened. "I can't. I don't have that kind of control, and I wouldn't know what metal to alter. Even if I did, I've never taken down something that moved."

"Sh-she's right. That takes training and her p-powers are too juvenile to handle that kind of c-control. I'll t-take out the scouts' vision with a s-sand storm. It'll l-look like an accident." Emery started down the walkway to the edge of town.

I pushed upright and we continued on along the backside of the buildings, but at a slower pace. Something didn't feel right. "Even if you could cause the scout to go down, it would damage the ship, and he'd have an opportunity to report mechanical failure which wouldn't prevent the queen's ship from going in that direction after the storm clears."

"If only I didn't have to steal life from people to help some-one," Ryker grumbled. A twinge of pain echoed in his voice. He pressed his lips together and shook his head.

I caught up to him. "You have to take him out, Ryker. It's the only chance we have."

We'd reached the edge of town. Ryker shook his head, his pupils dilated. "Don't know what you ask. You've never been haunted by the life of a person that you've stolen. You're asking me to do the one thing you were raised to hate."

I was no expert, but he'd given me advice on how to subdue my power; it should be the same for him. "We don't have a choice. You have control, I don't. Can't you incapaci-tate him for a while without killing him? When the ship is discovered as missing they'll assume a sermechtapede got it."

"She's r-right," Emery agreed.

"Mighty tall order. What if I can't control it?"

"Remember, Uncle t-taught you how. You c-can do it."

"I'm not like you, Emery. You are so good and pure. We both know something dark's inside me. You know what happened."

Three small crafts shot from the underbelly of the ship and raced toward the neverending sea of sand.

Ryker's jaw twitched and he shook his head.

My stomach rolled waiting for him to take action. It was our only chance.

Two airships zoomed by, and our robes blew in the wake. Another airship shot in the direction we hoped to travel.

Perfect.

I followed the object with my eyes until it receded into a bronze dot. Too much further and it'd look like another grain of sand.

Ryker altered his stance and lifted his arms.

I held my breath.

A chill radiated from his body. His fingers shook as if he was trying to pull the two-winged pod back with his bare hands. Silver current shot from his fingers and raced across the rolling hills. The light snapped back like a slingshot, sending him flying into the side of the general store. His head cracked against the wood planks. "Too much, too fast."

Emery moved to his side.

A plume of dust burst from the sand in the distance. He'd done it.

Emery tugged his robe tight around his face, but I caught a glimpse of his diamond eyes.

I moved to Ryker's side, knelt down and slipped my palm around to the back of his head. No blood. Warm waves brushed over my skin, up my fingertips, and through my body.

Darkness lingered for a moment. Cries echoed in my head, strangling my mind before the vice grip released, then peace.

Was that Ryker?

"You felt my power, didn't you?" Ryker lifted his head and met my gaze. "Now you know what I'm capable of. I see how repulsed you are. Go ahead and hate me. It's what you were born to do."

Opening my mouth to protest, I searched for the words to

explain why I didn't see him that way. He'd done what I asked of him, despite the obvious side effects. "I don't—"

"Hey, you need something over there?" A guard marched toward us.

"No, sir. Our p-priest is fasting in the n-name of the queen and became ill." Emery let her leg glisten in the light just for extra cover. Who'd ever believe a Mualite had an implant?

"O k-kay," the guard mocked.

I wanted to shoot fire at the man's heart for his cruelty.

Engine fumes came in clear ripples from under the ship. The guards scurried to the open door. A hunter struggled against his restraints as soldiers led him out of the hotel. The beast snorted in the air. His long fangs stained with blood. Black eyes narrowed in our direction.

The men restraining the savage beast paused at the edge of the gangway and looked straight at us. Ryker held tight to my hand. One guard stared as if he recognized me.

Ryker grasped my upper arms and captured my lips with his. Not the way the general had, but in a gentle yet passionate embrace. Strums of energy raced through my body. Hot, cold, and a mixture of both blanketed my skin. *What's he doing?* My mind blurred.

Strong lips urged me closer. This wasn't right. My heart quickened, hair rose on the nape of my neck, my palms turned sweaty. My body yearned for more, but my hands, resting on his chest, pushed—kind of.

He rose to his knees and pulled me tight against him. Earthy scents stoked the fire and when his tongue parted my lips, I only tasted juice and paradise.

"Ah, excuse me." Emery's voice broke the spell and I fell

back on my heels. Ryker sat across from me, his quick breaths matching my own.

I pressed three fingers to my stinging lips. "What was that for?"

"Th-that's called a kiss, but I must s-say, my first one was nothing like th-that," Emery giggled.

Ryker shook his head again. "When? Who?"

"I'm s-sixteen, dear brother."

I remembered the guard at the gangway and glanced back. The man ascended into the ship, dragging his right silver and black leg up the ramp.

Clutching the coarse sand between my fingers, I tried to comprehend what just happened.

Emery took my hand. "You okay?"

"Yeah, I—"

Ryker cleared his throat. "Priests often choose priestesses for sexual companionship."

Emery glared at him. "Yeah, right before th-they become s-sacrificed to the creatures of the w-wasteland."

Tugging my robe around me, I attempted to choke down the heat rushing to my face. My insides were mushy and warm. This wasn't right. Since he hated me, that meant he'd only used me to escape the guard and hunter. That kiss meant nothing to him, only one of a thousand. He'd obviously had a lot of practice. "Don't worry about it. It wasn't a big deal. We need to figure out how to retrieve the ship. But how can we make the several hundred meters in without a sermechtapede tearing us to shreds and slowly digesting us?"

The rumble of an engine drew my attention.

The ground shook beneath us.

Another small craft shot out from the ship, headed in the same direction that Ryker had taken down the other one.

"It doesn't make sense. The pod went down. Mother should be getting out of here."

Ryker crossed his arms over his chest. "Gluposti. So much for stealth escape."

I pushed up and paced the boardwalk. "There has to be some other way. Maybe someone in the saloon, a trader or scavenger, will help us—"

"Might be difficult for a princess to understand, but these people aren't goin' to bow down and do as you command."

"It can't end like this. I'd rather die than go back."

"Be careful what you wish for, princess. Many of those people in the saloon won't care if they turn you over alive or dead, and Uncle can only keep their minds busy for so long. We best find some place to hide until we figure out another plan."

Emery stood with her gaze transfixed on the horizon. I narrowed my eyes at the Wasteland but saw nothing.

Wait. Sand rose from the ground as if possessed by an angry god. It swirled and grew to a wall of brown, consuming everything in its wake.

I stepped to her side. "Emery, are you doing that?"

Ryker's mouth hung open. "Impressive."

We stood there watching the other airship plow into the wall of sand. There was hope yet. The corners of my mouth tugged into a premature smile. The sand didn't stop when it took down the ship.

"Emery, pull back," Ryker shouted.

The monster continued to roar to the edge of town, the sound of wind drowning Ryker's words. He grabbed our arms and raced for shelter. All the shutters banged shut. It was too late. No one would open for us.

The queen's ship fired boosters and rose to the sky, hovered a moment and shot in the opposite direction of the storm. It now seemed they weren't worried about what took the scout down. They thought they knew. But then, we wouldn't survive to retrieve it so the queen had no worries.

Sand blocked the sun and the sky darkened. I'd never seen a storm this close, it looked like a million desert beetles swarmed for an attack. I cringed, knowing coarse sand would buff our bones to a high shine.

"Emery, you can stop it. Concentrate." Ryker stooped to her eye level. "Come on."

"C-can't stop it. I c-created it, but now it's out of m-my control." Emery's forehead scrunched, her body trembled, and the storm continued.

Wind lashed at my face. Fierce grains of sand ripped through my robe and burned me like fire.

Emery stood with her small hands spread wide at the sky. Ryker grabbed her arm and mine and ran toward a building. As we neared the front door, I spotted a sign through the haze. *Boarding House.* We stumbled up the porch steps. I pushed on the door. It wouldn't open. The wall of sand barreled down the center of town. Ryker threw himself over us. Not that it would do any good.

His body shook, icy energy scratched at my skin. He placed a glowing hand on each of our backs. I looked up at him. I knew what he planned. His gift would end our suffering. For once I wouldn't have to face torture, just a quick end.

I gave a discreet nod ready to accept my fate.

His eyebrows rose. "You know what I plan?"

I nodded my head again.

"You're not scared?"

I shook my head and looked over at Emery; at least she'd be spared any more pain.

Emery caught on and shook her head. "No." She shoved us back and stood in front of the sand. Daring it to take her. It rolled over her like the ocean waves I'd seen as a child.

Before the murder of my father.

Before Emery's torture.

Before my own mother tried to turn me into a servant.

Funny the things one thinks of in the face of death.

CHAPTER SEVEN

A tidal wave blotted out the last of the orange sunlight. My legs shook as we huddled around Emery, waiting for death. The pounding of sharp particles never hit.

Ryker loosened his arm and we both looked to see the large mass hovering overhead.

"D-did it, but not for l-long." Emery remained focused, hands stretched out as if praying in a temple to the queen.

"That a girl." Ryker's eyes shined with pride.

How could power to save a life be a curse as Mother had said?

A head popped out from below the porch.

"Boaz here, save day. You come, or pummeled by sand."

My heart raced, overjoyed to hear that funny, raspy voice. I looked over at his scruffy head protruding from under the porch by my feet.

He pointed above his head. "Meet at door."

The frizzy red hair disappeared.

"Know you're a mite tired. Think you can walk and maintain the sand?" Ryker asked.

"I d-don't know." Emery tried to take a step but wavered. "No, I c-can't w-walk. S-sand's in my leg. It's frozen s-stiff."

My insides twisted at the sight of the metal leg frozen at an awkward angle. That hunk of metal was a forever reminder of her horrific cries that still haunted my dreams after four long years. I had to make it up to her. Somehow, some way. I scanned the metal levers and thought about blasting the sand from the crevices. Impossible; that was Emery's gift. If I tried to get the joints moving, I'd probably melt the entire leg.

Emery crouched down and tried to move one hand to her leg but the sand began piling around us and she stood again.

Gritty particles flew up my nose. I sneezed them out only to have new grains take their place.

A second later, Emery joined me in sneezing. A piercing, high-pitched sound echoed across the Wasteland. A golden light burst from her hands, sending the wall of sand back.

My throat raw, I sputtered and coughed, "Grab her!"

Ryker scooped Emery into his arms and charged for the open door. The sand fell from the sky like a brown apocalypse. I stumbled on the porch and collapsed. The dirt pummeled my back like Mother's metal fist.

Someone grabbed my hand and yanked me inside before slamming the door shut.

Boaz fell to his knees in front of me. "You almost desert scraps."

I spit the gritty sand and wiped my lips. Each inhale stung with the fierceness of a laser blast.

Boaz stood, thumbs stuck in the top of his belt. His mouth curled up in a reassuring smile.

I brushed my fingertips across my itchy eyelids.

"No, must not. Sand blind if don't stop. Here, let me. I free sand." He pulled a small round bottle from his belt. "Open eyes, I spray."

Forcing my lids open, I stifled a cry as the bits of dust, more like boulders, scratched the inside of my eyes. A small hand pushed my chin up. The swishing sound of a spray brought a soothing cool to my eyes. After a moment, the burning subsided and Boaz capped the top and plunged the small round object back into his belt.

For some reason, he always appeared when I most needed someone. The one person to watch over me since my father died. In a strange way, he felt more like family than Mother did.

I chuckled. A princess close to an engine rat. Wow, Mother would throw a gasket.

Yet here stood this little man by my side after saving my life, again. Shame filled me. How had I ever believed Mother's praises of my superiority to Boaz, a kind-hearted soul, full of spunk? Guilt plagued me. Now his life was upside down because he'd saved me. He'd never fit in with the Mualites; no work for his kind here. No way he'd fit in the scout ship with us either, not that we'd ever find it now.

Ryker squatted next to me. "You all right?" He stroked my short hair from my face and smiled as he said, "Life's never boring since you came round." His touch made the world alright in spite of the ascension of hell raging over the territory.

"I'm glad I keep things interesting." I returned his smile. "How's Emery?"

"Exhausted, she's resting on the couch. Everyone must be in the cellar waiting out the storm." He brushed sand from my head and robes. Even my ears itched from small crystals scratching at my eardrums.

"How's her leg? Will she be able to walk again?"

Ryker helped me up and we made our way to the living area. Emery was already fast asleep. Our talk would have to wait, but for how long? I couldn't keep our secret forever.

"She blasted the sand once the door shut behind you. She's a mite weak now. Other than the sand we dragged in, there's no Earth in here for her to drain energy from. She just needs sleep until we leave. Once outside, she'll be fine."

"All these rules about our powers. It's confusing." I huffed. "Powers…seems so strange to say aloud. Just hours ago, it would have meant execution." My heart ripped at the memory of Mother's scowl. My gut twisted in knots and tears welled up in my eyes as I recalled her words. *Your father would be devastated to learn what you've become.*

Collapsing on a green cushioned chair near the couch, I grasped my stomach and fought back the urge to scream or laugh hysterically. Slowly, I noticed the scent of meat and potatoes wafting into the room and my stomach growled. At Ryker's chuckle and Boaz's snort, I knew they'd heard it over the wind outside.

"I fetch food. When done, we find ship to fly." Boaz waddled toward two closed doors. They opened as he neared, then swooshed closed.

Ryker sat on the edge of the table, facing me. I tried to hide my tears. No one should ever see a princess cry. After all the years of *conditioning*, I thought I had my emotions under control. "Sorry."

I looked away, but he reached up and pulled my chin back

around. "No need for apologies. It's good you're not the heart-less Slag princess I believed you to be."

I sat up straight as if the corset still circled my middle.

"The queen didn't like emotion, I'm expecting."

"No, it's viewed as a sign of weakness. But I'm not weak." I shot out of the chair only to have him pull me back down to face him. My hands betrayed me as they trembled in his. He'd held my hand so often today. These people seemed to always be touching one another. Hand holding, hugs, and *kisses*. Without thought, I touched my lips with my free hand and he smiled.

"That be your first—"

"No, of course not." I lied. Well, not really.

"Yeah, who? When?" he challenged me.

"Back when I lived in the Resort Territory."

"The boy, who was he?"

"A servant." I laughed. "I didn't know back then the line between servant and indentured. My father caught us. Talk about awkward."

"So, I wasn't your first."

The pain in his voice made me want to share the truth. The *why* defeated me. But since I'd been following my instincts ever since his rescue, I decided to continue. "Well, he kissed me, but it wasn't like...that." I could feel the heat rise to my cheeks. His hand gripped mine tighter. It didn't make me uncomfortable as I'd expected. Also, the cool of his body was...pleasurable.

"Resort Territory, what's it like?"

"Green, rich with color. Of course, I didn't know how precious the land was at the time. I thought the whole planet looked like that. My father explained that it was the only area that had fresh lakes filled with fish which we ate. He said everything else was still too radioactive or the water was too dangerous to drink or swim in."

Ryker leaned in closer. "I know you didn't have a choice earlier, it was part of the cover, but now..." His mouth brushed across mine and the heat ran from my lips down my neck, through every inch of my body.

My back stiffened, my mind screamed for me to pull away, but when his lips pressed against mine, I didn't move. His hand brushed my cheek and left a frosty trail behind. My body edged toward him as if my heat craved his cold. I wanted more. The soothing calm that made all the madness disappear, if only for a few moments.

My body stayed rigid, frightened that if I moved the wrong way, I'd break our connection.

Pots and pans rattled in the nearby kitchen. Boaz would return soon. He leaned back and I blew frosty mist from my mouth. *More...I want more.* I reached up and ran my fingers through his hair to the back of his neck.

He shuddered under my touch. It felt powerful. I tugged his face to mine and kissed him. My toes curled and delicious shivers ran down my arms and legs. As our tongues brushed, I heard and felt our mouths sizzle and pop. Cold and heat melded and exploded. My body seemed to freeze and boil simultaneously.

He moved closer. When our bodies pressed together, a loud pop echoed in my head and we both flew across the room. I landed backward in the chair, knocking it over, with my skin covered in hot prickles. Ryker lay on the floor next to the sofa. Emery slept on. The flames in the fireplace shot up in tall streams and the illuminator next to me exploded into shards.

One of the pieces sliced through my robe, cutting my right upper arm and cheek. We both remained on the floor, gasping. My body reveled in the aftershocks. As I pulled myself together, I scanned the room. How had Emery continued to sleep through the noise of Ryker's and my life-altering kiss?

"I see you both have found the Art. Beware, opposites you two are, don't go too fast. Flames and ice mix, but passion makes unstable."

Ryker pushed himself upright. "What do you mean, little man?"

"Power core opposite in nature."

My heart leapt, beating faster than the sand blasted outside the window. I rolled out from under the chair, righted it, and dusted off my robes, buying some time to gather my thoughts. Boaz stood there with a goofy grin. He knew more about my life than anyone else from all the times he'd watched over me from the vents on the ship. He'd bring me water and food when I was in confinement for disobeying an order, or a cool compress after a "training" session.

Ryker settled back on the edge of the table. Neither of us spoke.

"Forgot forks and napkins." Boaz scurried from the room.

Tingles still danced over the surface of my body. I looked down at the shattered illuminator. How could anything that pleasurable cause so much damage? Worse, I wanted more, even after the illuminator broke. We couldn't do this again. It would draw attention or kill someone. Somehow, some way, I'd have to find my way back to the Resort Territory and stay far away from Ryker and Mother. Given that she hated it there, I might have a chance of surviving if I stayed in the old cabin I'd once shared with Father…and no one ever saw me.

Ryker pulled the sleeve of my robe open and touched the wound. I leaned back. "No, don't. I won't have you steal energy from someone else to mend a cut."

His eyes dropped to the floor. "Just going to take a look and clean the wound. It's not deep, won't be needing stitches. Besides, I don't always have to steal energy. Can use my own for small stuff."

My heart ached at the sight of how much pain I'd just caused him. His dark eyes showed the anguish of taking lives to use his powers. I grabbed his hand. "I'm sorry. It's just that—"

A surge radiated between us, as if our bodies knew what they could have and demanded it freely. The tools resting on the side of the fireplace clanked against each other.

He freed his hand from mine.

We sat motionless for a moment, his golden eyes pleading with my soul to let him in. I wanted to lose myself in them forever. Leave all this craziness behind.

My chest constricted at the thought of us never touching again. We couldn't. I didn't think I could stop next time.

Emery stirred. "Wh-what's going on?"

The doors swished again and Boaz dropped some white cloth napkins on the table. He pulled a wooden box up and sat. "Not much time before storm ends. Eat."

Emery staggered to her feet and limped to the table, dragging a chair behind her. She grabbed a fork and pierced a roasted potato. Her gaze flitted about the room. "I h-hope Uncle's okay."

Initially, the heat of pepper-coated meat burned my

tongue. After a few mouthfuls, I sighed. It reminded me of home and Father. This was the first time since his death I'd eaten anything with flavor. On the ship, I'd eaten a pot of yellow mush that tasted like steel for the past few weeks.

I bit back a smile as my stomach settled for the first time in days. I took a sip of my drink and almost choked. "What is that?"

Ryker smiled. "Just some wine."

"It's...strong."

"Actually, it's watered down. Not great quality, but it will help give us strength. Water is way too expensive here."

Emery took a drink from her cup. "Th-the w-wine makes th-the water taste better. If n-not, it t-tastes like chemicals."

I took another sip, this time prepared for the strong acidic flavor. It slid down my throat with a sting but warmed my belly. My lips and fingers tingled after half a glass. I cupped my mouth, trying to stifle a rogue giggle.

"Ah, I think you've had enough." Ryker took the glass from my lips. Berry flavors lingered in my mouth and my head felt light and happy.

"But it's good. I'd like more, please."

At my hiccups, they laughed.

"Princess find restraint." Boaz's belly shook up and down several times as he chuckled and looked at Ryker. "Yes, restraint something you both must use, but can manage with caution."

I redirected my attention to the food in front of me. Boaz didn't realize what he was urging me into. My body quivered with the thought of Ryker's mouth on mine, and another illuminator popped but didn't explode.

Ryker pressed his lips together and his cheek muscles flexed and tightened in an attempt not to laugh.

Great, now I was a joke. "So I've never been kissed. Who cares?"

Emery cleared her throat and averted her gaze.

Ryker pointed at the vibrating muted white box on the other wall. "Yes, I can see that."

"It's just my powers freaking out on me again."

Ryker chuckled. "Yeah, and what be the catalyst? No one's 'round threatening you. Admit it, you want—"

"To get out of here." I jumped up, knocking half the food to the floor. "Sorry, it's just that…oh, never mind." What was the point in trying to explain; no one understood me anyway.

Boaz scurried around to clean up the food.

I scooped some potatoes back onto a plate. "Stop, you're not my servant anymore. You don't have to clean up my mess or pretend to care about me."

"Pretend? Valencia thinks I only stayed to fix you drinks? I am friend and more." Boaz took the dishes to the kitchen, his head bowed.

"Don't know how I feel about you, but I reckon that man loves you and would do anything to protect you." Ryker picked up the remaining mess and went to the kitchen.

Standing by the window, I looked through the murky glass. What gave Ryker the right to scold me? It wasn't like I was a child. I was maybe only a couple years younger than him. Just because I didn't have the experience he did, it didn't make me a fool. Still, the way Boaz had looked at me broke my heart. He was the one good thing in my life over the past four years. He deserved more than a pouting, childish princess lashing out because she was frightened.

When Boaz entered the room, I knelt before him, my arms wrapping around his shoulders. "I'm sorry, Boaz. There's no excuse for what I said. I know you're my friend, my best friend ever, and the one person in this world who only wants what's best for me." My gaze slid to Emery and back to him. "I shouldn't have let my fear rule me."

He patted my cheek and nodded. With a smile, he walked to the stairs, grabbed the handrail, and hoisted himself up. "To your room."

I looked between Emery and Ryker. "Shouldn't we get out of here and go for the ship?"

Ryker shuffled to the stairs. "Empty that head of yours about leaving tonight. Sermechtapedes will devour you in seconds. Never no mind about the spiderats with their black-as-night wings. One bite'll kill you."

"And what about scavengers. They roam the Wasteland during daylight hours. I know my mother avoids them. If the queen's ship can be overpowered, we won't stand a chance."

Ryker paused at the top. "Don't rightly know about scavengers. We don't see much of them. They mostly scour for metal from what I hear. We ain't got no metal. Must take things how they come. First, rest. We'll need it before tromping up them sandy hills. You've never walked up one of those, have you?"

I followed close behind, helping Emery with the first couple steps. "No, I've only been to this territory once before. You've been outside the field?"

"Once." Ryker glanced down at Emery's leg and I decided not to pry any further. Not now, not until I could speak to Emery alone.

"But why are these sermechtapedes so dangerous at night?"

"Because they retract their million legs into their hefty bodies and plunge through the sand to attack from below. If on the surface at night, their owl-eyes let them see great distances. So when you hear their eerie clicks, you don't rightly know if it's the eyes or the feet shooting out at the surface. Do you aim up or down? And the spiderats use their bat-like sense to bounce sound off objects to find ya; the bird wings allow them to fly fast and dive bomb without warning, and before you draw your gun, you're caught in a web."

I shivered. So many creatures to learn about and so little time. "Where did all these creatures come from?"

"Some Mualites developed them to help catch fly-ships and steam trains during the war, others the queen created to keep us all imprisoned in the territories working for her." He shrugged. "There're lots out there."

Boaz opened the door to a simple room with three twin beds, a desk and a chair. It appeared homey with the white wood panel walls and dark brown rug on the floor.

Emery collapsed onto a bed. "I know it isn't w-what you're used to, b-but—"

"It's far better than what I'm used to, thanks." I didn't want to talk about it, but I was sick of everyone believing I lived a pampered life. If you could call the multiple trips a week to the medic and social isolation a dream life, then yeah, I'd lived like a true princess.

We all sat in silence, listening to the people stirring below. Boaz left without a word. With a full belly for the first time since Father's death, I longed to sleep on a real mattress.

Finally, an end to my sixteenth birthday, and we were all alive. Maybe tomorrow, no one else would have to die.

I removed the robe and collapsed on the bed. My short silver hair dusted my shoulders. The only amenity I wished to have from the ship was a sandblaster or steam shower. Every time I closed my mouth, the grit crunched between my teeth.

My eyes slid shut and dreams of happier times brought me comfort, but not for long. Pleasant memories morphed into familiar dark nightmares.

"Emery. Don't die. Please." My words echoed in the dark engine room.

Emery's tiny, frail hand lifted to me. I took it and wiped blood from her forehead where the neuro-alterer had been drilled into her skull. "It's better if I die. No more torture."

My chest constricted with grief. How could I sit and watch her die? The stench of infection told of a long, gruesome death. This young girl who'd been tortured for days coughed and grasped at my hand. I couldn't bear watching.

My insides fluttered as the ship descended.

Voices, guards, bay door opening.

Emery, on the edge of death, begged for me to end her life. No, no more suffering, please. I couldn't watch.

Guards stormed in. "Why hasn't she been incinerated?"

Boaz waved his arms. "No, better to leave in sand. Queen not happy if engine breaks."

"Fine." The guard stepped toward us. If Emery was found alive, the torture would begin again, and I'd be punished. I looked to Boaz, and I knew he saw my betrayal. I'd promised to help Emery. To get her home. Now I only wanted her to disappear.

The guard punted Emery's small body down the gangway. Her limbs flopped in all directions as her body rolled onto the sand. I wanted to cry out, cradle Emery to me, and demand medicine to heal her, but knew I couldn't.

As I looked down at her, I realized Emery was dead and was now no more than food left for the Sermechtapedes. That I was relieved filled me with shame.

Screams echoed up my throat and I bolted upright. Strong arms encircled me. My body was convulsing with the memory of my cowardice. Did Emery not remember what I did or didn't do? Had she romanticized our friendship? We were only children, barely twelve years old, and thrust together in impossible circumstances.

In the end, I'd let her down. I'd put myself first. I'd saved myself at her expense.

"Shh…it's okay. Just a dream." Ryker's cool breath soothed my burning skin.

This was wrong. All wrong on so many levels. I didn't deserve his comfort. I'd betrayed his sister and left her to die alone in the Wasteland. And when he discovered the truth, nothing would stop him from sucking the life out of me.

And I would deserve it.

CHAPTER EIGHT

Pressing my palms against Ryker's solid chest, I shoved him away. "I'm fine. I don't need your help." My arms shook uncontrollably.

Ryker reached out but I backed away. His eyebrows arched and he opened his mouth, but I was saved by several loud knocks at the door and leapt from the bed. Fire slid down the back of my throat, my ribs constricted, and I blew out steam.

"Calm down. W-we're expecting Uncle." Emery jumped from her bed and let him in. Boaz trailed behind, holding a round cake.

"I know day bad, but celebrate with cake." Dimples creased his cheeks, while his nose was red with excitement.

A cake and celebration was the last thing I wanted. But looking around the room, it appeared to bring the others a little bit of joy. Besides, I hadn't tasted a real cake in over four years.

"Thank you. That was very kind," I managed after a few long breaths.

Boaz's crooked teeth gleamed as he placed the white cake on the desk. Letters scribbled on top read, *happy birthday my litle princess.* My father wrote that on my cake every year. Tears began to stream down my face. I choked out, "Thank you."

Boaz pulled a single candle from his belt and lit it.

"Happy Birthday to you," they sang softly as I blew out the candle. For the first time in years, I had a family birthday party. They might not be my family by birth, but in this moment, they were in my heart. As for the future, maybe somehow, some way, I could stay with them. Maybe these foreigners wouldn't see me as a Slag princess if I stayed long enough.

No, I couldn't. Not after what I'd done. No one would forgive me.

"Uncle, how are w-we going to make it to th-that ship?" Emery asked. "And even if w-we do, how do we f-find it buried under all th-that sand?"

He looked at me. "With our walking metal detector," Fallon said.

What the turbine engines was he talking about?

" Valencia, you have the gift of altering metal, correct?"

Gift. Still a word I needed to get used to when it felt like a curse. "Yes."

"If someone can alter something, they can find it."

We looked at Fallon with wide eyes. At least I wasn't the only one out of the loop for once.

"Ryker, how do you think you found your sister out on the sandy planes at the edge of town?"

Ryker shrugged his shoulders.

"When they ejected her from the craft, her body was failing. Your gift is to take and give life force."

My stomach churned with his words. I stole a quick glance at Emery who shook her head in warning. Why did she protect me? I didn't deserve it.

"Each life force has a different signature. You found her because of your gift."

Finally, I understood how Emery had survived that day. All these years, I'd fantasized about her living, but I'd known it was impossible and was filled with guilt. Now, I understood. By rolling her out of the ship where we had, Boaz and I really had saved her. I glanced at Boaz and saw his knowing smile. Ah, so that was why he'd chosen where to push her from the ship. He'd known Fallon and about Ryker's gift, but why hadn't he told me?

Spotting the vein on the side of Ryker's temple throbbing again, I realized he didn't like talking about what happened to his sister.

I wanted to fall on the floor and beg their forgiveness, but how could I apologize if they didn't even know? What would happen when he found out the truth?

"Why didn't you explain that before?" Ryker snapped. He clutched his hair and paced, his gaze wondering. "Power can be used to help," he mumbled.

"Because you would've gone off and tried to save every Mualite lost in the sand. You can't save everyone, Ryker."

A loud gong sounded from outside.

"Boaz and I have to go. A mandatory curfew has been imposed on the town. They still believe the princess was kidnapped from the ship and Mualites have her. This could get ugly in a few days."

My hands shook. I remembered what happened to the Agriculture Territory when the queen ate a bad piece of fruit. Steam rose from my skin. "I can't be the reason your people suffer."

"Valencia, you are one of us now. You might not fully understand or accept it, but you need to start thinking as if you are." Fallon paused in the doorway. "Don't believe for a minute that if you sacrifice yourself it will save our people. I assure you, that wouldn't be the case. She searches for more than just you."

He closed the door before I could ask what he meant. Could he be speaking the truth? Yes. Yes, he was. The last thing Mother wanted was to have me back safe and sound. Should the council discover she had a parasite for a daughter, her crown would be challenged.

I crawled under the light blanket and relaxed my head against the soft pillow. Emery turned off the lights and I could hear the other beds squeak. Sounds of foot soldiers in the street, people mulling about in the common area, but no hum of an engine, or clanking footsteps from the hall. I'd even gotten used to Emery's leg. Her light weight created a different sound than Mother's when she walked. Then again, it thumped against the wooden floor rather than clanking against the hard ship corridors.

Closing my eyes, I tried to sleep. Images of my father in the Resort Territory filled my head. Memories of walking on the beach near the lake, teaching me to swim, and reading in bed drew me further away from harsh realities. *A flicker of something shone on a table. I raised my hand and the object shook. My father stood on the other side of the table, his silver eyes gleaming with pride. He smiled and ran to me, lifting me into one of his rib-squishing hugs.*

As if ripped from his arms, my eyes fluttered open to sun peeking through the window. The whine of a ship landing filtered through and I bolted upright.

A squeak drew my attention to Ryker's bed. He paced, his hand rubbing the back of his neck. "She's back. So much for having to be in Acadia."

I shuffled to the window, a sting of apprehension coursing through my veins. I clutched the lace curtains.

The bay door lowered. Council members and guards began to pour out onto the viewing seats. Humans gathered, curiosity etched on their deep-lined, sun-kissed faces. Cursed scrambled, but guards herded them back to the main strip. My breath quickened and I clutched my chest in an attempt to relieve the ache. "Why's she back?" I mumbled.

Scanning the street, there was no sign of Fallon. Hopefully he remained in the saloon, not that two swinging doors would protect him from my mother's wrath if she caught wind of his involvement in hiding me.

The tip of her bronze foot scooted into view.

Emery cleared her throat. "W-what is it?"

"Not sure," I managed, without tearing my eyes from the events unfolding only a few meters away. Why had she returned? She never kept the council waiting. Especially with the mumblings of there no longer being a need for a supreme ruler. Of course, my mother never spoke of these things. I'd heard them in hushed conversations outside my room, or in the infirmary when the medics believed me asleep.

Ryker lifted the window, then sat on the edge of the bed, his forehead resting against his clasped fingers. I knelt next to the small desk by the window, my fingers protecting my chin from its hard surface.

The crowd quieted as Mother descended the ramp. My heart pounded against my ribs, as if in protest at the sight of my mother's commands for respect.

Esmada stepped from around the seating area and addressed the crowd. "Her gracious majesty has returned on urgent business, the protection of all the inhabitants of the Mining Territory." She turned and bowed to my mother, as did the rest of the crowd.

"Bet she isn't here for a tea party," Ryker scoffed.

I lowered my hands to my side and leaned into the hot wind blowing through the small opening. Licking my lips to relieve the sting, I held my breath as Mother lifted her hand for all to rise. Slowly, each head popped up, followed by their bodies. A wave of brown and gray-clothed Cursed shuffled away from the ship, but guards only shoved them back in place.

Her gaze traveled over the Mualites to the humans along the boardwalk. "The gravest of circumstances have caused my return, despite urgent business in Acadia. My loyalty and commitment to all territories is as important to me as any royal business."

"Lažnivec!"

"Shh," I snapped. I hung on every raspy word, waiting for the inevitable fallout. Even though I knew it was a lie, a small part of me clung to the delusion that she spoke of true concern for all.

"There are never any secrets among my people. All of you have been a great wealth of information over these trying years. It's because of your commitment that we've begun to rebuild and replenish all that was lost during the war. The years that innocent humans were murdered in their sleep by parasites claiming to have special abilities are over. The war has ended, but we can never forget that these parasites sucked the life out of your loved ones and tortured the rest."

"Freaks of nature," a man with no collar shouted from the boardwalk.

"We thank your royal highness for all of her compassion and protection," a guard called out. Yeah, like he wasn't coerced into participating in the *I love the queen* song and dance.

Once again, Mother raised a hand to silence the crowd, and out of fear, they immediately obeyed. "I will continue to protect you, even when there is a traitor among you."

Gasps rolled over the crowd.

She lifted her natural hand into the air with dramatic slowness. In her palm rested a control collar. One of our altered control collars. I gasped and clasped my hands over my mouth to stifle my screams. My pulse erupted in a tympanic echo of double-time beats against my neck.

Whooshes deafened me and the room spun. "She knows," I managed.

Emery sunk by my side. "Knows w-what?"

Ryker slammed his fist against his thigh. "That we don't have our collars on. Our hiding in plain sight won't work any longer. Need to get movin.'"

I wanted to look anywhere but at Mother, but I tilted my head to watch as she threaded the collar through her fingers before she passed it to Esmada. "These are still dangerous times we live in. A fragile system has emerged from the ashes of hatred, murder, and conflict. Yet it is only in its infancy. As your ruler, I will never allow us to return to those dark days. I will protect you at any cost. That is why I have been forced to take action. One inhabitant of the Mining Territory will be punished each hour until the parasites that stole my daughter are brought to justice. I still cling to hope that my daughter will return to me, but make no mistake, my first concern is for all of you."

Heads turned left and right. Cursed scooted away from the armed guards, but they had turned their backs on the wrong executioner.

My eyes barely focused on what my mother held before a blast echoed down the sandy street and back to the boarding house. The entire world fell silent. Air squeezed in my windpipe and I couldn't breathe. I doubled over, but not before I saw a young Mualite fly sideways, arms flailing, until his head smashed to the ground. The rest of his body hit the packed dirt, only to bounce and slide until he landed in his final resting place.

My brain couldn't comprehend her execution of the innocent person only a few meters away. He unwittingly gave his life to keep me in hiding.

My hands shook. I stumbled back and landed hard on my butt. The walls closed in around me as I gasped for air.

The boy died because of me and he wouldn't be the last. *One an hour.* Mother's words echoed in my head, but my brain couldn't fully process them.

Movement swirled around me, but I only saw blurs of browns and tans. I trembled as I pushed myself up. "I have to stop her. I can't let anyone else die."

Strong arms shoved my back against the wall. Ryker dropped on one knee in front of me, saying something, but I couldn't hear. All I heard was the echo of the shot that had ended the boy's life.

"Let me go. I'm turning myself in. I'd rather be promised to the general than cause another life to be taken."

Better yet, I'd rather give my life instead.

CHAPTER NINE

Ryker pressed a cool rag to my head.

Emery sat at my side, holding my hands tight in hers. "N-not going to happen. N-need to stick t-together."

Fallon straddled a chair.

Emery shifted. "W-what can w-we do?"

"Unless we get her to safety, I'll have no choice. As a council member, I have to protect this town. They've announced the execution schedule. We only have one hour until another Mualite is murdered in the center of town. They'll find a reason to execute a human next."

I pushed up and ignored my spinning head. "I won't let that happen."

Emery crossed her arms over her chest. "N-not happening."

Ryker grabbed my arm. The bright blue shock startled us both, but he didn't let go.

"You can't turn yourself over to them, they'll turn you into...a—a—"

"Slag. Yeah, I know."

The whistle blew outside the Queen Enlightenment temple. Time had run out.

Emery shot up from the bed and stumbled to the window.

"I'm sorry the queen—my mother—did this to Emery, to everyone."

Ryker cupped my cheek. "No fault of yours. Don't let who raises you define who you are."

"Let's get you guys to the tunnels. We're trying to pull as many of us as possible underground without any humans or guards noticing."

We started to follow Fallon out the door, but something made me hesitate. "How will this help? She'll just keep killing until I'm turned over. I can't leave all those people to die. You think when she runs out of people to shoot, she won't search the tunnels?"

The front door burst open. Guards flooded the downstairs and shoved people down on their knees, pointing guns at their heads.

Fire bubbled inside my belly and seared my lungs. Ryker grabbed my arm, tugging me back to the shadows. Coolness surged beneath my skin and steam rose from my arms.

Screams echoed. Crying. Suffering. No matter how much I wanted to hide, I couldn't. There was no hiding from my destiny.

I swallowed hard and jerked my arm from Ryker. Straightening my vest, I stepped to the top of the stairs. "Spare these people. I was not a victim but a willing participant. I was curious about how others lived off the ship and chose to explore."

Emery whimpered behind me, but I knew Ryker would keep her hidden.

A guard stood at the bottom of the stairs. His eyes narrowed and he knew my altered appearance caused him to pause. "Princess, we are glad you are well. Quickly. Escort her to the ship. We will take care of these people for you."

"No. I will not allow them to be executed. They've committed no crime."

The officer's eyes narrowed. "You show...compassion for these people?"

It didn't matter. My punishment waited no matter what the guard reported. "You question my allegiance? I've discovered a new mining ore that could propel our ships and assist us with developing more powerful weapons. It's below ground and we'll need these parasites to retrieve it. The queen would be disappointed if her resources were cut off because of a hasty decision. Now, we must all return to the queen and share the good news."

Did the guards believe me? The look plastered on the faces below told me they did.

The officer didn't move. He pressed his ear implant and smiled.

The front door flung open and the general stood in all his ornate glory. His gaze traveled up my robe to my cropped silver hair; a disapproving snarl arched his lip.

A surge of pride over my little victory empowered me for a moment, but his glare indicated it would come at a great price.

"I'm glad you are well, Princess. I wouldn't want you to be ill for our wedding in a few days."

"Wedding?" I shrieked, my regal composure lost for the moment.

"Yes, your mother set the date. Only two moons until our

wedding night." He wiped his mouth with the back of his hands while his narrow black eyes scanned my body.

Rage consumed me. "I will never marry you."

"You have no choice. The queen has given me permission to treat you as a hostile." He turned to the guard. "Secure the prisoner." The general spun on his heels and went to the front door. "Then execute every being in this establishment. Do not spare any parasite, human, dignitary, or dwarf." He looked back and smiled. "Queen's orders."

The door banged shut behind him. A second later, the general's speeder roared to life before it took off through town.

One of the guards aimed his gun up the stairs. All hope drained from me, leaving only bravado. "You will seal your fate if you harm me."

He waved the weapon at the stairwell. I took two steps and swung at him. Before my fist could connect with his body, a hard object hammered the back of my head. It was the hilt of his gun. I fell to the floor, searing pain radiating from the back of my head. Consciousness threatened to abandon me, but bloodlust churned the energy inside my body.

My head spun as it battled for freedom. I blinked and pushed myself up on my hands and knees. Ryker bolted to me. I reached out to grab his leg but wasn't fast enough. His hands clutched the guard's face so tightly the man's cheeks squished together.

Darkness shot into me. The taste of decay lingered in my mouth. Ryker had sucked the life from him in less than a second.

Shots fired. Fallon grasped his shoulder and fell to the ground.

Ten beams of silver light streamed into Ryker's fingertips from the bodies of the ten guards in the building. Not one Mualite was hit. The guards collapsed, dead. Steam rose from their contorted bodies and wafted around the two-story room. The air reeked of burnt clothing and skin.

Clutching the back of my throbbing head, I stumbled forward a few steps to Ryker's side. He stared down at his hands, face twisted in grief. People cried around us and crawled to one another. Were they all Mualites, or were there humans among them?

"He's sealed our fate," a middle-aged woman whimpered. "We're doomed."

Their fear infected my emotions. Inside, my gift fed on the panicked energy. Did I feed on people, too? Was I the monster Mother always warned me about? The life-sucking creatures who mercilessly preyed on the innocent humans, stealing their energy in their hour of need. No. I wanted to help them. Ryker wanted to help them. Mualites weren't monsters.

"You were already doomed. Now you have a chance," I said.

"When the guards don't return, more soldiers will come," another woman with salt and pepper hair cried out.

I looked at Ryker. "You okay?"

"Yes, I-I—"

"Did what needed to be done or all of you would've been executed on the spot. You've bought us some time," I said.

Yes, he'd just annihilated ten people in seconds. Stories my mother used to tell to scare me into hating the parasites that murdered crowds of innocent people had turned into reality in front of my eyes. The decaying corpses sprawled on the floor proved the truth of the Mualites' power.

Too bad the general wasn't one of them.

I fought to control my powers—keeping my fear under control—while calming everyone else. If I didn't, they all would perish, and I'd be returned into the cold, hard arms of the general.

I shook off the burning disgust that rolled over me.

As I moved toward the stairs, Emery skipped toward me, humming, oblivious to what was going on around her. I shook my head. Yesterday, I was lost in naïve ignorance. Now I knew the truth. Slag, human, Mualite—they all could and did cause death and were capable of betrayal.

I looked around at the carnage fear had left in its wake. In that moment, I made my choice. Yet, I was left to wonder what kind of child joined a rebellion that wanted her own mother dead?

Ryker leaned against a support beam. "There is a resistance beyond this town that is building strength."

"You speak treachery. You'll bring Her wrath on—"

"Her wrath is already here." He glared at the cowering crowd. "If she would kill her own daughter because she suspects that she possesses Mualite powers, she will slaughter all of you to keep it a secret."

He was right. I didn't choose to betray my mother. It was a necessity to survive. I wanted to crawl beneath the nearest table, curl into a fetal ball, and make the world go away. But I was no longer a child; I had to face the truth. Mother wanted me dead, or worse, married to the general whom she controlled.

Squeezing the banister, my nails dug into the paint before meeting the resistance of hard wood. I needed to ground myself somewhere in this world. Somewhere far from Mother and the fate that awaited me. I wanted to scream at the people before me that at least they had each other. Who did I—a Slag with Mualite abilities, a freak of nature—have?

I inhaled then exhaled slowly, taking in the thirty or so faces etched with panic. They'd lived under Mother's tyranny so long they didn't know how to survive without her rule. Something I could understand more than they knew. They needed hope and direction, but how could I give it to them?

Mother may have been right that Mualites could murder whomever they wanted, but one look at Ryker told me that was only half the story. If he could take life, then he could give it.

"Do you have enough energy to help the wounded?" I asked. I knew the answer. Of course he did; he'd just absorbed the life force of eleven people.

Ashen-faced, Ryker nodded and went to his uncle and the five people crouched by the couch. Silver threads of energy flowed from his hands. Tan and peachy colors washed the gray from their faces.

"Fallon." I squatted by his side. "If I make it appear as if all perished in this boarding house, is there a place your people could hide until my mother leaves?"

He gave me a reassuring smile. "Yes."

I looked around the room and caught Emery's gaze. She deserved better, as did the rest of them. Now was the time I made amends for past mistakes. I'd protect Emery, but how? The building was wood, not metal. How could I make it look like they all had died in a tragic accident?

I ran my hand along the wood panels. Coughing at the smell of singed hair, I peered through the lace curtains. Whatever I planned, I had to work quickly. The guards outside the door were signaling the general back over. They must have heard the commotion inside. My skin crawled at the sight of my betrothed approaching on his speeder. Running a shaking finger down a flower pattern in the curtain, a dull burn blanketed my body and I feverishly scanned the room, grasping for an idea.

"Emery!" I swallowed hard and hoped she would be coherent enough to help. I glanced back out the window. No time left. I had to act immediately.

"Put a field over these people." I spun toward the others. "Everyone, go to the cellar. Hurry!"

Ryker kept working on one old lady near the cellar door. Fallon, pink and fit, pulled two others toward the back. Everyone descended the steps.

I grabbed Emery and we moved by the cellar doors as Ryker and the rest of the people disappeared. We'd have one chance at escape. It was an insane idea that could get us killed, but I had to try.

The engine of the speeder stilled in front of the hotel. The general's boots thudded against the wooden porch, echoing the finality of my future.

I glanced at Emery. "You ready?" At her nod, I closed my eyes and reached out. Heat surged through my body and down my arms. My fingertips tingled. The walls creaked. "Now," I said as I pictured the large, cut nails holding the structure together and the roof shimmied. Crouching on the first step, I watched with satisfaction as the support beams crashed, filling the ground floor. Walls caved on top of the second floor. The roof collapsed.

Emery tugged me down next to her, but I continued to

pull the nails from the entire building. The door flew open and everything tumbled down around us at once.

"I can't hold—"

Emery grabbed the back of my vest and tugged me backward. Together we tumbled down the stairs and slammed against the hard cellar floor. Looking up, I saw a wood spear impaled through the top step. A shiver ripped through me. If Emery hadn't jerked me to safety, it would have speared my body. Again, Emery saved me.

"Thank you," I whispered, but Emery had already checked out.

Ryker ran to us. "Seal the tunnel."

"I'm not sure Emery can manage any more."

"She'll be fine. Come on." Ryker pulled us both to our feet.

"We sealed all the tunnels they discovered earlier. We might have a chance." He led us to where people sat whimpering and holding onto each other.

Fallon greeted us. "That was magnificent, dear." He rubbed my shoulder and took Emery's hand. A—father's touch. I wanted to fall into his arms and feel the warmth and security my father always provided, but I couldn't. He was a stranger, in spite of his apparent open heart to Emery.

Ryker moved close to me. "You okay?"

"Yeah, fine." I shuffled away from him and picked up a doll, brushed it off, and handed it to a whimpering child.

The little girl clutched my hand and melted my heart with pleading eyes. "Mom?"

"We'll find her," I said, brushing her bangs from her red, swollen eyes.

"If this works, we can only hope the others will be spared. They need someone to do their mining," Ryker said.

Fallon nodded. "We've sent scouts to check. If not, we'll try to sneak as many as we can to safety."

"I'm sorry. I—" I choked at the thought of all the others being lined up in the street and shot in the back of the head.

Fallon clutched Ryker's arm. "You three must leave as soon as possible. Even if we all perish, you're the ones who could change the course of all Mualite enslavement."

Ryker leveled a hard glare at the man. "What're you talking about?"

"Don't you know?" Emery smiled. "Powers of three will merge, one earth, one fire, one ice, and free our people from the great price."

"That is just a children's story told to give us hope," Ryker said.

Fallon shook his head. "I always thought it was a myth, but watching you three together... Well, it gives the rest of us hope."

My stomach churned. No. This couldn't be true. Yesterday, I was a Slag princess, today a Mualite, and tomorrow a savior? Too much. Way too much.

The smell of body odor filled the small space. Cries echoed in my head.

Fallon clasped his hands to my shoulders. "You are brave and strong. You possess the mind of a Tertian, the talents of a Mualite, and the heart of a human, all the best qualities of each. You were meant to lead all to freedom. There are many Mualites and humans who support the cause, but most are overseas. We communicate through two Mualites with the ability to relay messages great distances."

I sucked in a shuttered breath. "How did you know this

about me? What if I'm none of these things, but a freak of nature?"

"I knew your father and mother a long time ago, before and during the war."

My stomach flopped. My vision must have been true. A man stood before me that knew both my parents before they separated.

Fallon glanced back at Emery and Ryker standing close by.

Breath hitched in my throat. "How'd you know them?"

"I was a great friend to your father." Fallon wrapped his arm around my shoulder and led me down a hall. "Come, we must speak in private."

I glanced around. Even in their misery, ears and eyes were firmly planted on the four of us. Emery hummed at the rhythm of each step. The hair on the back of my neck stood on end at her eerie cadence. Dust stirred up in the halls making the air thick and clouded. I wrapped my arms around my middle as the cold, damp feeling climbed back over my soul.

We reached a room similar to the one I'd woken in the day of my escape. A table, chairs, and a few luminaries lined the room. Vents in the ceiling allowed air to flow from above. Would the guards spot them and realize there were more tunnels, as I had when Boaz popped in and out of sight along the street? Though they appeared to be drains, not air vents. If they wised up, the guards would know drains were irrelevant in the Mining Territory. All the water had to be dug from below ground. No rain had blessed this area of the world since the war.

"Come, sit." Fallon pulled out a chair for me. Ryker sat to

my side, and Emery squatted in a nearby corner playing with her red ball.

I shifted, unable to control the excessive energy flowing through my body. After all these years, I finally had a chance to talk to an old friend of Father's.

I glanced down at Emery.

Fallon tapped a warm hand on mine. "It's okay. She still hears us. It's just, her brain shuts down when overloaded by emotion. But she'll store the information and use it when needed." Fallon sighed and leaned back. "At least that's what we believe."

"Valencia? You all right?" Ryker went to grab my hand but I shied away. Not sure why except it just seemed wrong to find comfort when so many suffered around me from the misery I'd brought down on them.

"I'm fine." I forced my best princess blank face and turned to Fallon. "How did you know my father?"

"We fought side-by-side during the war. Even after, he remained part of a hidden underground resistance against the queen."

After? That would mean he was in the active resistance while raising me in the Resort Territory? Father lied to me?

"No. My father couldn't have. I was there, with him, always." Was my time of a perfect life, before I was forced to live on a ship, a lie?

"It's true." Fallon grasped my hand.

I shot up, knocking down the chair behind me. All this touching. After four years of solitude, it was uncomfortable, awkward...wrong.

Stale, dirty air caught in my lungs. I coughed and wheezed

but couldn't catch my breath. Ryker appeared at my side. Hands pressed to my back.

"No." I shoved him away.

"I know this is a lot to comprehend. But if you will hear me out, you'll understand, and it might help you figure out exactly who you are."

I stood under one of the vents and tried to imagine fresh air entering my lungs.

Was this the hiding place I'd always dreamed of?

Lights popped, but nothing melted. I forced the anxiety down but still refused Ryker's help.

How could I trust these people? They wanted a war. That they wanted me to be the leader of a resistance was bad enough, but to think I could lead them against my mother and win was beyond foolish.

Yet how could I not?

"Before the war, your father was a researcher, a leader in the robotics engineering department at a top facility. He fell in love and married a brilliant woman with a heart of gold." His eyes stared off in the distance, clenching his jaw tight. "Your father kept a secret, as did everyone else who possessed gifts. History passed down from generation to generation warns of the hatred and fear of our kind."

"If my mother was so great, how did she become so...hateful?"

Fallon pressed his lips together and lowered his head. "The queen lost her arm and leg during the war and was left to die. She thought the man she loved had betrayed her. The general pulled her from a burning building, and he's been her second in command ever since. Valencia, she despises Mualites because she believes they turned her husband against her."

"I don't understand. The war started because Mualites attacked and murdered people. Why would my father side with them?"

"They didn't. The war started because of fear, power and money. Government against government, pitted against each other by a new race that called themselves Tertians and preached of saving the people from blood-sucking parasites."

I stared at him in shock. Who did I believe? My mother, who wanted me dead, or a man who I barely knew? My head swirled with conflicting thoughts. I didn't know who to believe anymore.

A winded man burst into the room. Deep, red blood stained his light brown shirt. "Must hurry. All executed," he panted. "Evacuating city."

Fallon jumped to his feet. "There's no time. Listen, Valencia, and know—your father was one of us. He blessed you with the gifts of a Mualite. You must choose what to do with it."

No, he had to tell me more. That couldn't be it. "But I'm also half Tertian," I blurted as Ryker retrieved Emery and raced through the corridors after the man.

Fallon paused at the door. "Yes, you have the brain of a Tertian."

CHAPTER TEN

We reached a group being herded into a small shaft. Ryker nodded back the way we'd come. "Emery, you know what to do."

I looked behind us. Dozens of people merged with our group and they all raced for the opening and crawled in. Shots were fired. Explosions shook the underground. Fissures shot through the ceiling.

Emery stopped at the edge of the opening and held her hands above her head. " Valencia, g-go."

I jumped into the small tunnel—so small the walls closed in on me. Gasping for air, I looked back at the illuminated area behind me and met Ryker's eyes.

"Sealing off this tunnel. Get a move on."

My hands shook as Ryker pressed me forward. "Sealing it?"

"Yes, so they don't know of the other area."

Emery charged in as the tunnel behind us collapsed. Screams of terror echoed as darkness fell around us.

Then silence.

No one spoke for a moment. I lay on my belly and closed my eyes trying to imagine myself in a large open field in the Resort Territory. But my mind kept returning to my confinement hole. The small box I'd been forced to crouch in for hours, if not days, when I disobeyed an order or when Mother was in a bad mood. Boaz used to massage my muscles as he unfolded each seizing limb. At least here, I could stretch out flat. Still, my heart thundered in my chest and my eyes tried to focus on an escape route.

A white glow came from ahead. Everyone began to shuffle forward. But each time I scooted ahead, the light moved.

I glanced over my shoulder at Ryker.

His face was barely visible in the muted light. "It's Billy's gift. Bet he's glad he finally saved the day. Always thought his power was useless. Billy always says no use in being branded a parasite if there was no purpose for your gift."

What was my father's gift? Was he really a Mualite? That made no sense. Mother hated parasites. She said they murdered him, they told lies. But then, Fallon had said Mother had a heart of gold.

Biting my lower lip, I admitted to myself my gifts started before I landed in the Mining Territory. Perhaps my father was Mualite, but why would my father keep his identity a secret from me?

A loud thump sounded ahead and the tunnel walls shuddered. Dislodged pebbles fell around us. "Sermechtapedes are attacking!" a woman screeched.

"Stay calm and keep moving. Try to remain silent. They home in on noise," Ryker called out.

Praise the gods, that shut the woman up.

Ryker touched my calf. Even through the boots, his

comfort penetrated the skin and calmed my over-heated emotions.

"The sermechtapedes won't break through the metal supports, don't worry."

Despite my elbows and shoulders aching, I pressed on. Every few meters, whatever lived outside the tunnel would ram it. I passed several bulges. Fear tensed my muscles, readying them for a fight should fleeing prove unsuccessful. But when I looked around, I realized I'd be useless. The only way I'd get the energy to fight would be to use the metal supports in the tunnels. That would be suicide. Without them, we'd be crushed or suffocated by the sand around us.

Twenty minutes later, a light finally shone in the distance. How far outside of town had we gone? Would we be safe once we reached the end of the tunnel, or did it dump into the middle of the sand dunes?

My nails raked against the metal ladder. Arms fatigued, I rested for a moment as others climbed out into the white blur ahead.

"You all right?" Ryker asked from behind.

"Fine." Everything happened so fast, I never had a choice, but once out of the tunnel, I'd take a breath and find out the truth about my father.

If only he were still alive.

I scooted to the edge. Two hands grabbed mine and pulled me from the tunnel. The light shone so brightly I couldn't see.

"You okay, miss?" a strangled voice asked from my side.

"Yes, thank you." Polite, even in my lie. I was so far from okay I doubted I'd ever reach it again. I blinked and shuffled forward until I found a solid wood object to hold onto. I drew in several deep breaths. Warm, humid air carried the smell of foliage and citrus.

A room came into focus and green surrounded me. Fresh air, flowers, and fruit hung from trees. Yet we were inside.

"This place? What is it?" I mumbled.

"It's a hydroponics garden. We've been smuggling our food in from here for years."

A tall, thin man in his mid-thirties grasped my vest. "You shouldn't tell her these things. It's a trick. She doesn't really have powers."

I balled up my fist and punched him in the mouth. He fell back against the wall, then approached again. Fire in his eyes. Literal fire.

I gasped but choked down my surprise.

Ryker jumped between us. "If I were you, I'd think twice before challenging her." His broad shoulders and muscular back flexed as he clenched his fists at his sides.

"Now, you're defending her? You'd fight your own kind over her? She's bewitched you with some sort of Slag device."

"No. It's because she will kill you with one breath of hot air."

"You're lying." The man stepped up and I knew Ryker wouldn't back down.

I pushed him to move out of my way, but his massive frame wouldn't budge, so I ducked around him. "Try me." I steadied my emotions and waited for his response.

Fallon stood behind the man with a smile. "I'd think again. I've seen her powers for myself."

"She's one of them. She's going to save us." A young girl with big green eyes scurried around the angry man, doll clutched in her hands. She tugged on my arm. "I knew you would come."

I looked back at Ryker. He stood still, his jaw clenched. Silver and black hair fell to his temple. Handsome and deadly.

"I have something to show you." The little girl continued to pull me through the room and up some spiral steps. She stared ahead and I turned to see a glowing orange ball in the distance. It was what was left of the town.

"Do you think everyone died and isn't—" Her small frame shuddered, tears streaking down her face. She fell into my arms and convulsed with grief, her long blonde hair soaked with tears. I slid to the ground and held her, the way I'd always wanted to be held.

"Y-you h-have to be the one," the child managed before a young woman came and retrieved her.

"Sorry, she lost her brother and parents today."

I felt the weight of the girl's grief on my shoulders, along with the young woman's who carried her down the spiral steps, as well as every other Mualite and human staring up at me from the bottom of the stairs. How could Mother have ordered the slaughter of so many innocents? According to her, they were deceptive.

No. I looked into their faces and saw the truth. Even if a plot existed to overthrow the world, none of these faces had a clue. All of them looked to me to save them. I'd been groomed from birth to lead the people, but not these people. Then again, if I truly was a half-Mualite, half-Tertian, wasn't it up to me to choose who my people were and to ensure they lived in peace?

Ryker ascended the spiral steps and sat cross-legged by my side. His muscular legs scrunched up against the rail. "Know you want to be alone, but these people need hope. We're the only ones who can give it to them." He raked his hand through his hair. "Hell, don't rightly know if we're destined to save the world or are just a symbol to give our people hope. Doesn't matter. Right now, we can give'em reason enough to go on."

I looked out the smeared windowpane to the distant ball of fire. My stomach churned, then steadied. I couldn't refuse to help the survivors of Mother's mercilessness.

CHAPTER ELEVEN

Fallon leaned against the wall and lowered his head to his knees.

"Is he okay?" I asked.

Ryker closed his eyes; his chest rose and fell. "No, his gift is a curse today. He hears the screams of those left behind."

My heart ached. Everywhere I turned, there was nothing but sadness and death.

Fallon climbed the steps to us and faced the crowd of desperate souls. The orange hue from their burning town reflected off the side of his face. He cleared his throat. "We did not choose this time to fight a war. We did not want this or ask for this. Now, it has been forced upon us and we must face it. Each of us will play a role in freeing all who wish to no longer live under the tyranny of a dictator. Once again, humans, Tertians, and Mualites alike will be free."

The crowd cheered. Fallon stepped aside and Ryker moved in front, his shoulders back. His solid jawline and deep voice commanded attention. He was born to lead. "Uncle Fallon had warned me of the great price of war. I should've listened. I've wanted to earn our freedom for so many years, but I had no idea the suffering that would occur. Now I understand, and I will do everything in my power to ensure the safety of those that have escaped—"

"We're still not safe. There are Slags here!"

Ryker held up one hand. "Now, that's a big concern. But, Valencia isn't one of them. Yes, she's a Slag princess, but she's also one of us in talent. Great abilities like our ancestors' course through her veins. Abilities that will help free all of us from the bonds of captivity."

This wasn't his fight alone. I needed to speak, but what could I say? Stepping up, I joined Ryker and lifted my head to address the crowd as I'd been taught. They needed inspiration, the will to fight to stay alive. "We have suffered a great loss. We all grieve. But in the name and spirit of friends and family lost to this atrocity, we will fight. And we will persevere."

Claps echoed off the sand-colored glass dome overhead. I had no idea where those words came from, but they rolled off my tongue as if I'd been born to say them. I followed Ryker's lead and raised my hand to quiet the crowd. Anxious faces stared, waiting for me to speak. "I've witnessed firsthand the loss of loved ones. The murder of innocent lives is never acceptable. There are those who doubt my loyalty to the cause. I am here to reassure you that I will never support the unlawful and unjust. I will always defend those who wish to live in peace."

I glanced back at Ryker, then offered my hand to Fallon. These people needed a united front, no fractures in leadership. No dictator. They looked to us for hope. "Fallon is right." I continued. "From this moment forward, we cannot afford to view one another as different, but must embrace each other for the greater good. Humans, Tertians, and Mualites no longer exist. We are not defined by our abilities but by our actions. We are now the resistance to tyranny, no longer its victim. As a first step, I will use my ability to remove all the collars from those wearing them."

Cheers erupted so loudly it rang in my ears. The words I'd spoken—they came to me in my father's voice. A memory? Was Fallon telling the truth? Was my father really part of a resistance?

We stepped back as the crowd continued to cheer and boisterous conversations continued.

"You are your father's child," Fallon whispered to me. My insides warmed at his compliment. "Once you fulfill your promise, both of you and Emery need to head out. Boaz is making preparations for your journey," Fallon said.

My dry lips cracked as they tugged into a smile. "He's here?"

"Yes, he couldn't return to the ship. The bombing came too quickly. He risked his life to save many. Distracted the guards while people were lined up for execution. They escaped before the queen ordered the bombing." Fallon's nostrils flared.

Ryker's hands clenched around the railing. It creaked. I saw the anger in his eyes.

Fallon led us down the stairs and through a narrow corridor. "She didn't even wait for her own guards to evacuate. A few of them made it through. I've given them clothes, but I'll have to keep an eye on them at night. Not many will accept them. Although, after Valencia's speech, maybe others will realize we are all in this together."

Fallon's hope for cooperation was an ideal, but he hadn't lived with my mother's guards. I had. "I caution you. Most guards will do anything to survive. They also want nothing but the rewards of the queen. Trust me. I've learned the hard way that they'll do anything to earn her gratitude. So don't let them see your people until after I've removed the collars."

Fallon only returned a forced smile, then continued to lead us through a long hall to a series of rooms full of sleeping bunks, a cafeteria, and an exercise and combat training room.

A handful of Mualites waited for us in the center of the cafeteria. Two metal boxes rested on the table. Without a word, I approached and pressed my right hand to one of the metal boxes, and my left to one collar.

Ryker joined me, pressing his hand to my shoulder. "Be here if you lose control."

Emery stood to my side and nodded.

I took a deep breath and harnessed the warm spark deep in my body.

Power surged without interruption between the box and the collar.

The Mualite's dark eyes shot wide as the collar bubbled then fell from his neck. "Triune," he whispered.

"You're welcome," I answered, assuming that meant *thank you* in Mualite.

After the fifth collar, it became natural. Ryker removed his hand from my shoulder. "You've got this."

After removing dozens on my own, it became an assembly line of blurred faces until the last little girl was brought in, the one who'd lost her mother.

"Knew you'd save us." Her tiny hands touched my elbow as I pressed my fingers to her collar. I was thankful for the many collars I'd already practiced removing. With little effort, the dark contraption fell from her neck. "Triune."

Someone escorted her out the door then I fell back into a chair exhausted.

Ryker's mouth curved up on one side as he looked down at me. "You be a hero now."

Before I had a chance to respond, he turned to his uncle. "Uncle, I've not heard any banging. Why aren't the sermechta-pedes attacking this facility? They must hear us here," Ryker said.

"Over the past several years, we were able to copy the technology surrounding the town. Boaz smuggled the pieces we needed. We're able to harness power from the sun. The only danger is when we have to lift the solar panels out of the sand to charge the facility." Fallon looked around and dropped his voice. "If the queen discovers this bunker, there'll be no place left for us to run."

Sizzles deep inside echoed in my eardrums. Why I didn't spontaneously combust at times, I'd never understand. Would my powers ever calm down?

Fallon pulled out a geo-map and placed it on a long wooden table.

Ryker snarled. "Wait. How'd you get your hands on a Slag device? Not touching that thing. We don't need their stuff."

"You want to carry twenty-two maps with you, be my guest. If not, listen up." Fallon touched the pocket-sized black device and a three-dimensional topography popped up. "There is some difficult terrain between here and the scout ship. Mostly wasteland. We've acquired sand surfers for you, but there will be sections that are too dangerous and you'll have to continue on sand boots. Once you reach the scout ship—"

"If we reach it," Ryker muttered.

Fallon ignored him and continued. "Once at the scout ship, you'll head east." He pressed the green button on the lower right side of the device and a new map displayed. "You'll arrive in scavenger territory here. You'll offer them a gift we'll provide you in exchange for supplies and fuel. Then continue to Old Chicago." His voice hitched. "It was a major city during the human reign. The city could still be radioactive. You'll have to use masks."

"Scavengers? Are you insane? They'll just capture us and do who knows what."

Fallon nodded. "Maybe, but for the right price they'll help you instead."

Ryker grumbled.

My mind raced remembering the few scavengers I'd seen from a distance. Men with alterations unlike that of the council. Ink patterns covered their bodies, and they walked around half-dressed with piercings and all sorts of other crazy alterations. I shivered.

"Why don't we just avoid Old Chicago if it's radioactive?" Ryker asked.

I stared down at the maps. The distance looked doable on them, but I knew different. I'd traveled to the other side of the Wasteland to reach the steam trains that joined the capital to other cities aboard my mother's ship. Even in her massive, well-gunned ship, we had to be cautious.

I did the math in my head. "We'll need fuel. Those are diesel-powered ships. The scout ships are too small for a reactor to supply nuclear power."

"That's right," Fallon agreed. "There are rumors of a fueling station there. It's your only hope. Only the northern regions and council ships are still using oil-based energy and steam power."

"Fine." Ryker looked over the maps, seeing, I knew, the multitude of dangers we'd have to somehow make it through. "But Emery stays here."

"You need her, Ryker. You'll never make it across the Wasteland without her and you know it." Fallon's lips drooped into a frown of obvious guilt.

My mind went over all the details, but one piece didn't quite fit right. "There's something you're not telling us," I said.

His frown turned into a wry smile. "Yes, refueling's not all you need to do in Old Chicago. You'll also find a valuable asset to our people. She's been a relay point between a spy we had on the Queen's ship and the ENR."

"ENR?" I asked.

"European Mualite Rebellion," Fallon answered. "Our spy was compromised and we believe has been killed. We need to reach our contact in Old Chicago before the queen discovers her location. The last communication we received indicated that our contact had discovered something that could swing power into our favor."

This was getting more complicated by the second. Too many things could go wrong. Mother could be en route to the same location we were headed. "If we find this person and refuel, then what? The scout ship won't carry four."

Ryker's eyebrows furrowed. "What kind of power?"

"We don't know, but our contact is one of the original fighters from the war. If she says it is important, it is." Fallon rubbed his chin. "She's...resourceful. You shouldn't have a problem. If she's still alive, rescue her and continue east through several other smaller, abandoned cities and one territory. From what we understand, the Horticulture Territory is run by humans. They don't want trouble because they deal in Verillian juice and Arvenati leaves. Scavenger activity is high there. If possible, I'd avoid contact. I'd advise you to study these maps as you go. Try to find alternate routes if possible."

Fallon clicked the green button again and old ruins on the edge of a large body of water appeared. "This is your ultimate goal. From there, you'll find a boat in the Trading Territory. We've sent communication to secure your ride. You'll have to make it to the coast in three days. After that, they won't wait. The council regulates all trade, and schedules are rigidly kept. It's at great risk they're smuggling you aboard. It's imperative you deliver our contact, or whatever information she has, to the ENR."

"If there's trade between the Horticulture Territory and Arcadia, why don't we stow on one of those ships?" Ryker asked.

"Their trade is via the train, but only twice a month. We don't have the luxury of time. Besides, they also don't enter the Wasteland. Scavengers usually deliver goods to the city outskirts in exchange for, well, company."

I shook my head. "You're talking about going to Acadia West and East. All the council resides there. We'd never make it."

"That's why you'll use the scout ship and divert around," Fallon said.

I shifted nervously by Ryker's side. "This is all great, but from what I understand, the sermechtapedes will devour us before we make it a meter in the sand."

A ventilation shaft flapped open with a bang overhead. Boaz dropped onto a tall metal storage unit, climbed down a ladder on the side, and grinning, stopped at my side.

My mouth curled into a smile for a moment then I pressed my lips together in a thin line. I wanted to scoop him into my arms and fall on the floor crying, but I didn't have the luxury of being a needy child anymore. "I am pleased to see you again, Boaz," I addressed him with a formal tone, keeping distance so that I wouldn't lose my composure.

He laughed and hugged my leg. I tried to ignore the feeling of comfort, to remain cold. It was the only way I could continue without falling apart. My shoulders tensed, but I patted the top of his head. "Um…yes…well, you have prepared something for our journey?"

"Yes, yes."

Fallon shook his head and opened the storage door. "First, here is the gift for the scavengers. It's all we could gather. There should be enough coins there to buy their help. Also, there is food, emergency supplies, and clothes for your task. Boaz even smuggled water from the ship." He placed the supplies on a nearby wooden table. "We have three each of goggles, pistols, and masks, but only one repeller." He set a metal chip on the table.

"That's an implant!" I yelled and stumbled back. "I…I won't—"

"It interacts with your thoughts and allows you to repel the desert creatures. It's the only way you can cross the sands, but it's not for you." Fallon looked behind him as Emery skipped to their side.

My head swam. "Emery? No."

"She already possesses the necessary metal in her leg to conduct the current. It has to be her."

"But she doesn't have the ability to process an implant," Ryker argued. "She's not a—"

"Her brain was altered during her captivity. We believe—"

"Believe! Believe? You're insane." Ryker stepped in front of Emery. "You're not going to touch my sister with that contraption."

I took the device from Boaz. It was the size of a thumbnail. Frowning, I traced the disk's smooth surface and serrated edges.

"She's the only one—"

"No, she isn't. I can." It was the least I could do. "I know how much you both despise technology. Your sister has suffered enough. Boaz, this is the only way we can cross the desert? You know this for sure?"

"Nothing for sure."

I analyzed the silver and bronze device. Four small holes, where the wires would shoot out and connect to my brain, dotted the center. It was so tiny, yet the significance of the device was greater than the room we stood in. "Is there no one in the group with the ability to repel these creatures? No back-up plan?"

Fallon pinched the bridge of his nose. "Yes, there was. He died in the fires back in town. This was the back-up plan."

Ryker crossed his arms over his chest. "I'll go alone. Maybe I can maneuver without sound and the sermechtapedes and spiderats won't detect me."

"You know that's not an option," I said. "Let's get it over with." I sat down in a chair and brushed my hair from my eyes.

"Wait. I could take the implant," Ryker offered.

"You don't possess the brain power of a Tertian. You'd die instantly. The chip inserts directly into the brainstem." My voice came steady and cold. "I'm the only choice."

Tears slid down my cheek even though I didn't feel like crying. Boaz placed the implant in a small device and pressed it to my skin behind my ear.

Ryker squatted next to me. For the first time, grief threatened to expose me for the coward I truly was. My lip trembled and I sucked it in, biting it to keep it still.

Ryker squeezed my shoulder. "It can always be removed once this is over."

"No, it can't. It's permanent." I straightened and wiped away the tears. "I'm ready."

He stood and snatched the map from the table. "Wait, we could—"

Snap...crunch...hiss.

CHAPTER TWELVE

Wires plunged through my skull with a loud crunch, the sound echoing as they snaked through my head and slithered under my scalp, binding human anatomy with technology.

Eyes stung. Ears popped. I smashed my hands against my temples and stifled a cry. Every nerve synapse convulsed at the intrusion, forcing me to breathe through the pain and the intimate invasion of the device.

I squinted against the searing pain in time to see Ryker turning his back on me and striding out the door. He couldn't stand to look at me. Heck, I couldn't stand to face myself in the mirror. For just a day, I'd thought I could escape my fate. Now, I realized fate wouldn't be cheated. It was inevitable. It forced me to finally face my greatest fear, trapped in the world of Mualites in the body of a Slag princess.

A metallic taste lingered in my mouth, and my head ached. I ran my fingers against the edge of the device, unsure what I expected yet surprised it had the same sense of touch as my skin, only amplified. I tapped my nail against the hard surface and it shot a current into my right eye, causing teary blinking.

How did Emery handle an entire leg with such intense sensations? Is that what caused her to slip in and out of reality? No, that was from the abuse Mother had inflicted on her. I shook off the feeling of dread. Unlike Emery, with her massive bronze appendage, the small device was hidden beneath my hair and behind my ear. Thank goodness I hadn't cut it any shorter. No one would ever know unless they inspected under my hair. And maybe, just maybe, I could master control of the implant to such a degree that one day I could remove it.

Boaz ran his oil-stained hand down my cheek, his calluses scraping my skin. "Things not as bad as you think. Those in need thank you, not condemn."

Emery hopped up onto the metal table at my side and laid her cheek on my shoulder. "I won't b-be alone now. You're like m-me."

"Yes, Emery . Just like you."

Fallon gave a reassuring smile. "We'll give you two a minute. I'm going to check on a few things." He and Boaz headed out the door.

This was my chance. "Emery, I...I don't want to upset you, but we need to talk."

Emery sighed and lifted her head. "I-I know."

"Do you remember me?"

Emery gave a half-smile, a haunted smile, and took my hand. It was identical to the way I had stroked Emery's that night Boaz and I had hidden her in the engine room. Her fever had been so high I'd feared the girl would die at any moment.

"You s-saved m-me and are m-my friend."

My heart warmed that Emery still thought of me after all

these years, but she was wrong. "I'm so sorry." Tears spilled down my cheeks. "I should've done more." Terror seeped in at the memory of that night. "I tossed you from the ship—" I broke at the weight of my words.

"You had no choice. Your m-mother was on her way."

Four years of suppressed guilt surfaced in one breath and the weight of it crushed my insides. "I should've stood up to her. Done something."

"Sh-she would've killed us b-both."

Emery spoke the truth. There hadn't been a choice, yet I knew the horrific thing I had done to Emery. "I never knew if you lived or—" I doubled over, unable to finish.

Emery hummed and stroked my hair. "I lived b-because of you."

My heart warmed at the thought, but I knew the truth. I'd dumped Emery in the Wasteland to die. "If you believe that, then why didn't you tell Ryker about me and my role in your leg being altered?"

Emery laughed. "Th-they say I'm the c-crazy one. Ryker's s-spent four years wanting to murder the one who did th-this to me. Reason isn't his s-strong s-suit."

My stomach knotted with the realization. "Ryker will not only hate me, but he'll kill me when he learns the truth."

"I think w-we should keep this s-secret. You're my f-friend, V-Valencia. M-my b-best friend. I-I can't lose you t-to my crazy brother." She locked pinkies with me and giggled before retreating into her world of humming again.

"And you've always been and will always be my best friend." A promise made between two naive twelve-year-old girls hidden in the dark of a dirty engine room had come true.

Fallon shuffled through the door with his arms full. "Gear

up and get ready. If you don't make it to the coast by the third sunset, all this will be for nothing."

I turned my head away to hide the evidence of my tears. Hopefully, if anyone saw them, they'd think they were because of the implant. Ryker joined us and gave me an awkward sideways glance. My belly flopped at his distance.

"You never mentioned how we'd return," I said. My head throbbed with each thought.

Fallon scrubbed his chin. "I don't believe you will. Even with fuel, that engine won't make it round trip. It's a short-range airship. The engine will be shot by the time you reach the ocean."

"If we reach it," I added.

No one protested. They all knew it was true. Ryker donned his gear, stuck the coin in his belt, and walked to the other end of the storage area. "Let's get this farce over with."

Sliding the goggles over my hair, I pulled on my jacket, lacing the hood tight around my ears. I grabbed the rough, four-foot sand surfer. I'd been on something similar in the Resort Territory, but wasn't confident I could maneuver it after all these years.

Emery pulled a large black sock-looking thing on over her slag leg, mounted her board and steadied herself with surprising grace.

The outer door opened. Hot sand blew against our bodies. Hearing a click behind me, I spun around only to realize it was the implant. With a sigh, I pulled the mask and goggles over my face. Between the mask, goggles, and hood, no skin was exposed. Surfboard in hand, I moved in front of Emery and Ryker.

I dropped the board to the ground, climbed atop it, and

positioned both feet shoulder-width apart. It wobbled slightly, but then I balanced. I lifted my right leg, snapped the back lever, and after a sputter, it took off.

I skimmed the sea of golden sand for almost sixty meters, then crashed. A wave of orange blanketed me. I pushed through the thick layer of harsh grains as Ryker crashed into my side, sending me once again face down into the grit.

Emery spun around in the air and landed gracefully next to us. Apparently, she'd mastered the device. The tiny, frail, one-legged girl never ceased to amaze me, be it now or four years ago.

Ryker freed himself from the sand. Straddling the board, he swiped his goggles clean, then offered his hand to me, his massive biceps stretching against black fabric. "Need help?"

"No. I've got it," I said, inching away from him. I didn't want to touch him—to feel something, even momentarily, that I could never have.

I mounted the board, shot forward, flipped several times, and performed another nose-plant. The mask slipped to the side and sand filled it. I removed it, shook the gritty particles out and repositioned the mask. I tightened it, my teeth grinding the coarse grains between them.

Determined to succeed, I straddled my board and looked at Emery hovering in the sky.

Sand rippled away from my boot pressed against the ground. My board vibrated. An enormous worm-like creature shot from the sand and bent in the air. Enormous pincers clicked and saliva splattered on my goggles before it plunged back into the sandy abyss. I jerked back and my board sailed out from under me, sending me backward into the sand.

"Sermechtapede!" Emery screamed through her mask, but only a muffled sound reached me.

High-pitched squeals. Searing pain. I clutched my head trying to keep it from exploding. The implant. It wanted something. I concentrated on the beast, then realized it wasn't just one. Dozens of creatures dove in and out of the sand.

Plates surrounded their heads like a Triceratops I'd seen in an old archeology book. Long wrinkled bodies were half hidden below ground. Yellow eyes with large black slits blinked at me from several meters away. Then thousands of small legs jetted out from its sides.

Every muscle in my body tightened. Wires fired inside my head, and I concentrated on the beast. It swayed back and forth in the air.

I met its gaze. Each wire vibrated against my skin and nerves. The electric impulses created an itch deep inside my head where I could never scratch.

Something registered, like the smell of ash in my brain, yet I didn't detect the odor through my nose. A snap and click between my ears, and a metallic taste, warned of invasion. My body waged war with the implant.

I shook my head and refocused.

Emery and Ryker joined me. We huddled together near Ryker and his board.

"Is it working? Get rid of it or we're all worm food." Ryker shouted through his mask.

"Trying to focus." Throbbing head. Burning eyes. Shaking hands. The sermechtapede jettisoned into the sky from our right. Its jaws spread wide. Thousands of razor-sharp fangs reflected the orange sun. Warm liquid with the aroma of a waste containment area dropped in large pools on my head.

"Odvratno! Awk!" Ryker wiped his forehead and flung the saliva to the ground.

The creature burrowed down and disappeared into the distance.

I held my head, wishing the throbbing pain away. After a moment, the implant returned control of my mind and body. Remnants of a metallic taste remained in my mouth along with a dull zapping sound in my ears. The constant hum, I realized, would be permanent.

Emery flung her arms around my shoulders. "You d-did it."

Ryker scooted off his board and sunk down. "Not sure it was her. Rumors say they don't feed during mating. They hunt solo but mate in groups."

Ryker held up his board.

"Looks like we're down to two boards." He ran his finger down a crack from lever to tip.

I scanned the horizon and saw mine resting in two pieces. "One board," I said, pointing at mine a few meters away.

"Guess w-we walk. It sh-shouldn't be too m-much farther to the s-scout ship." Emery pulled her sand boot on one foot and laced a tan material around the bottom of her other one. She pushed up from the dirt and shuffled ahead.

"You both could return and let me continue on alone," I said.

Ryker tucked the only surviving sand surfer under his arm. "No. If we ever make it to the rebels, you'll need me to help convince them you're not a spy. They'd kill you on sight with that...um—"

"I got it. Let's go." I pushed up onto my knees then stood and wobbled. Ryker grabbed me. Instantly, a shot of cool sting ran through my body and the connection was restored between us. I couldn't move—the humming of the implant, the horrible itch in my head, the feeling of a foreign object lodged in my brain disappeared. For a moment, I didn't feel like a Slag. I was just a girl who wanted to press closer against him and feel his touch against my hot skin. Instead, I forced myself to step to the side and join Emery.

Every time we touched, I remembered how much I now disgusted him. Distance? I needed to shut the door on this and stay as far away from him as possible. He'd never kept it a secret how he felt about Slags. I knew the only reason he tolerated my presence was to save his people.

The sun beat down on us as we trudged up a large dune. Rivers of sweat ran down my back. I pulled my mask to the side and took a few sips of water. We'd have to be cautious not to waste a drop.

A monstrous hill rose from the sand ahead. Groaning, I looked back at the embers glowing behind us. How far had we traveled? The sun dropped low in the sky and the moon was already a large sphere in the distance. I feared we'd traveled too far and missed the ship. At the top of the hill, I'd know for sure.

My thigh muscles burned with each step. The incline was so steep I had to crawl up the last few meters, clawing myself forward inch by inch. I stood up on shaking legs. Emery was already scanning the distance and Ryker appeared behind me, scanning the area behind.

I pivoted in all directions, surveying our surroundings. True to its name, the Wasteland was nothing but kilometer upon kilometer of sand, stretching behind, before, and to each side of us. Could my metallic senses have failed? Could we have walked right over the ship? Fallon assumed that my powers would work to locate the ship, but it was just a theory, so would I even recognize it if I stubbed my toe on it?

Gasping, I bent at the waist and rested my hands on my knees. Between the poor air quality and physical activity, I could barely breathe.

Ryker rested his hands on my shoulders. "Relax, think metal. See if your gift'll home in on it."

"I'm trying. It's not working." I winced at the frustration in my voice. Clearing my throat, I hoped he thought my raised voice was due to the mask.

I let my vision blur and released control of my body. A faint, deep roar sounded. Maybe I heard metal instead of feeling it or seeing it? Before I could say a word, Ryker rammed into me, sending us tumbling down the hill. My shoulder smacked against something hard, but I continued rolling.

The world spun. My hip connected with Ryker. Or was it Emery? With one final jolt, we three landed in a huddle at the bottom.

Metal. My body had come in contact with metal on the way down. It was the ship.

I tried to move from the huddle, but Ryker pulled me close and we sunk into the sand. His arms and legs wrapped around me, and Emery dug in close behind.

A craft buzzed overhead, paused for a second, then continued toward the village.

"Long-range probe. Probably been flying 'round here for years. Only reports if it finds something. We should be okay. I don't think it saw us," Ryker said in a muffled tone.

Emery pulled away and dug herself out of the sand. Ryker's arms remained around me, only our heads above ground. Eye to eye, our bodies pressed together, chest to chest. The world stopped as he rested his forehead against mine. My rapid heartbeat matched his.

Before I had a chance to enjoy the moment, he released me and brushed the sand off his body. "Mighty close call," he said.

Emery hummed and played in the sand. Our being nearly discovered was too much for her.

I sat up. I couldn't take the teasing anymore. Each time we came close, the implant disappeared and the world looked brighter.

Instead of taking his hand like I wanted to, I rolled on my side and let the sand fall off my body. Once it all flowed to the ground, I pulled my knees in and wrenched to the side to stand.

Somewhere up that hill was the ship. *But how will I ever get it out?* Even if I literally bumped into it, which I doubted—more likely my body reacted to it—the ship would be too heavy to pull out.

Ryker pushed the last sand surfer, now broken in half, and scooted over next to me. "You've sensed something, haven't you?"

"Maybe." I concentrated on metal and tried to visualize the sleek lines down the wings of the ship, but nothing happened. "I don't know."

"Your eyes, they...changed. You do sense something."

"I thought I did when we rolled down the hill, but now, nothing."

Ryker pinched the bridge of his nose. "Try to visual—"

"I already have!" I sighed. "Sorry, it's just that—" I tried to think of something to say, but no words came.

Ryker grasped my hand tightly so I couldn't easily pull

away. "This is difficult, I know." His eyes pulsed through the goggles. "Stay calm."

"Stop." I tried to tug my hand away but his grip tightened. Searing heat rushed from my body, replaced by soothing frost. His eyebrows arched, touching the bronze rims of the goggles.

"Stop what?"

"You know," I whispered.

"So my touch soothes you as yours does me." He pulled the mask down and smiled. "I wasn't sure it still did, but I'd hoped."

"It doesn't matter. Right now we need to focus on that ship."

Wind whipped through the sand dunes, sending grains dancing around us. Then I saw it, the bare tip of the wing, the color monochromatic to the surrounding dirt. My heart thundered in my chest as I scurried up to it.

Ryker dusted off more dirt and his mask rose as his cheeks tugged upward into a smile. "You did it."

"No, the wind did."

Emery's childlike laugh echoed. "No, s-silly. I-it's you."

Had Emery altered the sand? Perhaps Fallon was right and she never totally disappeared into her mind, just shut the world off from communication so her brain could process.

Ryker wrapped his fingers around the luminary at the edge of the wing. His feet plunged so deeply into the sand it looked as if his legs were amputated above his knees. His back muscles bulged and threatened to rip his jacket, yet the wing didn't budge. "I need something to brace my legs on so that I can excavate the ship." Finally, he admitted defeat and sat back.

I smoothed my hand over the royal gold emblem. The letter Q with an MS inside the circle. Queen Mordica Sade. My mother. The raised surface scraped my palm. A feeling of a dozen feathers swooshed up and down my arm. From the metal, or the thought of my mother, I wasn't sure.

The wing trembled. I gasped and yanked my hand away. Warm, stale air entered my lungs and I coughed.

The wing shook.

Ryker's eyes grew wide. "Don't stop now. Do it."

My body honed in on the ship until a hairy black stump protruded from the sand. A shiny tip slid out. It continued to protract until the stump morphed into a long leg that extended over the side of the ship. It raked across the bare metal with a loud squealing sound.

I let go of the wing and shifted to the implant. Another long leg shot up from the other side of the sand dune and then another.

Terror ripped through my body. There were four…no five spider-like creatures. I tried to concentrate on all of them, but couldn't. The implant hissed when I focused on two at once, but I continued and added a third. Each leg retracted.

A fourth spider scurried closer. I stretched my mind to stop it but lost the other two. The implant shocked me and my brain vibrated with one continual electric charge. A sharp tip on the hairy appendage shot at Ryker. I grabbed a knife from my belt and launched myself up on the wing, stabbing its leg.

Ryker rolled and jumped to his feet. "Watch out!

Another hairy appendage speared my thigh. Searing pain from my head collided with the burning in my leg. It dragged me several meters and yanked me down until I was half-covered in sand.

I screamed...head spun...stomach churned. My mask slipped off and dirt invaded my nose and mouth. I clawed at the sand, trying to find purchase, but the creature wouldn't release me.

CHAPTER THIRTEEN

Ryker straddled the ship's wing and plunged the splintered wood of the sand surfer into the abdomen of the spiderat. It screeched and convulsed. Brownish-gray liquid flowed from the edges of the board to the ground, making the sand into muck.

Several more dark hairy legs sprouted from the depths of the neverending sand. A massive round body emerged behind Emery.

"Help her!" I shouted. Kicking with my one good leg, I tried to keep the sand from consuming me. Then I noticed something shiny sticking out of one of the spiderat appendages. *My knife.*

Ryker yelled at Emery . "I'll lead them away. Get Valencia!" He slid down the wing, landed on his sand boots, and pumped his arms and legs with fury, moving away from us. The spiderat behind Emery chased Ryker.

"Emery, knife." I pointed. Sweat burned my eyes. My heart thrashed against my ribs. The creature continued to burrow down; I'd be under the sand in seconds. "Help!"

Emery tumbled down the sand and slid to a halt by one of the other spiderat legs. She snatched the knife out and tossed it to me. I plunged the blade into the spiderat leg still piercing my thigh. It shook and squealed below ground. Eight dark, glossy eyes peered up from the sand and focused on Emery. I grabbed the prickly leg and shoved the knife in again. Black wings sprouted up like wind sails on a trading ship, red veins in a maze pattern pulsing with each flutter.

I yanked the knife free and plunged it in again.

It squawked like a dying hawk. The wings billowed and the spider curled the spike in further. I cried out. Pain shot down my leg and up to my hip. I focused on the small middle eye. It had to have a brain.

It lifted its head up from the sand. Pincers snapped at me. Pain trapped air in my lungs, my head spun, vision blurred, but I refused to faint.

I clutched the blade in my right hand, keeping the creature's pincer at bay with my boot. Leaning up, I knifed it in that middle eye with all my strength. The claw retracted. Blood gushed from the wound in my thigh.

The creature opened its mouth and flapped twice, hovering over me. Glacial blue streaks shot over my head. I looked behind me to see Ryker climbing the sand dune shooting strings of energy at the spiderat.

"Hovno!" He gasped and stumbled back, but recovered quickly.

The blue streaks penetrated the spiderat and the animal screeched, flinging itself to the side barely a few paces away from me.

Ryker fell to his knees heaving beside my head. The creature frantically moved back and forth another meter before it collapsed. Warm, brackish saliva exploded from between two pincers all over us.

I struggled to stay conscious. Two more creatures flew overhead, flinging silk threads and ramming each other as they fought over the body of the one Ryker had killed.

"Over h-here!" Emery's voice echoed from the other side of the ship.

Ryker held me in his arms. Red stained our clothing. Crimson ran across the sand around us. So much blood.

He dragged me across the sand to the other side of the ship, fell to his knees, and pulled his mask away. "Listen to me, you ain't gonna die. You got that?" He ran his finger down my cheek. With one hand pressed against my thigh and one above the wound, he stared down at my leg. Swirls of silver spun in his eyes and the inside of my leg stitched back together with little pain.

Emery stood by our side, keeping watch on the creatures fighting over their meal.

He paused and lifted the pressure from my thigh. "Small fibers left behind from the spiderat complicate things. Fibers can't stay inside; they could cause severe infection." He wiped his forehead.

"Wh-why do you w-wait?" Emery asked.

"Need more energy. Must kill off the hair, but that'd drain me. If I don't heal, she'll die of infection."

"You m-must try." Emery grasped his hands, pleading with moist eyes. "Sh-she's s-special."

"Don't. Leave me. Get Emery out of here." I finally managed, barely above a whisper, but he only ignored me.

A sizzle sounded from inside and the smell of burnt spider hair flooded the air. Itching, burning, fire...pain. "Ah! Stop."

He pulled back. "Sorry. This isn't gonna feel too good. Don't have time or energy for the anesthetic part of my gift to work." He gripped down like an iron vice around my thigh.

I tried to pull away, but I was too weak to fight. Tears streamed down my face. Icy darkness shot deep into my body. I screamed and clawed at his hands.

Intense pressure mounted deep in my leg. I could hear bone crack and feel muscle fibers re-lacing. My tendons stretched and heat surged as they melted back together. "Can't seal skin all the way though." Ryker exhaled.

His hands shook.

I clenched my jaw, attempting to drive the piercing icicles from my body.

"It's over...rest," he rasped between labored breaths while stroking my hair.

"Emery, I—" he gasped, "—can't finish healing her." He lifted the water jug to his lips, then to mine. Smooth, cool water caressed my throat on the way down.

Aeek. The Spiderats sounded.

Emery nodded. "They finished their snack."

Ryker grabbed the supply bag and dug through it. "Really? Who would've..." He retrieved a first aid kit. "Uncle."

I chuckled at the thought of a guy who could heal anyone having a first aid kit handy.

With antiseptic, needle and thread in hand, Ryker faced me with soft eyes. I cringed and scooted away. "No, just bandage it. I'll be—"

Hot wind whipped through, stirring sand around us and he hunched over my wound. Coolness radiated up and down my leg, massaging my muscles until they relaxed.

"Ever done this before? I'm thinking no, since you can heal people," I mumbled.

"Never touched a needle and thread, but it's the same basic principle." His hands shook, betraying his confident tone.

Emery crawled to his side. "Here, l-let me." She took the supplies from him, ran the thread through the eye and handed it back to him.

If I survived all of this, it would be a miracle. He tore my pants and cleaned the wound. He studied the raised white skin on my thigh above the wound. "What happened?"

I wanted to shield my scars from him, but he'd already seen them. My mind slid back to the day the general had taught me a lesson, and I could only shake my head.

He poured the antiseptic over my wound. It bubbled a foamy rust color. Small cries escaped my lips, but the thought of attracting more creatures of the Wasteland empowered me to clench my jaw tight to keep from screaming.

Ryker wrapped his arms around me and held me tight against him. "Shh. Know it hurts, but it'll pass."

My mind whirled through the moments of hatred in his eyes, then to all the touchy-feely times. I knew it was just the Mualite way. A few days ago, I would have never believed a Tertian princess would end up wounded and in the arms of a Cursed.

His tan skin, rugged jawline, and muscular body drew me in, but his loyalty to his people and his compassion wrapped its tentacles around my heart and squeezed tight. Never had I met someone so strong with such a gentle and kind touch.

Ryker leaned back on his heels. As he pressed his hands against my thigh, a tingle danced across my skin, but it didn't last long. He wobbled and fell to his elbow.

Emery helped him upright. "You c-can't use your power anym-more."

Ryker shook his head. "Only want to dull the pain some."

"I'll be fine." I swallowed hard and stared over his shoulder, refusing to show my fear.

"I'm sorry," he said as he pushed the tip of the needle into my bare skin.

I sucked in a deep breath, refusing to cry or scream. The smells of alcohol and blood overpowered my nose, but I ignored them and continued to stare into the distance. My vision blurred into orange waves.

Skin pulled and stretched. My stomach churned when he pushed the needle up the other side of my tender flesh. It was no worse than the zap of a laser with no anesthetic. I'd been conditioned to take my punishment without screaming. This was no different.

"Should've protected you."

My heart soared at his words despite the little voice inside my head reminding me he was never going to be an option.

"Mission is to get you to Acadia. I won't fail again."

My chest constricted. *That's all I am, a mission.*

Thread laced through another piece of skin, burning as it pulled quickly through.

Emery squatted by his side and blotted his forehead. He continued for ten more stitches. "Should keep dirt and germs out. Must be more creatures around here. I'll try to steal some energy if I get the chance."

"Looks g-great." Emery wiped my leg clean and Ryker fell against the ground next to me.

Despite my ability to stifle my cries, I couldn't keep my head up. I fell back, my eyes rolling back in my head.

He pressed his forehead to mine. "I'm sorry," he whispered.

The sun would set soon. With me unable to walk, let alone lift my head, there would be no way to dig the ship out tonight, and we only had three days to reach the coast.

"No way to survive the elements and scavengers of the desert overnight. We don't stand a chance. Need shelter."

I heard Ryker speak, but couldn't pry my eyes open.

Ryker lifted my head. The feel of his strong, large hands, and earthy scent had become familiar to me. "Emery, your gift. Any way you could uncover the hatch of the ship enough for us to crawl in, then recover the majority of it?"

"How w-would we b-breathe?" she asked.

After a moment, he rummaged through the bag. "We'll leave the vents open; if we run out of air, we can use these recycling masks."

"Wh-what if we can't s-start the sh-ship t-tomorrow?"

"Let's worry about tonight. If we survive, then we'll tackle tomorrow."

I didn't want to be helpless while they worked on getting us safe. I needed to figure out how to lift the ship from the sand. I forced my eyes open, but still, the world spun.

Emery turned, one hand toward the sun, the other at the sand. A large tidal wave lifted and retracted. A wall of bricks formed from sand, erecting at the edge of the cockpit.

Aeek, Aeek.

My heart thundered. Spiderats.

The sky grew black in the distance. Not just a handful, but hundreds of them flew straight at us.

They'd come back for revenge. "Hurry!"

Emery turned and blew cyclones up like a wall of wind and sand, but the spiderats busted through. She tried again as

Ryker grabbed my hand. Despite the pain, I sat up and half-crawled, Ryker half-dragging me into the ship.

"Grab our bags!"

Emery didn't move. "Get in! Now!"

He let go of me, reached out and snatched the bags. Emery stood and stared at the fast-approaching beasts.

She was lost again. No one home.

I dug deep and lifted onto my one good leg. Clutching her boot, I yanked her in, her metal leg slamming against Ryker's shoulder. He pushed free and closed the hatch. Red spots dotted its edge and I knew what had happened to the scout. The same thing that almost happened to us.

"Emery, now. Cover the ship."

The darkness closed in; only a few rays of light remained as a tidal wave of sand covered the ship.

I held my breath as thuds and bumps echoed in the small two-man ship—the three of us barely able to fit inside.

I prayed the creature's legs weren't strong enough to smash through the glass. If so, we'd be impaled and ripped apart for the spiderats to feast on our bodies.

"Can they get in?" At the sound of my voice, spider legs clicked against the glass. A small crack etched down the side of the window.

CHAPTER FOURTEEN

The ship jolted. Glass cracked. I pushed my palm against the cold metal below me and grunted. A small vibration seeped through my hand.

Weak. So weak. Not strong enough to repel the spiderats with my implant, if I even figured out how. Too many of them. But maybe I could use my gift.

I tightened my stomach, ignoring the throbbing pain in my leg. Then took a deep breath and clenched my teeth so hard my jaw popped. Two quick, rapid zaps rushed from my core to my hand.

The ship hummed around us. Spiderats stopped for a second.

Ryker squatted by my side.

Sand ran down the sides of the ship, allowing more light in. Emery smeared the dirty glass. Eight midnight eyes shone back at us.

I cringed but kept my focus on the ship. A claw raked down the metal on the side of the small craft, sending shivers through my body. Hot lava bubbled and churned in my chest.

Thin lines of fire shot through my lungs, down my shoulders and arms, and out my palms.

We couldn't lift off, but I connected with the ship. Warm waves flowed through copper wires and into the console, a direct line to my mind. I searched for the right path to the ship's weapons, or some way of blasting the wretched creatures off. Colored threads of current pictured in my mind, taste of copper invaded my mouth, sounds of humming currents.

There. The shields.

"You can do it," Ryker whispered.

My mind sputtered. The implant fought my possession of the ship's metal components. Cracks and pops electrified my skull as if thousands of tiny explosions attacked my sinuses. I sneezed and coughed, trying to expel the singeing particles, but couldn't. Instead, I embraced and followed the path back to the implant. I could see the veins and wires crossing into one web and I allowed the implant's will to lead me.

The connection jolted my body, shoving all the air from my lungs. I clutched my throbbing head but relaxed my mind. With one last brain-splintering snap, the energy waved through the implant, back out, and through my body, electrifying the ship.

Horrific, long groans sounded from outside as the cabin jostled once then rested in the sand.

No dark, hairy legs pecked at the glass. No glazed eyes stared hungrily at us. Only a muted bronze hue from the shields. Hopeful the spiderats would not return, I fell back, exhausted. Every muscle twitched and wire complained.

Ryker pulled me tight against his chest. "That's my girl."

His words caressed my heart. *His girl.* Since my father's death, I hadn't been anyone's girl.

"Impressive." His lips pressed against mine, vaporizing the scorching heat from my powers. A cool mist danced around my mind and body. Bliss, as if I'd jumped in the lake on a summer day and floated on the surface.

My muscles calmed, his powers internally stroking mine. Lost for a moment in his arms, I gave in to his comfort.

Emery cleared her throat and sat at the control panel. "I-I don't th-think the s-spiderats will come back t-to play anytime s-soon."

"Long as shields hold, we should remain here 'til morning." Ryker scooped me up in his arms and settled me down behind the pilot's chair. He removed his jacket, folded it, and placed it gently under my head. It reeked with the bitter odor of spiderat venom, but I didn't care. Since my father's death, no one besides Boaz had cared for me like this.

"I can heal the rest of your leg slowly through the night."

The thought of him touching me all night sent a warm buzzing through my head. Would it be so bad, enjoying his touch for one night? Tomorrow I'd probably be eaten, shot, or executed.

"Just need my body to regenerate. I can steal that energy and use it to heal you." He arched a perfect dark eyebrow as he spoke. "Unfortunately, normal rate, without stealing energy, will take all night. If I could've gotten closer to the spiderats, I would've taken some. But for now, this should work."

"Do we have enough water and supplies?" I asked.

"If w-we fly out in the m-morning." Emery spoke with a blank stare at the control panel. She touched buttons and studied controls. "Th-this is a Boulton V25. I-I can fly it." Emery swiveled the chair to face me. "But for once, m-my brother's right." Emery gave a teasing grin. "We sh-should travel during th-the day. S-sleep for now." She swirled the chair back and pulled her knees to her chest.

Within a minute or two, her breathing changed from shallow, quick breaths to long heavy ones. Her nose whistled. How'd she close down so fast? *One minute she's planning to fly us out, the next she's off in another world.*

"She tends to check out on occasion, but if she says she can fly it, she can."

"But what if she 'checks out' while flying?"

"You'll be flyin' the ship, then."

"I wasn't trained to pilot. I mean, I know the basics, but flying was considered beneath a princess." Secretly, I'd always wanted to fly, but Mother would have never allowed it.

"Hate to break it to you, but you ain't no princess out here. Besides, you and machines will blend well with your power." He gave a teasing smile. "Now, lay back. I need to work on your leg." He shimmied down between me and the back of the side-by-side chairs, the space barely big enough for one, let alone two, people.

His skin pressed against mine and my body reacted with pleasurable surges. Lukewarm strokes raced up and down my arms. My heartbeat quickened at his touch.

He rolled on his side and pushed my hair from my eyes. "You did great."

Maybe he could get past the implant. Maybe he'd forget about it.

His fingers raked across the edge of the metal device in the back of my neck. I tensed and waited for his response. He looked away and let go then rolled over. "We should get some sleep."

Disgust, that was what he felt.

Tears stung my eyes, but I swallowed them back and faced the wall. Pain shot up my thigh and I grabbed my leg, sucking in a quick breath. Muscle spasms ravaged me from foot to stomach.

Ryker's strong hand pressed against the back of my thigh. Soothing vibrations rumbled over each fiber until they all calmed.

He scooted close and pressed against my back. Scent of cedar and musky earth relaxed me into him. His hand raked against my pants until his arm encircled me. Two fingers rotated around the wound with a soft touch and rested to the inside of my thigh.

His thumb continued higher until it stopped above the wound.

I shivered. No man had ever touched me in such an intimate way. Even if he only meant to heal me, I still trembled from his touch.

He didn't move for a moment.

"How did you get these?" he asked in a raspy tone.

"What?"

"Scars."

I didn't want to tell him. It was embarrassing, and he already thought of me as a Slag. "I, um, I've had them for a while."

He pressed his lips to my temple above my ear and whispered, "Tell me." His breath teased my resolve.

"I got them because I was disrespectful."

"Sounds harsh. To who?"

I swallowed hard. "The general."

"He did this?" Anger dripped from his voice.

"Yes."

"Your mother didn't stop him?" An arctic blast shot from his mouth across my cheek, bringing with it the chill of death.

"She ordered him to do it, while she sat back and watched."

The seats vibrated behind him. The temperature dropped several degrees.

"Razrušen kučinja! They'll never touch you again. You have my word as a Mualite."

White puffs lingered with each exhale. He needed to calm down before he froze us all. Why was he so upset about what the general and Mother did to me, a Slag? If he was that upset about a few scars, imagine how he felt about what happened to Emery.

My chest tightened, and heat steamed off of me.

My mind spun, and I laced my fingers with his and squeezed tight. He must never learn the truth. I couldn't bear it.

Our powers merged. We both calmed, and I relaxed back into him.

He let go of my hand, his fingers and thumb pulsing and massaging in tiny circles.

A burning chill radiated deep into tendons and bone. A steady charge surged into the wound and I knew, bit by bit, the skin began to heal. After each pulse, minuscule vibrations trailed up and down my leg—a side effect of the healing.

I closed my eyes in anticipation of the next wave. Slow breaths. Lips pressed together.

The soothing reached the top of my thigh.

He stopped and fell against me. His slow, steady breaths

left me in sensory overload, in the silent, dark night. Both Ryker and Emery slept, but I couldn't, not with my body craving more cool energy like a drug.

For hours I remained still, eyes wide, fighting the urge to pull his hand back onto me. Finally, I gave into exhaustion and drifted off to sleep.

My insides began to dance in anticipation. Hair rose. Goosebumps covered my flesh.

Dreaming?

No, I opened my eyes and realized Ryker's hand cupped around my wound, healing me again.

Small pulses...warm vibrations. He grasped my thigh tight and I tensed as one last electric current shot through my thigh to my stomach, chest, and scalp.

A thousand tiny strokes of pleasure ignited. I raked my tongue across my teeth. "More," I whispered, my mind ruled by my body. I pressed against him.

He moaned and kissed my ear. Lips traced up my neck until he reached the implant and stopped.

Emery started fooling with gadgets on the console. "I s-see you t-two are awake."

Oh God, I'd forgotten Emery was there. The deep throbbing pressure of his powers shattered, leaving only a cold sting. I shot up, still a little wobbly from my leg wound.

Ryker sat cross-legged, a boyish grin on his face. He pulled a compartment door open, flexing his biceps. "We should try to dislodge the ship and be on our way."

I pushed up onto my knees. Dull pain pulsed in me, but I refused to mention it. In the grand scheme of things, a little discomfort was better than acting like a spoiled princess.

No. Instead, I'd prove myself to him. I scooted forward

between Emery and Ryker, seated in the pilot and co-pilot chairs, and I pressed my palms to the console.

"What are you doing?" Ryker asked.

I didn't answer. I concentrated on the ship.

"I got it," Emery mumbled before her arms waved stale air into my face.

Somehow, Emery always knew what I had in mind. We had connected in the engine room four years ago. My heart warmed at the thought of Emery, my friend, working by my side.

A golden snowstorm erupted outside. Engines stuttered, cogs and wheels grinding from behind. The ship shimmied and jolted. A controlled stream of hot energy exited my hands into the ship's console. Two light indicators popped. Glass shards flew in all directions, yet I remained calm and focused on the engine.

Orange and blue swirls became clear from the rising sun. A dirt wall remained around us, but nothing covered the ship as Emery remained in control of the earth.

My chest tightened when I scraped the wings against the wall, causing sand to trickle down in long, thick tendrils.

I changed my focus to the gears and clucked my tongue at the overwhelming taste of lubricant. The smell of oil gave me confidence that I controlled every gear, cog, and lever of the ship.

Ryker whistled from my side. "Impressive. Only two days, and you can control an entire scout ship."

I didn't answer. Instead, I continued to ascend the ship until I could see over the top of the dune.

Emery fell back into her seat as the roar of sand below the

ship jostled it to the left. I compensated and pulled us further into the air.

Distant screeches sounded over the engines. It was time to go. Who knew when the next creature would attack? Even with the shields up, we could still be forced down. Was there time to land the ship and relinquish control to Emery safely?

A sermechtapede bolted from the sand and plunged back down. No.

I wavered and Ryker grabbed my waist.

"Enough of this. You need to rest." He stood by my side, but when three more sermechtapedes lunged into the sky and landed only a few hundred meters away, he shut up and sat back down. "Go, go, go!" he urged.

Two rose and dove at us, missing by a few meters. It was almost as if the ship attracted them.

Of course. That was why the scout ships flew so high. Too high to see a single straggler, but low enough to detect activity. That was also why the queen wouldn't travel in the direction a scout ship didn't return from.

My index finger traced the raised surface of the booster gauge and the ship propelled straight up. I fell and slammed my head on the storage bin. Higher and higher we ascended.

Ryker offered his hand to pull me back to the control panel. Before I could grasp it, the engines shut off and we plummeted in a downward spiral.

I ricocheted off the seat, storage bin, and levers, until I lodged between Ryker's seat and the bulkhead. Red lights flickered. Low-pitched warning alarms clambered all around.

I hooked two fingers onto the ledge of the control panel and pressed my thumb against the wires leading to the ignition button. Sparks flew and the ship pulsed twice, sending us faster to our death.

I grasped the back of Ryker's now empty seat and caught a glimpse of his contorted body between the two chairs. Everything continued to spin and my stomach twisted and felt hollow. I steadied myself and planted my palm flat on the ignition button. The engines sputtered, we stopped our descent and rose into the sky, then they cut off.

CHAPTER FIFTEEN

Ryker reached for Emery, who clung to the side of the hatch whimpering, but the force of gravity pinned him to the bulkhead. She grew white and her eyes rolled back in her head.

My stomach floated somewhere up in the sky while my body catapulted to the ground.

Smell of burning flesh drew my attention to the ship's controls.

"Valencia!" Ryker clung to the seat but tilted his head to my hands. Crimson spread from my palms, still pressed to the console, to the side of my hands. I hadn't felt it. Staring down at my seared flesh, it took a second until my brain caught up to the sound of my skin sizzling.

"Ahh," I cried out. A jolt of fire exploded against the console. Instinctively, I pulled the hand away. Somehow, I managed to concentrate enough to keep the connection with the ship. It tilted up and my knees slammed to the steel floor. Emery thudded between Ryker and me. She moaned but smiled at me.

My eyes burned from the pain, and tears streamed down

my face, but the ship steadied. Ryker crawled over and lifted my left hand. Blisters formed in white bubbles, rimmed in red.

Shaking his head, he frowned. "How can you hold on? Even now…grown men would crumple from less." He stroked my wet cheeks. I could see my pain reflected in his wide eyes. He pulled my palm close to his chin. His nose crinkled and he coughed.

"Smells bad." I tried to make light of it to keep from showing how much it really hurt.

The blisters swelled and he blew a long frosty breath over my wounds. Each small water-filled bump oozed then shriveled up.

I sighed and relaxed under his breath, almost forgetting about my other hand still burning against the console. He doubled over and fell against the pilot chair.

"Stop. You don't have the energy after working on my leg all night."

His facial muscles twitched in reprimand, but he pressed on until I pulled my hand away.

"Enough; you need your strength. Don't waste energy on small things."

With the distraction, the ship wobbled. Emery jumped into the seat and took control. She fidgeted with some buttons and moved the throttle handle forward. The ship gained altitude and sliced through the sky, leaving behind a tangled mess of creatures.

Peeling my damaged hand from the controls, I relaxed for the first time in twenty-four hours.

Ryker collapsed against the steel wall.

I gave him a reassuring smile. "Thank you," I whispered through steamy breath.

"You're the heroine. Saved us all from mutant creatures and busting into a million pieces."

"I shouldn't have...I almost killed us—"

"No. You were perfect." He smiled.

The ship continued east, toward the rising sun. Hopefully, we'd make it to scavenger territory and retrieve the necessary supplies to continue on to Old Chicago and ultimately, to the coast.

My stomach tightened and I looked between brother and sister. Yes, both possessed powers. One fell in and out of reality. The other was hot-headed and damaged. And me, I had only discovered my powers two days ago. They would be volatile at best for months, if not years.

He continued to hold his hand out, waiting for me to take it. "Not even a seasoned Mualite could've maintained control with her flesh burning. Instinct would kick in and cause them to pull away."

Did I impress him? Could he understand that I wasn't a murderous Slag princess? If I told him the truth, would he forgive me and know that I wanted nothing more than to help Emery?

Clank. Emery's foot banged against the floor each time she spun back and forth, manning all the controls solo.

We both glanced at her, and when he looked back, I saw it in his eyes.

Hatred.

His hand slipped back to his side and he looked away.

The bright sun glared back at us as if to warn of the hell

we were about to enter. No one had ever gone this far and returned alive.

Many could only guess at what resided in the old, abandoned cities. I'd been through that region. It was desolate, a breeding ground for wild animals. Fallon could've been fed bad information.

Emery's morbid humming and rocking drew Ryker's attention. "What—"

Dread slipped down my spine one vertebrae at a time. "There. Look!"

Large black masses sped toward our ship in a head-on collision course.

"Spiderats?" I asked.

The black billowed in the wind, bronze and gold reflected below it.

Ryker shook his head almost imperceptibly. "No, not—" He leaned forward, narrowing his gaze. "Sranje! It's scavenger patrols. Might complicate things."

He looked over at his sister. "Sis, not now. We need you." He shook her shoulder but she only pulled the little red ball from her pocket and rolled it in her palm. "Valencia, chair —now."

I guided Emery out of the chair onto the floor behind us and jumped into the pilot's chair. "Why does this complicate things? We brought the gift—"

"Hoped we'd make it further into the territory. Not sure these lowlifes will be agreeable to our gift. Scavenger patrols are outsiders, even to the scavengers"

An explosion sent our right wing up and we banked left. Another one ahead. I pulled up and over.

"Time to see if Uncle's gift will be enough." I slowed the craft.

Scavengers were soulless creatures who roamed the Wasteland, stealing and pillaging anything they could. My stomach twisted in knots at the thought of them scrapping the ship and probably Emery's leg.

"I'll do the talking. I'll tell them I'm the Tertian princess and—"

"No. Can't let them know you're Tertian." He scanned my body. "You're dressed like a Mualite yet could pass for human. Scavengers detest the queen. These scavengers of the desert are the closest thing to a resistance in the territories."

"Then we'll tell them we're part of the rebellion."

"No." The ship came to a sudden halt. "They only care about one thing. Scavenging for materials and gifts."

The massive, round, bronze and gold-trimmed vessel with large sails circled around and landed in front of us, casting a shadow of doom. Guns pointed in all directions. Skulls hung from the sides of the ship as prizes of their conquests.

Ruthless creatures who enslaved or murdered everyone they encountered.

Like Ryker, I hoped the gift was enough.

A rhythmic tapping caught my attention. Emery sat with her metal leg extended, bouncing the ball in front of her.

Three scavengers landed on the top of the ship with a thud. "We know ya in there. Open the hatch or we'll knock it in and cook ya inside." The scavenger's voice sounded hollow through the hatch.

Flames licked at the windows. Orange fire blasted from the end of a large silver tube. The man stuck his face to the glass. Gold teeth, hook hand, and a missing eye. They were what I had feared.

"This here's ya last warning."

Hair stood at attention on the back of my neck at the sight of the silver pack on the man's back sputtering to life.

Another larger man with dreadlocks, body piercings, and orange-colored eyes straddled the main window and raised a large anvil overhead. A battery acid junkie. Another tale whispered about to scare children away from the Wasteland. Only it wasn't a story. The man stood over us ready to fry and serve us to the crew for dinner.

CHAPTER SIXTEEN

Ryker shoved me to Emery's side. "Stay behind me."

Adrenaline spiked electric pulses through my brain twisting and turning through my veins and wires.

Ryker punched the hatch button.

Emery bounced her ball with more vigor.

He leaned back on his right leg and lifted his glacial blue hands to the runt of a man with the gold teeth and silver pack. "Requesting some supplies in exchange for a gift." Ryker retrieved the small satchel Fallon had given him and jingled what was inside.

"I'll be takin' that." The man lunged for the opening. The smell of cool rain rushed by and the man screamed. His feet flew up in the air and he flipped back.

A burly man rested his arm on one knee against the hatch opening. "Might want to rethink that."

A hiss sputtered from Ryker's hands and he collapsed to the floor.

"Warned ya. Don't use ya powers, or we be stoppin' ya."

"We brought a gift." Even while I stated the words, I readied to defend us. I concentrated on pulling energy from the metal hook of the runt and opened my mind for a rush of energy I hoped to blast at the conceited animal in front of me. If not, these scavengers were going to gut us before we had a chance to deliver our gift.

A dull burn coated my senses, traveling through every nerve. I switched gears and opened the floodgate for the eruption of burning hatred to singe him, but instead, it stayed trapped, exploding like a dwarf star in the sky.

I screamed and collapsed by Ryker's side. His eyes glowed blue and I knew the same had happened to him. Scorching current assailed my innermost essence.

"Enough!" The deep voice ordered. "I want them alive. I'm taken' that one back to Oasis. Hand me the gift."

The inferno inside me started to boil. Ryker panted by my side. Emery's ball kept bouncing. I was thankful she'd checked out and hoped Fallon was wrong about her knowing what was going on around her.

Steam escaped my mouth and the heat ebbed to a dull burn. "What—"

"Have me own Mualite." The oversized man winked at me. "He be power of all powers. No one can harm me long as he's 'round. I be takin' ya gift back to Oasis. Malvak decide what to do with ya."

Veins on Ryker's face still pulsed blue. A crystallized look of death. His knee thumped against the floor as he moved to stand.

I scooted to Emery's side and pulled her dress down over her leg in hopes we could keep it concealed.

"Little too late there, girly. Already saw that treasure."

Ryker lunged forward but fell to the ground with his legs sprawled in an awkward, frozen position.

I wanted to reach out and defrost him but didn't. I couldn't use my powers while my head pulsed with a sharp pain. "Let us go."

The man slapped his red coat, sending sand raining down on us. "Spunky. Like that." He laughed heartily and waved some other mutant scavengers over. "Best be gettin' outta here before the Wasteland discovers us." He moved back and looked out toward the vast nothingness as if he saw something coming their way.

One man leveraged himself on the console and grasped my forearm to pull me up.

Ryker smacked it away. "Don't touch her."

"Now, ya ain't in no position to be makin' demands."

My stomach tightened at the sight of the two scarred and maimed faces pulling me out and up to the pirate ship. "It's okay, I'll be fine. Help Emery ."

Never had I seen so many scars. My mother had forbidden anyone looking so deformed in her presence. She would have ordered them altered immediately. That most of the scavengers were self-mutilated wouldn't have made a difference.

Trying to maintain control, I took a few steps across the deck and rested against a mast—the sails now drawn tight against the bronze post. I looked at the deep purple lines etching a path down the dreadlock's face from temple to lip and back up to his eye. It matched the pattern on my left thigh from the general.

The captain smiled, revealing crooked teeth. "Ah, I think she likes ya, mate."

"That mark. Who gave it to you?" I asked.

"Don't matter. Not much left a him."

I ran my hand over the rip in my pants, not ready to reveal my own mark.

The captain smacked him on the back. "This here is Josheb. He'll be escortin' ya to the cell below deck." The captain bowed mockingly. "Not often we get such distinguishable company."

Ryker moved to my side and squeezed my hand in warning.

"I was a tutor back in the Resort Territory," I said.

"Yeah, sure ya were. Maybe some time below deck'll alter that lyin' tongue."

With the barrel of a gun pressed to my back, I moved forward, keeping Emery and Ryker in my sight.

I stumbled over chains and rope. An open-air ship in the desert? How could they survive the heat, dust, and *creatures*? What powered a ship this size? Too small for a reactor. Too big to run on the limited water or fuel in this region.

I pushed those thoughts from my mind as we shuffled down the stairs to two small cells. The gun nudged me into one and the door clanged shut behind. Metal! I could melt it. But what then? Escape where? Even if the Mualite who kept our powers under control didn't know I was melting the cell bars, we'd never make it off the ship unnoticed. And if we did, we couldn't walk across the Wasteland with no supplies or gear. Our ship was secured and would probably be scrapped when we reached Oasis. The realization made my knees weaken, and sighing, I slumped onto the floor, alone. The door to the cell next to me swung open and Hatchet shoved Ryker in.

I jumped to my feet and raced to the cell door. "Wait, where are you putting Emery?"

"Capt'n has special plans for her."

Ryker spun around and punched his face.

Josheb shoved him away and lifted his gun.

"Watch out!" I was too late. The butt of the gun struck the back of his head. He fell to the floor.

"Get in there and stay quiet."

I rubbed the bars, my body burning to kill Josheb, but my head still protested from using my powers. I crumpled to the ground with my hand outstretched, hoping to touch Ryker and make sure he was okay. My heart ached for his contact.

Two men raced down the stairs at Josheb's command and dragged Ryker's seemingly lifeless body into the cell.

Emery rushed over and hit her head against the cell door several times while she sang.

Josheb pulled her back from the cell. "What's she doin'?"

"She's sick. Can't you see that? Please, put her in the cell. Take me instead."

"Can't. Cap'n's orders." He grinned. 'Sides, he's got other plans for you." He grabbed Emery by the arm and pulled her up the stairs as she cried and scratched at the walls.

"No." I lunged at the bars and pressed my body against them. The smell of iron brought me back to Mother's ship. Emery's pale body strapped to the gurney, saw grinding against her bone.

What would they do to her? I clutched the bars and concentrated on melting them. Piercing pain knocked me back to the floor. I scrambled to my feet and tried again. But the invisible knife pierced my skull and cut through wires and arteries.

"Please." I clutched my knees to my chest. "I can't watch her suffer again," I choked.

"Watch what?" Ryker mumbled.

I froze. No, not now. "They took her." Tears gushed from my eyes. Pain and guilt plagued me, and I struggled with what to do next. I couldn't sit there and let Emery's leg be ripped from her body.

Ryker pushed toward my cell, holding the back of his head. Blood smears remained on the floor. "We need to find a way to get that Mualite traitor."

I scanned the holding area for a way out and noticed a vent. I half expected for Boaz to pop his head out and give me some encouraging advice I didn't understand. Never had I missed the little man so much.

Ryker crawled over to the edge of the cell and reached his forearm through the small slats between the bars. "Did they hurt you?"

"No."

His dark stubble-covered jaw twitched. There would be no way of stopping him from attacking the guards when they returned.

His fingers circled the top of my hand. The touch didn't become cool or push the anxiety away, but it warmed my heart.

He was hotheaded and dangerous, yet kind and gentle. My chest tightened with confusion. Should I tell him the truth? The weight of the secret crushed my soul. Besides, maybe I was right. The Mualite who helped the captain could be a captive. I had to make him understand and hope to find whoever interfered with our powers. Get him to realize we could help him if we joined together to escape.

"How do you know the Mualite's a traitor? Maybe he's being forced to help them."

He turned his head; silver and black hair fell over his narrowed right eye. "Doesn't matter. He's a traitor either way."

"I don't believe that. We might stand a chance if we can get to him. Convince him to help us."

"Not the time to be talking. Need to fight."

"You stubborn fool. It's always a fight. Never another way with you. All or nothing, right? Everyone is either bad or good." I jerked free of him. "Sometimes people are forced to do things. Things they never wanted to be a part of to stay alive—" A lump rose in my throat.

"All of us have a choice. Those weak humans back in the Mining Territory. They could've helped when Emery was taken four years ago. No. They sat back and let it happen. Nothing worse than a coward."

"Try to imagine—"

"No. I can't begin to imagine. You didn't betray Emery, you refused. The daughter of the queen."

He thought I'd saved his sister. "It's not like what you think. Nothing is. You want to help someone but the queen demands you follow orders." My voice cracked but I forced the words to continue. "If you don't, you both will die."

"I'd choose death."

I wanted to scream at him. Tell him what happened. Make him understand I had no choice, but his hatred-laced words kept me from the truth. "You say that, but if you were faced with a choice between someone else and your sister—"

"I'd never torture my own kind, and don't respect those who would. They don't deserve to call themselves Mualites.

Should be thrown to the Wasteland and abandoned for what they done." He spoke deep with hatred. "I can't even look at one of them. They disgust me."

CHAPTER SEVENTEEN

Ryker paced around the cell, running his fingers over the floor and walls. "Has to be a weapon."

Iron bars, a barrel probably filled with water or Verillian juice, a chain connected to the dirty brushed silver wall, but nothing sharp.

The muscles in my shoulder relaxed. If he didn't have a weapon, he wouldn't get himself killed.

I sat quietly, listening for Emery's screams when they ripped her leg off, but all I heard was the swishing of wind through the sails and the hum of an engine.

Fallon had to have known, or suspected, what would happen. He never would have risked Emery like this. He loved her too much. So…maybe these scavengers wanted her for some reason other than scrap metal.

"I'll wrap the chain around a neck the next time someone opens the cell door." Ryker mopped the sweat from his brow. "Heat's strangling me like the tamer collar."

Footsteps echoed overhead and I held my breath, waiting for them to take me away. "No, Fallon wouldn't have risked us like this. Once they open the gift, they'll grant us supplies and safe passage. It has to work. Just remain calm. It'll all work out."

Ryker slid down the wall and sat with his arms resting on his knees. "Fallon didn't know we'd get caught so far out. Scavengers must've seen our fight with the spiderats or something."

"We'll get out of this. We just need to convince—"

"No time to waste convincing some traitor he'd be better off on our side."

"Even if we could escape the cells, what then? Hundreds of miles of nothing between us and the next territory. We'll starve, dehydrate, or become food for the creatures of the Wasteland. Fallon wouldn't have sent us if he didn't believe the gift would secure our safe passage and supplies. Keep faith." I tried hard to make my voice sound as if I believed my own words.

"Don't worry. I'll get us out of this."

I spun and faced him. "How? By beating everyone to death on the ship? That's all you want to do, fight. Sometimes there are other ways. You're going to get us all killed." I gestured to the stairwell. "You're over there formulating a plan to take down the next person who walks down those stairs."

"No. I...well, yeah, of course. You don't get it. They're gonna kill us first chance they get." He bolted to his feet and grabbed the back of his head with one hand while he clutched the bars with his other.

My voice softened. "You don't know that."

"Scavengers are no better than the creatures of the Wasteland. Trust me."

I spun and stalked across my cell, then pivoted and faced

him. "You know everything. Yeah, I get it, but what if he didn't have a choice?"

"You think this Mualite has no choice? I wouldn't turn my back on my people for anything."

"Not even Emery ?"

His grip tightened on the bars. I narrowed my gaze, daring him to lie. Could he sacrifice his sister if he had to?

He clutched his head and collapsed to his knees.

"Ryker. You can't use your powers. Calm down." I rushed to his side, reached between the bars, and brushed his soft hair from his forehead. "Your anger will be the death of you." I pulled his chin up to face me. "You have to stay calm."

"I didn't even realize. Vo pekolot."

My hands shook as I watched him bang his head against the bars. I knew how it felt—searing pain raced through fissures and down to his brainstem. I wanted to soothe him, make him stop.

Instead, I pressed my lips to his cool forehead through the small slats, and my mind swirled faster, to a new level of flight. Bone-marrow-soothing-pleasure rippled through my body.

"Enjoying ya confinement, I see." Josheb's voice broke the moment and my desire recoiled, replaced by gut-punching fear.

Ryker backed away, leaving me empty inside. "Where's Emery?" he rasped.

Clunk...tap. My stomach unclenched at the musical cadence of Emery's steps. They hadn't taken her leg.

Maybe I was right. We could try to reason with them.

I presented my warmest smile. "Josheb, we just want to leave. We won't cause any trouble."

"Not gonna happen. Ya got some worth to ya. We gonna take you to Malvak."

"Malvak?" I asked.

"Yeah, ya never heard of Malvak? Gesh, ya have lived a privileged life there, lady."

He took the keys from his jacket and shoved Emery in the direction of Ryker's cell.

"What is this Malvak going to do with us?" I asked.

"Don't know."

The key rotated in the door, clicking not only the lock but Ryker's restraint. He charged and rammed his shoulder into Josheb's abdomen. They flew back and smashed the barrel, sending green liquid all over the floor.

Ryker drew back his fist and pounded it against Josheb's cheek. Then readied for another punch but slipped on the green fluid and knocked the back of his head against the wall.

Emery took out her ball. Curling her good leg under her, she sat in the corner next to my cell.

Josheb slammed his knuckles against Ryker's jaw, sending him sliding on his back through the narrow corridor.

"Ryker!" I screamed.

He clutched his head, then looked up only to have Josheb's fist connect with his chin. Grimacing, Ryker leaned back on his elbows, drew his knees to his chest, and drove his feet into Josheb's stomach.

Stay down, Ryker. Don't do it. My fingers clutched the metal bars so tight my nails dug into my palms.

He scurried to his knees but kept slipping in the liquid. "Not gonna touch my sister."

"You be wrong about that, mate." Josheb spun around and grabbed Emery by the hair and shoved a blade to her neck.

"Care to spar some more?" He pulled her around like a ragdoll, her head flopping in every direction. "Now get back in your cell."

With her hair hanging over her eyes, I couldn't see if she'd checked out or was dead. No humming, no ball, only silence. "Emery?"

He pressed the blade harder against her neck. "Now."

"Please, Ryker. Listen to him," I pleaded.

"Put the knife down. I'm going." Ryker skated on the slippery deck. Entering his cell, he fell on his back with a thud. The door clanged shut and he spun to check on Emery.

My cell door opened. I raced to catch Emery as Josheb shoved her in. We both fell to the floor. "Emery, you okay?" I brushed the sweaty, dark hair from her face. No bruises or scrapes.

Emery rocked back and forth and pulled the ball from her pocket but she didn't hum.

I nodded at Ryker to let him know she was okay. Well, as okay as she could be under the circumstances.

He blew out air and ran his hands through his hair.

"You sure made enough mess down here. Cap'n's gonna be none too happy ya spilled his juice."

"Tell him to send us the bill," I snapped.

Josheb tossed a frilly pink dress into the cell. "Put this on, gal."

I glared at him. "I don't think so."

"Maybe this'll change ya mind." Josheb pulled a gun from his belt and pointed it at Ryker. He stumbled but recovered and pushed his chest out.

I carefully propped Emery against the back wall and stood straight, facing Josheb. "So, the stories are true, scavengers have no honor. Nothing but animals, lowest on the food chain."

"Ah, ya flatter me." Josheb gave a half-sarcastic grin. "Now put it on." He cocked the gun and took a step closer to Ryker's cell.

"No. Don't—"

"It's only a dress. I've worn worse." I held it up in front of me. "Maybe not." I unhooked my belt, pulled my vest off and unbuttoned the undershirt. The thin dark shirt clung to my skin and rivulets of sweat dripped between my breasts.

"Turn around," Ryker growled at Josheb.

I peeled the brown pants down my legs.

Josheb stepped away from the cell and lowered his gun, mouth hanging open.

Ryker rattled the solid cell door. "Don't you even think about touchin' her."

"Those marks, how'd ya get them?"

I pulled the dress over my head. "Does it matter?"

"I know these marks. But the maker be dead." Josheb's eyes fixed on my leg, but his look wasn't lustful, nothing like the ogling the general used to enjoy.

I yanked the strings tight and knelt down for Emery to tie them in the back. "How would you know where these marks came from?"

"Swirl's a brandin' mark. A letter G."

I tensed under Josheb's stare. "You do know the general. He gave you those marks."

"Yeah, he be a mean son of a whore."

I half chuckled. "You do know him."

We stared at each other with knowing eyes, like we shared some sort of experience.

"You two have nothing in common. Trick, that's what it is," Ryker barked.

"You never no mind." Josheb shot him a glance. "He still be livin' then?"

"Yeah."

"How? I gutted him like a sermechtapede f'r breakfast."

The thought of eating one of those creatures churned my stomach. "So, that's why he's got the chest plate. You did that?"

Ryker scowled. "You know it's a trick."

Josheb ignored Ryker. "Yep."

"I like your work." Yards of material swayed as I glided to the cell door.

"Ah, ya flatter me. I should've made sure he be dead. How you know the general?"

I froze. Did I tell him the truth and risk our lives? I searched his eyes for an inclination and saw a man of honor, someone who shared a hatred for the same enemy. "I'm betrothed to him."

"Ya what?"

"Po gavolite." Ryker ran to the bars. "Nothing, it doesn't matter."

"It's all right, Ryker. I was ordered by my mother to marry him. I chose to run away and join the rebellion instead. Please, you have to help us. The queen has cut off trade, declared you enemies of the council, and murdered your people. Don't you want to fight back?"

"You're the princess." He stumbled back. "Princess Valencia?"

"Sranje!" Ryker grunted. "Dang woman never listens."

Josheb smiled. "Scavengers have 'eir own way of rebellin'."

Ryker's hands froze against the metal. "No. You can't."

Josheb shot him a sideways glance. "Kill the rulin' class. Startin' with the queen and princess."

"You what?" My hands shook. Emery hummed and rocked faster with her palms pressed to her ears.

That was why Ryker had warned me to keep my secret no matter what. He knew, but why didn't he tell me?

Ryker pressed his fingers to his temple and I knew he'd lost control of his powers again. The pain was etched in the blue lines crossing his face like a web.

"Why'd the general give you those wounds if ya gonna marry him?" Josheb asked.

Ryker was in no shape to fight. It was up to me. "I'm not like them. I am a Mualite."

"How can that be? You be the princess of the Slags. Heartless wench who sacrifices people for the fun of it."

"No." I reached through the bars and clutched Josheb's callused brown hand, ignoring Ryker's groan. I had to maintain control of my own powers, and watching him suffer only made it worse.

"I was imprisoned because I wouldn't sacrifice a Mualite." I gestured to Emery. "The queen ordered total Slag conversion and gave me to the general. The world thought as a wife, but in secret I...I was supposed to be," my throat burned at the words, "his servant."

Josheb squeezed my hand. He understood. His orange eyes showed compassion.

The ship shifted and he pulled away. His forehead glistened from the gold piercings. "How I know what ya say be true? Ya could be plannin' on takin' the ship. How I even know ya have such powers?"

"If you could get the Mualite not to kill me each time I tried to use my gift, I could show you."

"Lies. Ya be speakin' lies to me." Josheb shook his head and the long locks swayed across his muscular back and shoulders.

"We both have his mark, Josheb. You know I speak the truth."

"If ya were imprisoned, how'd ya make it here?"

"Ryker rescued me." My chest warmed at the sight of the small smile that creased Ryker's lips. I wanted to hold him in my arms again and make the world go away. Make him understand what I'd done. Maybe if I showed him that the Mualite really had no choice and I got them out of this mess, he'd forgive me.

Josheb glared at Ryker. "Why'd ya do that?"

"Sister demanded I save her. Most likely I wouldn't have except she told me Valencia saved her life. Felt like I owed her for that."

Owed me? His words made me cringe.

"How'd ya end up here?"

Ryker shifted onto his knees and managed to get to his feet. "Mining Territory was blown to bits. Didn't have much choice."

My hope rose at his words. Ryker was trying to reason with him. This was my chance to show him people could change. "We were on our way to meet a contact for the rebellion. My uncle gave us that gift to offer in exchange for supplies. It's our only chance to free our people. If we joined forces, we could—"

"I beg ya not to go speakin' of such things. Malvak will feed ya to the nearest spiderat."

"But why?"

"Cause, he be responsible for many. Found Oasis and started a life far from the council's reign. Just wanna live in peace."

"Peace? If the queen finds you, she'll strip you of all your resources in the name of the council, then enslave you."

"That's why ya never gonna leave Oasis."

"Then we can't reach Oasis. Set us free now and we'll leave without knowing where Oasis is. That way your secret is safe."

"Can't do that." Hatchet paced the small area outside my cell. His brows furrowed.

"I know you want to help me...us." I tried to speak in my smoothest, sweetest voice. The one that used to work on my father to get what I wanted as a child. "I promise. I'll repay the favor someday."

"I can't free ya or I'll be executed. I got family back at Oasis. Can't be riskin' their lives."

My heart fell deep into my belly. All hope drained from my determination.

Josheb pressed his lips together and scrubbed his face. "But I'll talk to the cap'n. Maybe I can convince 'im to free you before we reach Oasis."

Ryker shot across his cell and reached for Josheb. "You can't—"

"I won't. Ya've got my promise. Listen here, pretty face. You need to follow his lead. No tellin' anyone about ya being a princess. I'll plea for ya release another way." He turned to face Ryker. "Don't go doin' anything stupid now. Ya hear me? If I go beggin' for ya release and ya shoot a guard, ya be sealing all ya fates." Josheb holstered his gun and stomped up the stairs.

"Do you think he can do it?" I asked.

Emery stilled, bouncing her ball in a calming rhythm. She was still out of it, but at least she wasn't agitated anymore.

Ryker leaned his head against the bars. "Didn't kill you on the spot, so I guess that means something."

I wrapped my fingers around the bars near his head. "I had to try something."

He looked up at me and covered my hands with his. A spark raced up my arm and I took in a long breath. Sweat dripped down his temple. His eyes penetrated my soul. "I know."

In spite of the burning temperature, his touch cooled my skin and the weight of the heat lifted.

Ryker inched his face closer to mine. "Do you feel that?"

"But how?" I longed to be closer and pressed my body against the bar. "How can I feel your gifts if our powers are blocked?"

He shook his head. "Don't rightly know, but I feel stronger with the connection. Your warmth is touching every inch of my body."

"That's a good thing in this heat?"

"The gift's blocking the heat around me. Blocking anxiety, fear, and anger. All I feel is you. As if you are the entire world around me. The sole purpose I breathe." He panted and leaned closer to me. "It must be different. Not connected to our gifts."

"How can that be?" I could barely focus on the words. His soft, deep voice begged me to move closer. His full lips parted and I met him between the bars.

The room disappeared around me.

No bars.

No guns.

No Scavengers.

Only lips.

His lips.

"Hey, you two. Cut it out." A guard's voice broke our connection.

Fire erupted in my core and I collapsed to the floor. "Ahh," I cried. Loss flooded me. Unwanted tears streamed down my face. Or was it sweat? I couldn't tell. The heat suffocated me. I clutched my throat.

The guard smacked the bar with a rod. "Pull it together. Cap'n's on his way down here."

I forced the emotions into abeyance. Ryker reached out for me, but I moved back, knowing there was no way I could handle losing his touch again. Not right now. It was as if my heart had been full of love and happiness only to have it ripped down the middle and drained of all hope.

The captain's sandaled feet descended the metal stairs. I narrowed my eyes to focus as his plump yet muscular body came into view, followed by his head. No neck, just a head on shoulders.

"What've ya got to say about this new weapon?" The captain's words hung in the air and I looked at Josheb for answers.

Josheb arched his eyebrows. "Don't play dumb. I overheard you. You know how to get uranium."

I caught on quick. We had information that could help us, but why uranium? "Yeah, um—"

Ryker stood but still clutched the bars. "No. Not saying until you promise to let us go."

"Ya tell me first," the captain ordered.

"Tell you and I've got no leverage."

The captain smiled with his golden-toothed grin. "So ya ain't so stupid."

Ryker jetted his chin out. "No, I assure you I'm not."

"We'll promise to tell you where to get the uranium," I offered. "Although, I'm not sure why you want it so badly."

"To pilot me ship."

I glanced around but couldn't determine the energy source for the ship. "This ship has a reactor? But it's too small. The queen managed a reactor small enough for her ship only a few years ago."

"She managed it? That what she be tellin' everyone? Ha. She stole the technology from us. Glad to know she ain't got the new stuff, though." The captain's brows furrowed. "How ya know so much about the queen's ship?"

"Doesn't matter," Ryker interrupted. "Want the uranium or not?"

A speaker crackled overhead. "Cap'n, Oasis straight ahead."

"Think ya smart? Well, ya take it up with Malvak once we get there."

My stomach flopped.

"But once we're in the Oasis, he'll never let us go, even if we tell him where the uranium is." The ship came to a stuttering halt and I knew it was too late. We'd reached Oasis.

"No need to fret, lady. We'll find out what ya know. You just might not live through our...questioning."

CHAPTER EIGHTEEN

I shielded my eyes from the burning sun and tried to look out over the land but only saw a blur of orange. Stumbling toward the gangway, I clung to Emery, keeping her close.

The captain handed ropes to a guard. "Don't want ya gettin' any ideas."

The guard wrapped them around Ryker's wrists.

One of the men pulled me and Emery apart and bound my hands so tightly the rope cut into my skin. Then he shoved us single file down the narrow metal plank. Once halfway up the narrow walkway leading to the top of the city wall, I saw Oasis.

A labyrinth of boardwalks and skyways, twisting silver tunnels supported by wood beams circling around buildings, and small wooden houses formed a massive town. People hustled through the streets. Black smoke plumed from a far-off greenish-brown building and I wondered if it was made of copper. I'd never seen so many resources in one place. Not even in Acadia.

They were somewhere in the Wasteland yet had managed

to build a thriving town. Animals were penned in stables and loaded wagons were pulled by horses.

Then I realized why no one ever escaped the town. Tall walls lined with barbed wire secured the perimeter. Heads impaled on spikes above the wire stood every few meters as a constant reminder of what would happen if someone managed to scale a wall. An execution stand rested in the center of the town. Blood stains etched in the lines of the wood.

The captain shoved a gun in Ryker's back. "Move it."

We reached the bottom of the gangway where we were met by ten inhumanly large men. They were the size of assassins Mother sent to murder escapees, and as ugly, with their scarred, pierced, and tattooed bodies. The place reeked of oil, rancid body odor, and manure.

Ryker gestured to Emery and me. "What you planning on doing with them?"

The captain lifted one eyebrow. "Got plans for the pretty one over there."

I tensed against my bound wrists. Scanning the men leaving the ship, I wondered who the Mualite was that prevented the use of our gifts. I had to figure it out and find a way to escape. If not, Ryker would be executed, Emery would be scrapped and enslaved, and I would be used and abused by the captain.

The captain stepped to my side and pulled my hair to his nose. "Ya smell sweet, too."

Ryker shook the guard off and charged for the captain. A guard lifted his gun to Emery's head and he stopped in his tracks at her whimpers.

"Cap'n, I be thinkin' Malvak would be disappointed if you took her for yourself. He prefers 'em fresh."

Ryker turned on him. Josheb gave a warning stare and Ryker remembered the gun pointing at Emery.

A young man in what appeared to be sack cloth ran across the street and stopped before the captain, panting. "Cap'n, sir —" he huffed. "Josheb be ordered to Malvak. These three be placed in holding cell."

"Josheb? Why?" The captain looked at Josheb with a furrowed brow. He puffed his chest out. "Ya mean he wants to be speakin' to me."

"No, sir." The boy shuffled back a few paces. "He be waitin' on Josheb."

"Be off with ya then."

Josheb pushed past.

There was nothing I could say in front of the captain and his men. I had to trust Josheb and hope for the best. He was our only hope. I saw our gift hanging from his belt, and hoped it would straighten all this out.

Josheb continued across the street.

Ryker stuck close to us while the mutant humans escorted us to holding cells. It was no more than a small wooden building with a few metal cells. If we could use our powers, there wouldn't be a problem escaping.

We were each shoved into a separate cell.

Emery squatted down in the corner. "W-we need a p-plan," she whispered.

"Oh good, Emery, you're with us."

Ryker's face lit up at the sound of his sister's few words. Of course, the minute things got tough, she'd check out again.

The world sped by outside with the sound of machine

gears clanking, animals barking and mooing, and heavy wagon wheels crunching through the sand.

Ryker scrubbed his chin. "Emery, stay with us. Need your help."

"Y-yes?" Emery smiled like a child full of mischief and spunk.

He cleared his throat. "Listen, there's a chance I can incapacitate the Mualite who is holding us if we discover who he is."

"How?" I knelt near his cell, my hands clasped in my lap. Exhaustion had to be setting in. My calves were cramping and I knew if we didn't get water and rest soon we'd be in no condition to fight.

"Think the reason we haven't seen him is because they need to keep him hidden."

"Yes, so?" I leaned toward the bars.

"So, that must mean he can't protect himself."

"I g-get it." Emery clapped her hands and stood on her knees. "He c-can keep you f-from using powers b-but not against him."

"You mean if you direct your powers at him, he can't use his?" I asked.

"That's the theory, but the only way it'll work is if I hit him without warning. Duel-like attack to the death. I've gotta zap him quick and hard before he zaps me."

"That's great. If we knew who the Mualite was."

His muscles tensed at my sarcastic tone. "You got a better idea?"

"No, it's...how can we figure out who it is?"

"M-maybe you can ask J-Josheb. He l-likes you, Valencia."

"What?" Ryker cracked his knuckles.

"V-Valencia could f-flirt with—"

"No, too dangerous. I'll figure it out," he said.

I took a deep breath. "She's right."

Ryker froze. "They're a bunch of ugly monsters. You want to get close enough to find out?"

I smiled at him. "He's not that bad. Actually, he's kind of sweet."

"You like that freak? He's gotta be ten years older than you." Ryker paced the small cell and looked out a half-circle iron-barred window. "You know what he would do to you?" His body visibly shook and his hands changed to a pearl skin tone.

"Ryker?"

"What?"

"Your hands."

"What about them?" He looked down.

Emery breathed out and giggled at the sight of the puff of smoke. The room had dropped at least ten degrees.

"It's Josheb. He's the one who's been with us since we were captured."

I stood up and spun around, my hand pressed to my forehead. "No, it couldn't be."

"What? You trust this guy? Seriously? He's a traitor to his own people. Don't you see? He's not out there negotiating our release. He's insuring his own life."

My mind whirled at his words. "No, it's not true. I won't believe it."

"Why would you protect him? Can't you see? People will betray and murder the ones you love to save their own skins. Are you that naive?"

"No, it's just that..." I faced him, wanting to scream and

make him see things didn't always happen the way it seemed. "Never mind. You'd never understand."

"Understand what?"

"Nothing." My voice cracked.

"Fine, stay here and be his mate. I don't care." He stomped to the window.

Was he jealous? Upset? "No, it's not that."

"Do what you want, but I'm getting my sister out of here." He marched to the bars. Steam rose and his fingers cracked when he closed them around the bars.

"N-no!" Emery screamed at him.

Alarms clanged and men raced in through the far corridor, guns drawn, tamer collar in hand.

Josheb walked in behind them, his eyes glowing orange. Ryker screamed and clutched his head.

"No. Stop!" I screamed.

The cell door swung open and one of the men snapped the collar around Ryker's neck.

He fingered the tamer collar secured around his throat and his posture sagged.

"I warned ya not to try anythin', now ya've gone messin' everythin' up."

"Why are you doing this?" I asked.

"Have no choice." Josheb's voice faded.

Ryker rubbed his temple and managed to rise onto his knees again.

"You do have a choice," I insisted.

"Give it up. He'll always be a Mualite traitor." Despite the pain etched on his face, his eyes challenged Josheb.

Josheb spun on his heels and headed for the door, but

stopped. "Ya was gonna receive a trial, but now ya'r execution is set for one hour.

I pressed my palm against the wood wall to steady myself and looked sideways at Josheb. "But you said you'd—"

"That be before he tried to murder us." Josheb's eyes pulsed orange.

"But you're one of us."

"I've never been a Mualite. Was born here, me loyalty falls to these people."

"But you—"

"Can't interfere with Malvak. He'd kill me family for treason." Grief revealed in his eyes, but his narrowed stare showed his determination.

"Told you he was a traitor," Ryker snarled at Josheb.

Josheb's face tensed and he wrapped his fingers around the gun holstered on his hip. "I can't betray people who never wanted us 'cause me mother was deformed."

"Deformed?" Emery asked.

Josheb lingered as if contemplating what to say. "Yeah, me mom was an outcast 'cause she had a mechanical eye. She be one of the first experimented on."

I sauntered over to Josheb standing outside the cell door. "Then you know how Emery feels. We are all outcasts."

Josheb's nose rose into a snarl. "Not, him. He be one of them. I do what I can for the wee one there and for you, ya pretty face, but he hangs."

"No, please! You can't." I fought against the rising flames licking my lungs.

Josheb didn't respond before he marched from the room, slamming the door behind him.

I took a stuttered breath. "We have to do something." Ryker didn't respond. "Emery, tell him."

Emery didn't respond either. She only sat, bouncing the little red ball in front of her.

"Emery. Listen to me. You can't check out now."

"Nothing's left to be done." Ryker's words sent a wave of hot fear through my body.

"Come on, you wanted to fight back. I'll do whatever you want. We have to think fast."

I couldn't lose him. We had to figure out what was between us, what made our touch so powerful. The way pure happiness consumed me when he came near, his strong lips pressed against mine. So many unanswered questions. I refused to give up on the first thing since the age of eleven that made me feel whole, worth something.

Even if he never forgave my part in Emery's torture, I couldn't bear the thought of him being executed.

"No," Ryker said in a monotone voice.

"You can't give up." My voice cracked from the weight of never feeling him near me again.

Ryker finally strolled to the bars. "Not giving up. Not on you two." His hand slid down my cheek sending shivers through my body.

"What're you saying? We need to figure out a plan."

"Shh." Ryker pressed his lips to my forehead. "I have a plan."

My heart soared. "What is it?" I stepped back to look him in the eyes.

He cupped my hands and kissed each knuckle. "Plan is for you and Emery to live."

I reached for his collar. "I can remove—"

He backed away. "No, there's no time. This is the only way."

"And you?" My hands shook. "You, too."

"No. You heard Josheb. You'll both be spared. If I try anything else, you'll both die, too. Won't let that happen."

I stormed the bars. "You'd desert us? Abandon us to our fates here? A life of servitude and prostitution?"

"You'd be alive," he whispered.

"I'd rather be dead because it wouldn't be a life worth living. Ryker, I'd rather die fighting by your side than live like that. It'll be no different from being the general's pet to do with as he wishes."

"Nothing to be done."

"And you call Josheb a traitor. You're the traitor." The words flew from my mouth before I could stop them, but I didn't care. My hands burned and I wanted to melt the bars between us and shake him until he'd listen.

I reached for the bars and he lunged at me, grabbing my wrists through the openings.

"No. Stop." Ryker pulled my body against the bars and he stared me down. "Valencia, listen to me."

"No, I won't." My muscles fatigued as I struggled against his grip. "I won't lose you. Not when I've just found you," I sobbed.

"I don't want to lose you either," he said, his voice softening.

I wanted to tell him how I felt something for him the first time I'd woken in his arms. How my body longed for his touch every minute of every day.

Ryker released my wrist and brushed my hair from my eyes. "Know this sounds crazy. A Tertian princess and a

Mualite, but I thought we had a shot." He half chuckled and his eyebrow arched.

He'd said Tertian instead of Slag. That had to mean something.

Ryker's chest rose and fell with a deep breath. " Valencia, I think I'm—"

The door swung open and four guards entered before Josheb stormed in. "Malvak orders ya all to the platform now."

My stomach flopped. "No. It hasn't been an hour."

"Malvak's orders changed."

"You said they'd be spared," Ryker argued.

"They be ordered to watch."

Josheb's words stung like a laser through my heart. "No, please. You can't. It's too soon."

Ryker still clutched one arm and wouldn't let me go. "Valencia, listen to me."

"No, I won't. This isn't going to happen. I'll tell Malvak who I am and order your release."

"Not wise." Josheb shoved the key into Ryker's cell door.

I had to do something, anything to stop this.

"We need you, Valencia. You're the only one left in this war-torn world who can protect Emery. Please, I promised my folks before they were murdered I'd take care of her. Once I'm gone—"

"Don't say that." Tears stung my eyes and I wanted to pull him against me and disappear.

Ryker reached through the bars and held the back of my head so our foreheads touched. "Once I'm gone, you are her only family."

"Enough, it's time," Josheb ordered.

The guards rushed into the cell, bound Ryker's wrists,

and dragged him from the cell. One guard grabbed Emery by the arm and did the same to me. Josheb stood at the outside of my cell, door open, waiting for me to exit.

"I did all I could," Josheb said with a heavy, deep tone. He bound my wrists and stepped back. "Sorry, Malvak ordered—"

"You could do more. Trust me, you'll regret this later. You'll go to sleep each night with Ryker's face haunting your dreams. I'm still tortured by making a wrong choice when I was only twelve."

I shoved past him and went out to the center of town. Acid rose in my throat at the sight of the noose hanging from a wood beam. It had to be wood. If it had been metal, I could've melted it and bought some more time.

Maybe I could try Ryker's plan and incapacitate Josheb before he stopped me, then get his gun and take a few down. If we could find cover and some metal, we'd have a chance.

I watched Josheb out of the corner of my eye as we approached the platform.

"Don't try it, pretty face. I've trained for years to be a faster draw with me powers. Ya don't stand a chance. All you'll accomplish is ya own death."

I lifted my chin, determined to fight. "I can't stand by and watch him die."

"Ya don't have a choice. None of us do," Josheb insisted.

"You do. Let me use my powers and the three of us escape. Otherwise, you'll have innocent blood on your hands," I pleaded.

Wind whipped through the village. Creaks echoed from the skywalks. Water swished through the steel waterways above. Cannons and barbed wire lined an exterior wall. It was a fortress.

Mother had been right to fear them. Even if I freed Ryker, how could we get out? I suspected the walls were electrified. Maybe I could short out the wires, but I'd need Emery's help to demolish the wall.

Even if we managed to break through the wall, then what? We'd have to get a ship and figure out where we were.

There had to be a way to save him. I had to be missing something.

A horn sounded and people came out of homes and buildings, flooding the street to watch Ryker's execution. Didn't they see they were no better than the council?

I wrung my hands and pulled at my rope bindings that rubbed my skin raw.

The smell of animals and desert sand carried on the wind.

A tall man appeared on one of the skywalks with a fluffy cape of animal fur lining his huge frame. I couldn't make out his features, but he definitely had a tattoo running across his forehead. A reflection of sunlight off his face indicated some piercings.

"This here Mualite is charged with bringing the council's wrath to our land. Do we wish to sacrifice our way of life and be enslaved to the council?"

"No," the crowd yelled back as if in a trance.

"Terminate the prisoner and send his body as a gift to the queen."

"No!" I cried out and ran for the platform. "You're wrong. We only wish to go in peace. The queen doesn't know we're here. We brought a gift!"

I ran up the steps, but a guard snagged my hair, knocking

me down so hard the wood cracked against my shoulder. A pain shot down my arm. Ryker shouldered the man and raced to my side. "Valencia, please, don't do this."

"I can't watch you die," I managed through sobs.

The guards tore us apart and placed Ryker on top of a box.

I fought with all my strength and drew heat from my core to my hands, but the mind-splitting pain made me collapse. I lay on the floor of the platform forced to watch the noose being secured around his neck.

"Proceed with the execution."

The guard kicked the box out from under Ryker and the rope snapped tight around his throat.

CHAPTER NINETEEN

The tamer collar protected Ryker's neck from breaking. Unfortunately, it also pressed against his esophagus, cutting off his airflow. His feet flayed about trying to find purchase on something…anything.

Noise swirled around me, loud chants from the crowd that lusted for his death.

The rope swung and turned with his fight. He reached for the rope but his wrists were bound too tight. His limbs convulsed, but the crowd continued to cheer. Finally, his joints froze in place and his body stiffened.

"No!" I cried out. Heat radiated through my body. The world moved in patterns, but I only made out Emery storming the platform. We clutched each other close. Heat soared through me.

Josheb shot back off the platform. Emery shouted, but I couldn't make out her words through the thunder in my ears. My breath plumed in smoke.

Ryker's body smashed onto the platform, vibrating the

wood beneath me. His body lay limp, sprawled out across the planks.

The thunder subsided and I realized the cheering for his death had stopped. Instead, the only sound permeating the air was water swooshing through the steel overhead waterway and machine gears grinding away at their jobs. Everyone else was face down in the sand with arms outstretched overhead.

I swallowed despite my throbbing throat. Did they figure out I was a princess, and they bowed out of fear?

Ryker lifted his head and crawled to our side with his eyes wide and questioning.

"Wh-what just happened?" Emery asked.

"I don't know." The words tore like knives slicing my windpipe. Even to my ears, my voice sounded raspy and faint.

"Look." Emery pointed up at the skywalk.

Malvak stood with his hands grasping the wood railing. His face twisted in obvious disdain.

The people prostrated in front of us were breathing, but none moved.

"Did we do this?" I whispered.

Ryker rubbed his red and bruised neck but didn't release me. "Looks like the temple monks back in the Mining Territory during one of their worshiping ceremonies."

I clutched his hand in mine. "If I didn't know better, I'd swear they were worshiping one of us."

Malvak cursed overhead, smacking his fists against the railing, and then stomped off down the skyway into the greenish-brown building on the far side of town.

I looked around for a clue about what happened but only found singed rope threads littered around the sand-covered, cracked wood platform.

The smell of burnt rope sent a chill through my body. Ryker tugged at the collar.

"Let me," I whispered, placing two fingers on the tamer collar.

Emery kneeled by my side. "Sh-shouldn't we run or s-something?"

"Run where?" he asked.

"Yeah, I know." I gestured at the wall.

Another whistle blew. No one except Josheb moved. His head popped up and he glanced our way before placing his forehead against the sand again.

Ryker struggled to stand with Emery's and my help. Something had happened. My powers had worked somehow, and by the sight of frost on Josheb, Ryker's had too. Not to mention the sand covering the platform and the bodies of those on the ground below. Emery must have done that.

Were the people of Oasis scared because we could use our powers even with Josheb there? This could be the opportunity we had been waiting for. Yet, the look on Malvak's face before he stormed away meant he wasn't frightened, merely annoyed.

"Josheb, you will help us leave this place," Ryker ordered in an authoritative voice, but Josheb didn't move.

I let go of Ryker's hand and went to Josheb's side, kneeling next to him. "We need your help. What is going on?" I glanced back.

Emery leaned Ryker against the half-splintered post he had swung from moments before. "Rise Josheb, I order you t-to t-take us to M-Malvak."

Ryker grabbed Emery's arm. "What're you doing?"

"T-trust m-me brother." Emery maneuvered the two steps

down and rested her hand on Josheb's shoulder. He rose from the ground, but no one else followed.

Ryker crawled to the end of the platform and stumbled down the stairs into my arms. "She's crazy."

Emery smiled. "Not at th-the m-moment."

We followed Josheb through the still crowd and into the brownish-green building. Sulfur and oil nearly choked me. Ryker coughed, still clutching his rope-burned throat, but the bruise was already fading.

We walked through an assembly line of weaponry before we headed up two flights of stairs.

I clung to the cold, smooth metal railing and hoisted myself up each step. Fatigue was setting in along with lack of food and water. I needed something soon or I'd collapse.

Josheb pushed open a heavy green door with iron bars on the window and entered a room. Guns and swords lined the walls. A large desk stood at the end of the room, where the satchel Ryker had brought rested.

Malvak sat at his desk with his face pinched tight. "What be the meaning of this? Ya dare bring these traitors to me presence? It be a trick. The lot of them overcame your weak mind."

"No. You're wrong. No one entered me mind," Josheb argued as he stepped back away from the oversized gorilla behind the desk.

"W-we demand th-that you release us."

"Demand? Ha! Ya do be a fool."

Emery stood with shoulders back, staring the man down. "W-we are no f-fools. W-we're worshiped by your people."

"So, what if you are? Ya be of no use to me. Send them back to jail."

"Wouldn't advise it, sir. They'd still be praying for the Triune to deliver them."

"Triune?" Malvak pounded his hand against the metal desktop, sending a ripple through the floor and up my already weak legs.

Triune?

"No such thing as Triune. It's an old folk tale made up to give people hope."

"I saw it with me own eyes. Their powers mixed to one." Josheb lowered his head and half bowed to us.

These people thought we were some sort of mythological being that brought the dead back to life? Something called a Triune? The Mualites weren't saying thank you when I'd removed their collars, they thought we were this thing, too.

"You fool." Malvak shoved his chair back and stomped around the desk. Josheb stood straight and prepared himself for punishment, but Malvak stopped. His right eye twitched and I knew it was nothing good. "They only used gifts to stop 'im from dying. Nothing ya couldn't do."

"Just let us go, Malvak. We won't make trouble for you," Ryker said.

"Once at Oasis, ya can never leave, but that doesn't mean ya can steal me people away. They follow me and will never worship ya." One half of his mouth curled up in a grin, the other scarred half with a silver hoop didn't budge. "I know what I has to do now." Malvak lowered his hand and stepped away from Josheb.

"Me people need hope, so I'll give it to them. I think it be time for a celebration. Go ring the bell. Let the people know there'll be a grand ball in honor of Triune tonight. Everyone should wear their finest."

Josheb didn't move. His gaze darted between us all. It wasn't a good sign.

"After the celebration, you will free us?" I asked.

"No. Ya see, the gift ya brought was fine. Would've let ya leave with that payment until the queen sent word. I keep ya here and she'll leave us alone forever. If I let ya leave, she finds and destroys me town."

My chest tightened, the world swayed under my feet. My mother. Always my mother following me to the ends of the Earth. I glared at him. "Then there is nothing to celebrate. She'll only betray and murder you."

Ryker stepped between us, but Malvak shoved him away and grabbed me in his grubby hands.

"Oh, but there is. I be making sure me people still worship me. I be taking a wife. One of the Triune."

CHAPTER TWENTY

I shoved Malvak away from me. "I won't marry you."

He grabbed Emery and stuck a blade to her throat. "Then she dies. I tell the others it be an accident."

"People won't believe that," Josheb interrupted.

"Trust me. They'll believe me."

Ryker leapt at Malvak, but Josheb yanked him back. "He not be joking. That blade'll tear her from ear to ear before ya get to her."

Emery's eyes grew wide.

I scanned the area as heat surrounded me, my powers igniting into a ball of fire.

Josheb shook his head. He'd stop me. I slanted my glance at the weapons in the case. If I could find a way to get to them before they could stop me...

The captain pressed the blade deeper into Emery's neck. "Ya won't be using those weapons, girly. They not be working. Prototypes."

"You're no better than the queen or the general." I couldn't let Ryker and Emery die if there was something I could do to save them. "At least this time my sacrifice will earn their freedom."

"What ya speak of there girl? I said nothing about their freedom."

"Then this talk of marriage is a waste of time and breath." I hated the word *marriage*. It meant nothing more than a contract that gave a man power over me. The idea of his meaty hands groping my body nearly made me vomit.

"No. I won't let you—" Ryker pushed free of Josheb and took me into his arms.

"Don't be touchin' me bride like that or I cut off ya hands."

Ryker pushed my hair from my eyes and I lost myself in his gaze for a moment. "Don't do this. We'll find another way."

"There is no other way. You need resources and transportation, not to mention a way out of this place."

"We'll figure it out."

"Ya think ya be escapin' me kingdom? Ah, not likely there, mate. Agree to ya terms there, girly. Ya be my wife and I free ya friends."

I'd fled from one heartless wretch into the arms of another. Why was it always marriage or servitude? "How do I know you speak the truth?"

"I give me word as a Scavenger."

Ryker had talked about always choosing a Mualite no matter the price. This was my chance to do that, and make up for what I did to Emery four years ago. To make a choice to save instead of mutilate someone. I had the power to free them. How could I not? "Deal," I rasped.

Malvak let Emery go and she raced to my side. Ryker wrapped his arms around both of us.

Malvak's deep laugh echoed through the room. "Enjoy ya self. This be the last time ya be touching me bride. Prepare the girl for me wedding. I'll be tellin' the people what be goin' on." Malvak marched from the room and Josheb followed quickly behind, leaving the three of us alone.

Reality hit, and my shaking legs wouldn't support me. As I pushed Emery into Ryker's arms, I slid down the wall, pulling my knees to my chest. I shivered at the memory of his foul breath against my face. I'd come so far, risked my life, only to end up betrothed to a man just like the general—heartless and evil.

Ryker released Emery, who had returned to her own world, bouncing her ball, then sat by my side and took my hand in his. "I won't let you do this."

"There's no choice. It's your only hope. This is bigger than the three of us. Your people back in the Mining Territory suffer. They won't survive much longer. You have to get to Old Chicago, pick up the contact, and make it to the coast in order to help the rebellion." I remained firm despite the voice in my head screaming to run.

"Don't care. None of it matters if an innocent life is taken. We'll find another way."

Innocent?

"Don't care if we all die here. It's wrong to let this happen."

"What happened to you sacrificing your own life so that we would be enslaved instead of dead? At least in my plan, you two get out of here."

"That was before."

"Before what?" Something different reflected in the way he looked at me. His face appeared less tense and his body leaned more into mine.

Ryker rose and paced the floor. "Just watch, I'll take Josheb down when he returns. Then you and Emery make your escape. It would be better to die than to see that monster's hands on you."

He'd never give up. Fight to the death to save my honor. That was who he was, a fighter. I'd been cornered. The decision made for me. I had to stop him before he did something stupid.

I took a long deep breath and braced myself. "I'm not innocent."

"What're you talking about?"

"I was there when they tortured Emery four years ago. I stood by while they took her leg."

Emery sucked in a quick breath and scurried next to me. "N-no. Shhh."

Emery had heard. Fallon was right. She checked out but still heard what was going on around her. She put her finger over my lips but I batted it away.

Ryker looked down, brows furrowed. "What did you say?"

My insides twisted and turned. I wanted to fall on my knees in front of him and beg forgiveness, but I wouldn't. This was my chance to make up for what I had done. If Ryker hated me, he would leave and save Emery. It was justice that I remained and paid for my crimes.

"It was after my father was killed. I was brought to a mother I never knew I had. I'd been raised by my father in the Resort Territory and I thought that was the reality of the world. For eleven years I lived like no other Tertian, Mualite, or human had ever lived." I sniffed. "My father loved me and everything was perfect. I assumed my mother would be like him, only she was nothing like anyone I'd ever met."

Ryker fisted his hands, refusing to meet my gaze, and stared at the wall over my head. While relieved he didn't look at me, I swallowed hard and continued.

"After a few months of brutal reconditioning, the queen and the general felt safe taking me with them. I was twelve, like Emery, when she was captured during my first trip to the Mining Territory. The queen was experimenting on Mualites, something about perfecting a weapon to ensure the safety of all those who survived the war. I didn't want anything to do with the research. That drove her to send me for more reconditioning." I thoughtlessly stroked my cheek. "She thought that if she forced me to watch and participate, I would toughen up. She thought I was weak and pathetic."

Ryker punched the wall, then shot up, pacing the floor. My heart raced.

"One day, I was ordered to a prison cell. That's when I met Emery. I hadn't seen anyone my own age since I'd boarded the ship."

Emery tugged at my sleeve. "S-stop, no need to d-do this."

Ryker glanced at Emery. "You knew? You remembered her and you wanted me to save her anyway?"

"Y-yes." Emery grasped my arm. "P-please, V-Valencia. You're my b-best f-friend. Don't do th-this."

"No, you fantasized about our friendship, made it into something it wasn't." For once I wished Emery would check out so I wouldn't have to face the pain in her large brown eyes.

Ignoring Emery's pained expression, I focused on feeding Ryker's hatred. There would have never been a chance between us anyway.

"I sat by and watched as they removed her leg, then—" My

voice cracked. "I dumped her body in the middle of the Wasteland."

Ryker raced back and grabbed me, sending Emery to the side. Her whimpers tore at my heart.

"It's not true. I know what you're doing."

"It's true. I'm the one that threw her out like garbage in the desert."

Josheb's unmistakable heavy steps drew close. My mind spun with theories of how to escape. No, this was where I belonged. I wouldn't risk their lives to save my own. There was no future for me. A Slag princess, disowned by my mother, and an outcast.

Ryker shoved me away and pulled at his hair. "You tortured my sister to the brink of insanity, then allowed me to rescue you, risking her life again?"

"N-no. Sh-she didn't ask to b-be s-saved. And sh-she s-saved—"

"I opened the gangway and rolled her body out," I said, fighting back the sobs of regret.

Ryker marched over and slammed his fist against the wall next to my ear. His eyes cold and distant. "Tell me it's not true."

"I can't," I whispered.

Josheb entered and cleared his throat. "Not much time. Ya need to follow me. Malvak's not be keeping his word. He's going to enslave Valencia after the wedding and kill the wee one and ya. This will put the people of Oasis back under his control. I've got to get ya out of here while he's busy. It's ya only chance."

No. I'd just confessed to save us. How could he offer help now?

Josheb looked back down the hall.

"You're risking your own family by doing this," I said.

"I be no better than a servant if I don't do what's right. Whatever goes on between ya two, let it go for now. No time to be fightin' if ya wish to save the wee one."

Ryker pulled away with a deep snarl still on his face and took Emery's hand. "Come on, Emery. Time to get out of here."

No, I'd just accepted my fate. Confessed my sins, resulting in hatred from the one man who ever had a gentle touch. "Josheb, leave me here. I won't risk your family."

"You won't risk his family, but you'll torture and try to kill mine?" Ryker twisted a dagger of condemnation through the center of my heart.

I steadied myself and walked past him and Emery to Josheb's side.

A chill pierced my back. I knew his ability to manage his anger was only because of Emery.

Josheb handed my clothes to me. "Change, that dress'll be noticed."

With no time to waste, I stepped behind a half-wall and quickly ripped the dress from my body and shoved back on the soft pants, undershirt, and vest.

Josheb took my hand and led us down a winding staircase in the corner of the large factory. "Josheb, listen," I whispered so Ryker couldn't hear my words. "We can manage if you tell us where to go. Tell Malvak we overpowered you. The whole Triune thing. Then—"

"No, I've stood by too long and watched innocent people die. Ya might not believe it because he be power hungry, but he would give his own life to save Oasis. He believes in a dream of a better life. I only know what is here, but he speaks of the old world and how he plans to rebuild it. Once the Mualites and Slags finish hashing things out."

"The Mualites are not the ones fighting. The queen ordered their extinction in the Mining Territory. She blew the entire town to bits. If there was a way to join forces, we could all stand a chance to live free again."

"Ya be a strange one, pretty face. How can ya be a princess of Slags, yet have powers of a Mualite?"

"All I know is my dad was Mualite and my mom was a Tertian. He never told me, though. There's a lot he never told me." Sadness crept in despite the danger that lay ahead. Why hadn't my father prepared me for how life existed outside the Resort Territory? Why hadn't he ever warned me about my mother? He never said a word, not even a hint about them being married. Mualite and Tertian.

"Get down." Josheb yanked me to his side. His dark muscles glistened in the light of the luminary.

We edged further down a corridor and exited behind the skywalk. The sun had fallen in the sky, the orange moon shining in its stead, revealing a small walkway.

Josheb barely managed to shimmy down the path sideways. "Ya ship be docked at the end of this. We must climb the wall. I will stall long enough for ya to get out of range."

"No, you can't. He'll suspect and kill you." I didn't know why, but this man with a conscience was someone I could understand, a person who had faced many wrongs in his life that he only wished to make right. I didn't want to see any harm come to him.

"Gonna stand there all night, or is this a trap like I suspect-ed?" Ryker accused.

"Ryker, he's risking his life." I snapped.

"It be okay, he has reason to suspect me. Promise, no trap." Josheb said.

I shuffled behind Josheb. Malvak's voice boomed some-where overhead. I pressed my sweaty back to the wall and listened to him announce the union between the two of us until Ryker nudged me forward. When we reached the animal pens, the smell of pig and manure choked me. I stifled a cough.

Josheb handed me a small swatch of cloth. "Here, this helps."

I pressed it to my nose, wishing I still had the desert mask.

"There's the stairs. Ryker, ya first. I'll hand the wee one to you, then the princess."

"W-what about th-the electricity?"

"Powered it down."

Emery smiled at him.

Ryker narrowed his gaze. Josheb bent down, picked up a pebble, then tossed it at the wire. No spark.

Wind whistled through the long, narrow path. We froze. The stink of our fear surrounded us. People mingled out in the courtyard, but I didn't hear Malvak's voice, which made me more anxious to escape.

Josheb gave me a quick, knowing glance and grabbed a cloth from a box near the animal pen. "Take a feed bag and place it over the wire.

Ryker snatched it from Josheb's hands then climbed the ladder with caution, put the feed bag in place, swung a leg over the barbed wire, and stepped over cautiously. He sat on the other side of the wall and looked below, then signaled for Emery to follow.

Emery struggled with the angle of her mechanical leg. It wouldn't bend far enough and Josheb gave her a push from behind, helping her up each step. She managed to make it over the barbed wire with both of their help.

Josheb returned to my side.

"Come with us," I said.

"I can't abandon me family."

"I knew you weren't evil. I think we could be friends if we had a chance." I longed to have another friend in life, especially now that Ryker would never let me be near Emery again.

"I believe the same, pretty face."

I flung my arms around his middle and he pulled me close.

"Let's get ya to ya ship before Malvak discovers ya're missing.

I climbed the steps and waited for Ryker to offer his hand, but he'd already helped Emery to the ground, leaving me behind.

"Don't worry. Don't know what ya said to him, but he'll forgive ya. He's sweet on ya." Hatchet winked.

Heat rose to my cheeks. "Me? I think you're mistaken."

"Nothing gets by me. And ya feel the same." He winked.

"Please." I maneuvered over the wire and halfway down the ladder. "He hates me and always will."

"I don't believe that." Hatchet threw one leg over the wire and pointed. "Ya ship be down there."

"Get them!" Malvek shouted over the loudspeaker.

A mind-numbing sizzle shot down the wire indicating someone had turned the power back on. Before I could warn

Josheb, he jolted about like a turkey getting its neck broken. His large body fell limp against the wall, his leg hanging from the wire.

"No!" My heart pounded so loud I couldn't hear the electric current anymore. I grabbed the ladder, but Ryker pulled my hands free. "You can't help him now."

CHAPTER TWENTY-ONE

Ryker shoved me to the side and climbed the few rungs to Josheb hanging upside down on the ladder. Ryker pressed his hand to Josheb's chest then slid back down. I clutched the ladder, but Ryker's arms were like vices around my middle. "No more time. I restarted his heart."

I kicked and dug my heels into the ground, but he dragged me to the ship.

"He m-might be okay," Emery tried to comfort me.

I thrashed in Ryker's arms, but he shoved me into the co-pilot seat and hit the hatch button, cracking the glass.

"Why didn't you just leave me behind? I know you wanted to," I lashed out.

"Ryker. Sh-she didn't t-tell you everything." Emery grasped the steering handles.

Ryker turned and glared at me. "Not the time. Sit down. Know you didn't want Josheb to die. But if you don't help, he sacrificed himself and his family for nothing."

I swiped my tears so I could see. Connecting with the reconditioning of my youth, I grasped the throttle with my shaking hands and straightened to my perfect princess posture, storing my grief into another little compartment deep inside.

We zoomed away from Oasis. The Scavengers would be close behind, and if we didn't put enough distance between us and them, we would never make it.

Emery flew the ship low, skimming the dunes. Hopefully, we'd blend with the sand and the Scavenger ship would stay high, away from the sermechtapedes.

I checked the nav and entered the coordinates to Old Chicago.

Ryker shook his head. "Malvak will be on top of us any minute."

"We change our course th-then." Emery pulled up on the handles sending us straight up to maneuver over a tall dune.

"Can't. Only have enough fuel to reach Old Chicago from here. No way we can alter our course," Ryker warned.

"We wouldn't have to alter it far," I said, my throat so tight I wasn't sure anyone heard me. "Only enough to hide."

"See anywhere to hide? We're in the middle of the Wasteland." He sounded cold and distant. His eyes darted to me but quickly refocused on the path ahead.

I ignored his tone and glare. "We cut the engine. Glide down from the top of a dune to the bottom. Without the engine hum, the creatures under the sand won't know we're there."

"Glide down?"

"Yeah. I think I can manage my powers to keep us from crashing."

"We don't have much ch-choice," Emery reminded him.

"Go for it," Ryker agreed.

Emery banked right. She focused on the next long rise and soared high into the sky.

"Now," I said, pressing my palms to the dashboard, one hand still sensitive from the last time I'd tried this.

She cut the engine and I worked the controls. The flaps banged and bells whistled until I cut power completely. Wires hummed at the nape of my neck, connecting with the ship. A binary conversation took place in my brain.

An orange hue illuminated the cockpit. The ship glided on an air current and for a second, I was weightless.

I glanced over and Emery held her arms in the air and smiled. It wasn't just me. We were headed down too fast.

Once I cut the lights, all I saw out the front was darkness.

"Sure you got this? No time to power up now." He gripped the back of my seat.

My insides wrenched as I realized we were about to plow into the sand.

Ryker pressed against the seat.

The ship slowed.

We slid silently down the sand dune to a halt.

The only other light seeped through greenish clouds from the orange moon.

The roar of the Scavenger engines echoed and I held my breath, waiting for the ship to fly over the dune we'd surfed down and take us hostage again.

None of us made a sound. We knew if we dropped so much as a bead of sweat on the floor of the ship, a sermechta-pede or spiderat would find us in minutes.

The Scavenger ship passed, the rumbling of the engines fading.

"Ryker. I know you could never understand...but I'm sorry," I whispered.

"Can't talk now, the creatures could hear."

We sat in uncomfortable silence. Once in a while, he opened his mouth, only to shut it again. He'd sworn only a day ago to avenge his sister. Now the culprit sat next to him.

"Why'd you save me? You want me dead, yet you pulled me into the ship."

"How could you let it happen?" he mumbled.

"I-I..." The words wouldn't flow. I didn't know how to answer him.

"Sh-she didn't torture me. Sh-she t-tried to help me," Emery said.

"How?"

The door I had shut on the internal compartment of my mind cracked and tears spilled down my cheeks. I only hoped no one could see them in the dark. I clutched the small cloth Josheb had given me for strength.

"By disobeying her m-mother. Sh-she was discovered t-trying to c-comfort me. W-we were only little girls. I'd never s-seen a m-mother treat a child the way the queen did V-Valencia. Brutal."

My head throbbed at the memory of her body bouncing down the gangway. "I should've risked it and gotten you off the ship instead of dropping you like garbage."

"Risk more? I'm th-the reason she was promised t-to the general as a bride. She t-tried t-to help me escape and was caught. Queen ordered m-me to die and Valencia to be given to the general."

Ryker dropped his head in his hands.

The light shone in the distance again, this time in the other direction. "Must've given up and turned back. It's too risky to be out here at night."

We all sat in silence as the scavengers passed by again. I clasped my hands in my lap. "I think we should go."

Ryker stood hunched over. "Emery, you rest. I've got it from here. I can fly a straight shot. If anything happens, I'll wake you." Gripping the steering handles, he slid into the pilot chair. "You're right. First light, they'll return. This time of year, that'll only be in a few hours."

The engine revved and Ryker quickly got us in the sky before any creatures ate us for a night snack.

It would take us twice the time to reach Old Chicago without the power of the Scavenger ship. For four hours, I ran through everything in my head. My father's loving embrace. Being torn from the only home I'd known at only eleven, alone on a ship with a bunch of strangers until I met Emery.

The morning light crept up the eastern horizon. The fuel gauge danced at the middle, warning us we were cutting it close.

"We have a couple more hours, you should get some sleep," Ryker murmured.

I stared out the front window. "I can't sleep."

"You're still thinking about Josheb, aren't you?"

Fear clawed at me. "You judge him because of his circumstances even after he risked everything to free us. How do we know that Malvak isn't back there torturing his family now?"

Emery stirred on the floor behind us.

He shifted in his seat. "You said you tortured my sister."

His words shot like a laser through my chest. I struggled to catch my breath. "Yes, my mother forced me to participate in the interrogation after she caught me nursing Emery. I know you think everyone has a choice. But sometimes you don't, or it's between bad and worse. That's when people are forced to do things. It isn't always easy to stand up for what you believe in."

"You were only twelve. Josheb was a man."

"A man with a family—a wife, and child. Can you tell me you wouldn't risk everything for Emery? I think you've already proven you would when they tried to hang you."

A puff of white smoke blew from between his lips.

Knowing I'd never be able to make him understand, I sat rigid in the chair next to him for the next few hours.

The sun rose higher in the sky and the gauge dropped dangerously low. "We need to land soon," I said.

Ryker leaned forward and scanned the horizon.

I couldn't stand the silence another second. "Even if we find a place to land, we won't make it to the city and back before nightfall."

"Uncle spoke of panic rooms installed by the humans back before the war. They were terrified of the Mualites sneaking in while they slept or breaking into their homes during dinner to drain them of their blood."

"Blood?"

Ryker huffed. "They were obsessed with vampires and shapeshifters and thought we all wanted to drain their blood so we could live forever."

"Really?"

"Idiots. Bunch of mindless humans needing someone to lead them. Well, they got what they wanted."

A clearing between the rubble caught my eye. "Over there."

"No, we need to make it a few more kilometers to make

sure we're out of the desert zone. If we let her down near those beasts, the ship will be gone by morning."

"Morning? But we—"

"Don't have a choice. Face it, we're kilometers from the city. Even at the fastest speed possible, we'll never make it back in time. And from what I know, we don't want to be out after dark. We'll freeze or be devoured by hungry animals."

"Animals?"

"Once the population was gone, animals ran wild in these parts."

"Let's fly until we can't go any longer," I agreed.

"Good plan." The fuel lasted another few hours until the sun crossed and began to descend behind the ship. We were further than I'd figured based on the geo-map, and we wouldn't have long to find shelter.

"We're not going to make it, are we?"

"We'll make it."

I didn't say anything to keep from freaking Emery out. The last thing we needed was her becoming comatose. Ryker would be slowed by the weight of carrying her. Even though she didn't even weigh forty-five kilos, it would still hinder our progress.

The landscape turned from miles of orange sand to rubble, spurts of weeds, and busted asphalt.

The ship jumped and sputtered and the red line spun around the gauge.

"That's as far as we go," Ryker announced.

I opened the flaps decreasing our speed, and Ryker glided toward the ground.

"Steady. We don't want to damage the ship or we'll never get out of here," I warned.

Glancing around, I saw everything had been blasted to oblivion. Why would Old Chicago be any different? We needed to find the panic rooms. Assuming they still existed.

"There." Ryker pointed to the other side of a tall grass field.

The ship dipped lower and skimmed the tall green and brown trees. A scratch from a branch down the belly of the ship made me cringe. Beyond the last line of trees, the ship sputtered and we sailed down without power.

I sprang into action and controlled the flaps as needed, keeping the ship level as we descended. My heart raced at the realization the wind picked up. If we didn't die landing, we had to be close to Old Chicago. Fallon had said there were great radiated lakes on the other side of the city that created the wind, and it had been called the windy city before the war according to my history instructor.

The ship bounced twice and then halted after a few hundred meters. We all sighed and Ryker fell back in his chair.

"Sorry, too much wind. Wasn't sure I could handle it with my powers. The Wasteland with soft sand is one thing, wind another."

Emery took out her ball and bounced it a few times. Good indication she'd be back with us soon.

"No time to rest." Ryker stood hunched over and retrieved the radiation masks Fallon had given us. Not sure if any of the radioactive fallout still remained. I donned the mask and handed one to Emery. Then we each snapped on our belts with the few drops of remaining water nestled in a slot. Ryker helped Emery with her mask.

I loved the smell of worn leather. But when mixed with scented pine, I coughed and sniffled. Grimacing as the mask straps dug into my temples, I adjusted them higher on my head.

"Hatch opening." My voice echoed in my head.

I shoved Josheb's small cloth in my side pouch and pressed the button. Holding my breath, I waited for some mutant creature to attack.

Nothing moved.

Nothing swept through the sky.

Nothing scurried or squawked.

Only eerie silence. Until another gust of wind brought a cool breeze through swaying charcoaled trees.

Ryker bolted over the side and landed on the ground.

I flung my leg over and tumbled down. Ryker caught me before my head smashed against the side of the ship. I straightened and moved to the side so Emery could come down. "Do you know where we are?"

"Not exactly, but I believe we aren't too far from what remains of Old Chicago."

Emery sat on the edge of the cockpit dangling her legs.

"Jump." Ryker held out his arms.

She launched from the ship.

He hobbled back as he caught her. "Which way?"

I glanced around the desolate area and compared it to the terrain on the geo-map. Sparse, gnarled, naked tree trunks littered the area. Moss snaked up and around rocks and rubble of buildings and homes that once stood erect on this site.

I turned and studied the inviting landscape full of lush foliage behind us, then turned back to the crumbled remains ahead.

"Looks like we're abandoning a garden for a graveyard," Ryker muttered.

His words sent a shiver through my body, leaving a trail of doom and fear. "Well, if there is one thing I've learned, looks don't mean anything in the real world." I took Emery by the arm. "Come on, we'll walk together."

"You have such a way with her. How can you be so different from your mother? The woman who murders, pillages, and destroys without thought."

It was a rhetorical question. He brushed by and pressed on. The watch in my vest ticked in a loud beat. A constant reminder of the deadline we were under.

Emery's leg jammed and she wobbled before Ryker took her by the elbow.

"P-please, need to r-rest a moment."

"I could use a quick rest." I pulled my water from my belt, squeezed my eyes shut, and pulled the mask from my face.

"Here, you need to drink some." Ryker held the container out to his sister. "Make sure to keep your eyes shut and hold your breath. We don't know how the air could affect us. No one's ever been out this far…except for our mysterious contact."

"Ahead! There's a few buildings still standing." My insides jumped in hope we'd reached Old Chicago and despair at the ruin before us. The sun, only a third above the horizon, an hour left of daylight, shone from behind us down a rocky path.

Ryker rushed ahead and grabbed his viewfinder. My heart soared at the sight of the broken hell that lay ahead.

"Yes, that's it. It has to be." He handed the viewfinder to

me. "Over there, the lime green. It has to be the water Uncle spoke of."

"Yeah, too bad it's on the other side of the city and it's too contaminated to drink." I shook my container, the small amount of water sloshing inside.

"We'll have to find something to drink and shelter. Tomorrow morning, we'll look for our contact and fuel for the ship."

"I don't know if I can make it," Emery said faintly through her mask.

Ryker took her hand and helped her down the hill. "You have to. We can't stop now."

She grabbed him as her metal leg weighted her down. Losing her grasp on Ryker, she crumbled to the ground.

"Don't worry, I've got you."

I quickly took Emery's other arm. "I'm here, too."

Emery tripped and her metal foot clanged against rocks and tree roots all the way down.

By the time we reached the bottom, rivers of sweat ran down my back. I grabbed the cloth from my side pouch and dabbed my forehead. "See, told you we'd make it." Using the rag, I blotted Emery's cheeks and brow.

Emery reached for her ball.

My hand covered hers. We couldn't afford for her to check out now. "You did great, Emery. You're faster than a desert beetle," I teased.

Emery placed the ball back in her belt and walked arm-in-arm with me.

Bombed-out buildings came into focus. "We should head to the nearest building that looks habitable," Ryker urged.

I swallowed hard. The massive mounds of gray and black

piles looked like they weren't going to stand much longer.

I pointed. "Look. A street." There was a long, cleared path through the middle of the rubble.

Ryker passed us, leading the way into Old Chicago. "Must've been cleared sometime toward the end of the war." Ryker turned left and right glancing down the side alleys. "I never understood why the queen didn't drop the bomb directly in the heart of the city. Why only outside?"

"She never wastes resources."

"If that's true, she has something here. Some sort of mining or factory." Ryker tugged at his mask strap.

"I agree."

The hair rose on the back of my neck as we maneuvered down the rocky path. Shadows covered us in cool darkness, almost as if to warn of the evil ahead.

Snarls echoed down the alleyways as the light faded. A green-eyed beast blinked only a few meters away.

A light shone so brightly it blinded us. "Who's out there?" A hoarse woman's voice echoed from behind the light.

"Our ship ran low on fuel," Ryker shouted.

The sound of a gun being readied to fire sounded from behind the light. "Go back to it, nothing 'round here for y'all."

The lime green eyes reflected from the alley to our side.

"Please, my sister has a bad leg. We won't make it."

Silence.

"What's your business here?" the woman asked.

Ryker shielded his eyes. "Trying to get to a new territory. Our resources are running out, but our craft didn't make it."

I held my breath, hoping and wishing she'd help. The sun continued to lower behind us.

"Fine, this way," the woman shouted.

Emery collapsed to the ground and covered her ears.

"Grab 'er and follow me. They ain't stupid, ya know. Besides, temperature's about to drop like ya never felt," the woman said.

Ryker scooped Emery up in his arms. "Valencia, go."

I glanced back. More eyes shone behind us.

"Hold on," Ryker managed through labored breaths.

"There." The light shut off, revealing the woman, but a blue haze surrounded her face. I continued to blink away the remnants of the light in my vision.

"Behind the building. Go right."

Scared to say anything that would change the woman's mind, I followed her directions in silence.

After several turns, stairs, and a few metal doors, we entered a home in the middle of the rubble. The blue spot had faded from my vision, revealing a sofa, tables and chairs.

"Take her in that room." Her wisps of gray and blonde hair reminded me of my own. But the wrinkles on her face looked more like a human or Mualite. Strange, until the Mining Territory, I hadn't seen wrinkles. But then, no one on Mother's ship was allowed the disfigurement of the deep lines of age.

Ryker laid Emery on a gray couch with sunken cushions.

I collapsed into a fluffy chair and pulled the mask from my face.

The woman studied Emery with eyebrows pinched together. "What's wrong with her?"

Candlelight flickered around us. Emery retrieved her ball from her pocket and rolled it in her hand.

"She's been through a lot," Ryker said softly.

"Y'all not right smart, are you?" The old woman leaned

back in a white chair, tilting it against the wall behind her.

I cleared my throat. "We thank you for the assistance."

The woman slammed the two front legs down onto the floor and stood up. She glowered at the three of us, then left the room. "Couldn't let y'all be dog food. Guess I gotta feed ya now, too." She disappeared into a doorway in the back.

I reached out and took Emery's hand. "Can we trust her? Do you think that's our contact?

"We don't have a choice. No reason not to since she went out there to save us. But I'm not sure we should reveal why we're here just yet. We're not going anywhere before morning anyway."

I stared after the woman, then back at Ryker. "I guess so."

"Just glad we all made it this far." He caressed my cheek. I loved the way his hand cradled my face. I never thought I'd feel his touch again. He still had a hint of the earthy scent from the day we'd met. It soothed my nerves. I closed my eyes and allowed myself to enjoy it for a moment.

The woman returned with tray in hand. "I only have so much to spare. Huntin's scarce 'round here."

"Why were the eyes of those dog-like creatures green?" I asked.

The woman snickered. "Drank from the lake."

"You here alone?" Ryker asked.

The lady placed the tray of food on a hardwood table in the corner.

My stomach churned. The smell of whatever she brought was unlike anything I'd ever experienced, but I knew I needed to eat.

Ryker stood. His body swayed for a minute. As with Emery and me, exhaustion had overtaken him. Probably worse given he'd carried his sister most of the way. How he could even talk was beyond me.

Emery reached out. "I l-love soup. Thank you s-so much, Mrs...?"

"The names ah, well, what is my name again?" She huffed a half laugh. "It's been so long I'm not, um...it's Maggie."

"It's a p-pleasure to meet you, Mrs. M-Maggie." Emery took her spoon and blew on the gray liquid.

"Have you lived in Old Chicago all your life?" I asked.

The woman laughed from her gut this time. "Shoot no, I'm from the south. I moved to Chicago when I got married." Her gaze shot between us. "Old Chicago? Who are you people?"

"We're from the Mining Territory." Ryker slurped from his spoon.

I moved the spoon to my mouth, but I swore I saw hair floating on the top of mine, white fur to be exact.

Maggie slurped some of her own gray creation. Guess it wasn't poisoned. I forced a few spoonfuls of the liquid down and a few pieces of what appeared to be vegetables.

"What's a mining territory? Sounds like somethin' out of the old west."

I stirred the remaining bits left in the gray liquid. "It was one of the surviving territories that currently support the Slags and humans."

"What amagiggy?"

"Slags," I repeated. "Don't you know about the queen and the war?"

"Shoot yeah, I know 'bout the war. We were told about those creatures that could suck our blood."

Ryker flinched.

"Emery, I-I'm Emery." She fluffed her vest and smiled.

"That's Ryker, m-my brother, and that's Valencia. She's a—"

"Our friend," Ryker interjected.

"Have you been here since the war?" I asked.

"Yep."

"How'd you survive the bombs?" Ryker leaned forward.

"Myself and a few others were below ground when it hit. We were lucky to have plenty of food and water where we were. Actually, a few hundred survived. All the people who were in the cafeteria." Her eyes glazed over as if she returned to that exact moment in time. Tears welled up. "Some decided to go out and see what happened. They never returned.

"It wasn't a nuclear bomb?"

"Shoot, no. I wouldn't be here. The green slime eventually ran into the Great Lakes. Water supplies mostly come from the plant."

"The plant?" Ryker raised his spoon again.

"Yeah, scientists worked on a saltwater-filter-a-bobber. It turns fresh into salt. Never knew why they'd want to make saltwater."

"I do." I cringed. "The queen wanted to power her ships with it, but it never worked right."

"Queen?" The woman dropped her spoon and splattered gray liquid onto her already stained shirt.

"Yes, she rules the territories now."

She glared at me. "Who's this queen?"

"She was a scientist and founding member of the Council of Citizens against Mualite Crimes," I said, trying to hide the emotion in my voice.

Maggie's cheek rose on the left side of her face in a snarl. "That woman that always hemmed and hawed on the TV 'bout aliens taken over the planet?"

Here we went again. I sighed and forced a smile. "No, not against aliens, against Mualites. She called them parasites, individuals that have gifts."

"You mean like suckin' people's blood."

I smiled over at Ryker. "No, like the gift of healing. So, this plant, where is it? Were you a scientist there?" My hopes rose for the first time in days. If we could find fuel, we'd be able to power the ship to the coast, or at least a lot closer.

"Me? Nah...I was a janitor. My husband owned a bakery in downtown. We didn't have much, but we was happy."

I set my bowl back on the table. "How far is this plant?"

"Aren't ya gonna eat, girl?" Maggie snapped.

"I'm a little too queasy at the moment. Thank you, though. Please, the plant?"

"Well, aren't you proper? Yeah, well, it's across the other side. I tried to find a home closer, but the bombs blew out most everything." She snickered. "Always thought them rich people were paranoid for buildin' them rooms for doomsday. Guess I'm the fool."

"Can you give us directions in the morning? We need to leave at first light if we're to make it back to our ship."

"You sailed a boat here on the lake?"

"No ma'am, we flew here." Ryker tipped the bowl up to drain the last few drops.

I pointed to my bowl and he retrieved it from the table.

"Planes don't work no more."

"Not exactly a plane."

"Ya mean like from that old remake of a Star Wars movie?"

"I don't know what Star Wars is, but yes, we flew," I answered.

"Dang it all. Now I've heard everything. Nope, been

waiting too long for company. Y'all staying here with me." Maggie grabbed the empty bowls and bolted from the room.

"Wh-what are we g-going to do?" Emery asked before she yawned and rested her head back against the wall.

"We'll find it ourselves. We made it this far." Ryker shifted to face me. "You can detect a large amount of metal. I'm sure that plant is constructed utilizing metal. We'll go to the other side of the city and you should be able to detect it. We can only hope there's fuel there."

"Come with me, child." Maggie appeared at the door. "We can get ya cleaned up and in some new clothes." She offered Emery her hand, but Maggie's eyes remained on Emery's Slag leg.

Ryker stood.

"Don't worry. We can't go far. There're only three rooms here."

He sat back down. "Don't like having her out of my sight."

"Maggie can at least distract Emery from the harsh realities for a while."

Maggie walked back in the room. "I don't have runnin' water, but there are several barrels full. Some washcloths and soap on the shelf back there." She pointed at two tall cylinders and a wooden shelf in the back corner of a small room off the main one.

"Thank you, we appreciate your help."

"Didn't have much choice. Couldn't let ya get eaten or freeze. Ya just kids."

Emery cringed at her side.

"Oh, don't worry, sweet girl, I've gotcha. Nothings gettin' in here tonight."

CHAPTER TWENTY-TWO

Ryker stood near the wash barrels, waiting. The candlelight danced around the walls. I steadied my shaking hands. This was his chance to lay into me for what I'd done. To ensure Emery would stay out of it, I pulled the door shut behind me.

Emery and Maggie's footsteps echoed in the silent three-room metal structure. Someone once took great care to build this place. Although, it hadn't done them any good. They obviously weren't around.

"Let's get you cleaned up." Ryker went to the barrel and scooped out some water with a ceramic pitcher and poured it into a large bowl. "Take your shirt off."

I sucked in a quick breath. "What?"

"Your shirt." Ryker removed his vest and reached both arms across his body to pull the black shirt over his head. His muscles ran for miles. A long bumpy road from clavicle to dark pants resting low on his hips.

My gaze remained on the strange tattoo on his chest. I hadn't seen it since he'd healed me.

He smiled. "It's my family's Mualite mark."

I gulped and took in slow, deep breaths. He was sure different from all the pasty-white thin males that worked on the ships. As if my eyes had a mind of their own, they trailed from his broad chest down to his belly button.

Ryker cleared his throat and heat rushed to my face. "Sorry. I—"

"It's okay. I'm flattered."

His strong arms flexed and his chest moved up when he placed his fingers on the buttons of my vest. My breath shot from my lungs as if the buttons were the only thing holding it in.

He leaned in. His pupils wide and inviting when his hand wrapped around my neck. His fingers brushed the implant behind my ears.

"You don't have to—"

"I want to. It's just a piece of metal." He pulled the vest and shirt from my body and tossed them on the floor next to his, leaving only a thin white lace undershirt. "You aren't one of them."

My pulse quickened, mind spun. "I don't understand. You hate me. My mother—"

"You're nothing like her." He brushed his lips down my cheek, then my neck, leaving tingles in his wake. "I've never met a woman like you."

A smell of damp earth wafted from his hair. A reminder of where we'd met, where he'd saved me.

He turned to the water bowl and dipped a rag in. The sound of water trickling into the pool below echoed in the room. The overpowering scent of two days of sweaty travel was softened by the smell of fresh flowers and aloe from the rag.

Long, soft strokes swiped from my shoulder to fingertips. He gathered my hair and pressed the rag to the base of my hairline, around the implant and down my spine, leaving a trail of heat in its wake.

His skin didn't touch mine, only the warm, damp rag. Soapy water trailed down to my waist and he caught it along the band of my pants. So gentle. No man had ever touched me in such an intimate, soft way.

He pressed his lips to my shoulder and my legs shook beneath me.

A knock sounded at the door and Ryker sauntered over, bare-chested and shoulders back. I ducked behind a partition and crossed my arms over my lace-covered breasts.

"Your sister's asleep on the couch. You two can sleep in here. There are *two* beds. Blow out the candles, they ain't that easy to make, you know. Pass me her shirt and thing-a-ma-giggy she had on."

"Vest?"

"Yeah, what else ya think I'm talkin' about?"

Ryker stood at the other side of the partition. "Pass the rest to me."

I tugged the pants down my legs and removed my undergarments. Standing there naked, I crossed my arms over my chest.

"I'll wash these. For now, there's a gown back there on the hook you can sleep in."

The door clicked shut and Ryker returned with a smirk on his face.

"What?"

"Nothing. Just that you're strong and scared of nothing

that attacks or tries to kill you, yet you cower behind a large divider."

I retrieved the gown and slid it on, dropping my hands and pulling my shoulders back in defiance. "I wasn't cowering back here. It's—"

"You're shy?" He brushed my hair behind my ears. "I like that. You're complicated, not obvious like the girls I usually know."

Usually know? How many girls had he known?

"You're smart yet compassionate." His eyes traveled down my chest. "And you're beautiful, yet you cover it as if you don't realize how inviting you are."

I concentrated on calming my heart to keep things in check. I didn't want to melt the entire home.

With a deep breath, I focused on how my body hummed in his arms instead of my fear. I opened my eyes and saw such intensity in his.

He wrapped his arms around me. My heart pounded so hard, he had to feel it against his bare chest.

We had to talk, but I didn't want to break my few moments of bliss. I wanted him to be mine. A man worth losing my soul for, but I couldn't hide from what I'd done.

I tried to form the words. My arms began to shake. The thought of ruining this fractured my heart. But if I opened to the possibility of us and he refused, I'd shatter into a million shards that could never be mended.

His strong hand stroked the back of my head. "Shh, we're safe."

I leaned back. His eyes glistened in the candlelight and a reassuring smile calmed me. His sexy dimples tugged at my determination. Of course, this was the first smile I'd ever really seen since meeting him. I traced a finger along his jawline.

He lowered his lips to mine. Pressing his bare stomach to my thin nightgown, his cool energy surged into me.

At first, only small circles and soft kisses, then more urgent powerful strokes of his tongue left me breathless and trembling in his arms. His hand ran down my back and up my side.

The room spun and I clutched him tighter so I wouldn't fall.

The harsh realities of the world disappeared and my body longed for more. He suckled on my bottom lip and his thumb brushed against my chin. Lost, swirling in a pool of escalating excitement, waves of desire threatened to drown me. I captured his lips again, and electric currents ran through my arms and legs.

He tore his lips away. "What's that?"

The smell of a blowtorch tickled my nose. Breathless, I stepped back. Steam rose from the barrel of water. If we didn't stop, I'd melt the room to a pile of silvery goo.

He winked. "I'm glad you liked it."

I didn't know much about intimate things. Only the groping I'd suffered at the hands of the general. This was nothing like that. Something in me longed to connect with him in a deeper way, but how far could I take this before the truth separated us once more?

"Don't know I've ever wanted someone so bad in my life."

His words thrilled and frightened me all at once. "I don't...um—"

"Shh." He pressed his finger to my lips. "Not like that. Someday, but I just want you in my arms for now.

I wanted to meld with him, become one, never to be separated again.

He guided me down to the old bed. The springs squeaked under us.

Fear vanished. I trembled at his touch. For the first time, a man wasn't groping me. Instead, he shared the gentle touch of a lover. I wanted the harmful world to vanish and allow me to live eternity in his arms, below the trees and golden sunlight of the Resort Territory. Never to be parted from him again.

Bang. Ryker nearly fell out of the bed at the knock. The door creaked. "Think I'll leave this here door open 'til morning." The old lady's voice broke the spell.

I sighed, His breath caressed my ear. I pulled away, and while I wanted to wrap my arms around him and never let him go, I had to.

Ryker slid to the side of me on the bed. He tapped his finger playfully against my nose. "I'll respect Maggie's house rules, for now."

"Good night, y'all." Footsteps softened in the distance.

I felt for the woman. She'd lost everyone she loved. My muscles tightened at the thought of losing Ryker or Emery.

"Are you okay?" Ryker pressed his palm to my chest.

My heart beat faster than a spiderat's wings flapped as I nodded.

He leaned up and blew out the last candle.

In the darkness, I found my courage. "I hope you can forgive me someday for what happened to Emery ."

"Already told you. Not your fault. You were a child at the time. No way you could've done anything to stop it from happening. Just, my temper got the best of me. Made a promise to my parents, and I failed to protect her. Blame myself."

"You did save her. If you hadn't found her…" The words caught in my throat.

Ryker snuggled my head against his chest. "Don't go there. Not now. Let's have our moment together tonight."

He stroked my hair and kissed my head. For the first time since childhood, I was hopeful for the future. The calm energy pulsing from him awakened places in me. Had he used his gifts before, with other women?

"I guess you've done this a lot with other girls."

He froze. " Valencia, I lived like any man in the mining territory, and I shouldn't be judged for it."

"I get it." My body tensed, but I didn't pull away. "Look, we both know I haven't been with a man. I'd been promised to the general on my seventeenth birthday. Part of that promise was that I remained pure until our wedding. But if I'd had the chance…" My voice cracked. "Just forget it. Not important."

I flipped over. He turned and pulled me to him. We fit together like a well-oiled cog. Perfect. Not a space between our bodies. His fingers traced a line from my shoulder to my elbow. "I want to know."

"Part of me wants to be with someone. Because if I was, the general wouldn't want me."

"That's why you want to have sex with me? To not have to marry him?" Ryker asked.

The pain in his voice etched a permanent tattoo on my heart. "No. My mother would still force me, if only as a servant." I huffed. "My body chose you. I have no control. I know it sounds ridiculous. You wouldn't understand."

"You're wrong. I feel a need so intense I think I'll die if I don't fulfill it."

My head spun, then my body. "Yes. I've never felt that way, and now that I have…I can't bear the thought of giving myself to another man."

"Like the general or Malvak."

"Yes."

"You don't have to worry about that no more. Won't let them take you back."

My lips brushed his, as my salty tears moistened his face.

"Valencia, can I ask you something?"

My finger trailed down his forearm. "Sure."

He tensed. "Did you suffer a lot on that ship?"

"It doesn't matter. I'm free now."

"Are you okay with that? Queen's still your only family."

"No, she was never my family—only a woman who gave birth to me. I haven't had a family since the day my father died."

"You do now."

"I appreciate it, but we both know that the Mualites will never accept me. Just like they won't accept your sister."

"I'm not talking about Mualites. I'm talking about Emery and me. Family's people that care about you."

"You care about me?" The words flew from my lips before I could stop them.

"Yes."

"In what way?"

He raked his lips across my earlobe and I drew in a long breath. "In every way. I can't explain it. You have a way of mixing the words up in my head. No one has ever done that."

"What does that mean?"

"It means I want you in a way that's more than friendly."

"So this is physical. A chemical response between us, like my mother said. No such thing as love, just hormones and tools."

"Po gavolite," he rambled. "Tools?"

"Never mind."

"Don't know what's going to happen. I do know I don't wanna keep fightin' unless you and my sister are by my side. It's not just physical or hormones. I'm not sure what it is yet, except that it's amazing."

I yawned and nuzzled my face into his neck. "Ryker?"

"Yes?"

"Do you think we stand a chance of making it to the rebels?"

"We will. Somehow, someway, we'll make it." Ryker stroked my cheek. "For now, we're safe, so get some sleep."

My body relaxed. I closed my eyes in hopes the morning would bring new light to our situation.

The mattress bounced as he settled in and I rested my head against his shoulder. Only a thin sheet to pull over us, he pressed me closer into his chest.

I fit perfectly in the crook of his arm, as his free hand caressed my hair.

My breathing slowed to a steady rhythm and happy dreams from the Resort Territory ebbed into my consciousness. I wasn't sure if it was part of the dream, but I swore I heard the words, "I love you, Princess Valencia."

Sounds of someone stirring in the other room woke me. My muscles were stiff from not moving for what must have been hours, but Ryker didn't release me when I went to move. Instead, he clutched me to him tighter.

Never had I slept so well. Usually, my mind raced the minute my head hit the pillow, but not last night.

"Ya'll gonna sleep the day away?"

I rubbed the crust from my eyes and pulled my numb arm from around Ryker, careful not to wake him. Our damp skin clung together.

The smell of fresh meat cooking in the other room made my mouth water.

"You need to eat something." Ryker startled me. "I won't let you out of bed until you manage to get some food down."

He jumped from the bed and sauntered out of the room, only to return with two plates in hand.

Maggie peered in through the door. Handing Ryker two glass bottles of water, she glanced at the still-made bed and tsked, "I'll get your sister up and fed. You two get a move on. First light, we gotta skedaddle."

"Got it." Ryker sat by my side and handed me the plate and water.

I sat up and the covers spilled down to my waist.

He pressed a kiss to my cheek. "Oh, how I'd love to crawl back into bed next to you."

"Did you sleep?"

He sat on the edge of the bed. "Like I haven't in a long time." He stabbed the slab of gray meat with his fork and brought it to my lips.

I turned my head away. "I don't know if I can eat that. Think about it. Not much around here but rats."

"Then don't think about it. Eat."

I opened my mouth reluctantly and took a piece, chewing it slowly. I grabbed the bottle of water from the floor and chugged half of it.

He stood and lit some more candles while I choked the piece down with a loud cough.

"What do you think will happen when we reach the coast?"

Ryker returned to the bed and shoved another bite in my mouth. "We join the rebellion."

I shielded my full mouth with the back of my hand. "What if we don't reach them?"

"We have to."

"Why? What if we went back to the Resort Territory? You, me, and Emery."

Ryker shook his head. "Can't do that. The rebellion needs us."

"But we could—"

"We've got a problem." The old lady's words shattered our few minutes of peace.

He shoveled a few bites down and shot up from the bed. "Finish that. You're not to get up 'til you have some food in your stomach."

He followed Maggie out the door.

"Something's out there." Concern oozed from her voice.

I bolted from the bed, clutching the sheet to my chest to follow them.

Maggie waved her hand frantically for Ryker to follow.

She raised a panel on the outer wall and rays of light flooded into the room. "Look, down there."

A shiny object pulsed across the sky, then landed at the edge of town. "What is it?"

"Don't know, but heard it fly over when I cracked the viewer." Maggie stepped back and Ryker leaned out the small hole.

He pulled back, concern etched on his face. I ran over and looked out.

My pulse raced and I held my breath. A sense of dread crept out from the dark hole I'd pressed it to a few hours ago. Whatever it was, it couldn't be good out here.

Ryker rubbed his forehead. "Might be a scout or something. We need to take a closer look."

"Thought you'd say that. Got just the thing." She shut the view and walked over to an old screen leaning against the wall on a table. "It's a direct feed."

"But you don't have any electricity."

"Not powered that way. It's linked through the water factory. After the bombs, there were some strange ships flying in. They must've connected these direct views. One of the scientists figured it out before…well, a long time ago."

"Thought you didn't know about the flying ships."

"Well, might not have been completely honest about that. Not sure I should trust you and such."

What else wasn't she completely honest about? Of course, we hadn't been completely honest either. "Could you see us last night when you helped us escape?"

"No, there's no camera there. Just at the edge of town and at the factory," Maggie said.

I bit my bottom lip. "Does the queen know about you?"

"Don't think so."

"What do you know of the queen and what she's been doing here?" I asked.

Maggie adjusted the screen for us to see. "Only know she rules with an iron fist, literally. Been here trying to figure out what they left behind. Then people dressed in strange suites took out two-thirds of us when they came after the bombs."

Tears filled her cloudy eyes. "Lined 'em up and shot them all like animals. After that, the rest of us hid whenever something else came to town."

"Until we arrived."

"Yeah, ya'll didn't look too threatening, and besides, it's been awhile since I had someone around to talk to."

A buzzing sound drew our attention to the flickering screen. The feed rolled in rapid white and gray lines until it slowed to a stop.

"Dear all things holy, what the..."

I saw a large creature with pipes twisted around from the back of its head to its chest and around to its spine. It walked slowly but with purpose, dragging its massive legs along the street. A large single-barrel gun with two side cylinders was secured to one gloved hand while the other held something out. A green light blinked, then he lowered it and continued to shuffle forward.

"It's an assassin sent by the queen." My voice quivered despite my best intention of hiding my terror.

"That thing looks similar to the suits the men wore when they came here after the bombs."

"It's no man...at least, not anymore." I wrung my hands. "We need to get out of here."

"No, should stay here where we're safe. We'll have to wait it out," Ryker said.

"He won't find us here," Maggie added.

I clutched my neck. "It already has. That's a Seeker he's holding in his hand. It will distinguish us from animals and buildings within a couple kilometers." Dread snaked through my body.

Emery bolted up from the couch. "W-we need to g-get out of here. N-Now!"

I snatched my clothes off the edge of the couch and bolted for the bedroom, changing clothes and returning seconds later.

I looked between Ryker and Maggie. "That gun will tear us to shreds before we make it to the plant."

"We've got to try." Ryker grasped my shoulders trying to reassure me that everything would work out. His shaking hands betrayed him.

"Boy, y'all sure do bring trouble." The old woman's eyes narrowed, etching deeper lines between her brows. "Maybe I ought to stay here and send y'all on your way."

I stared the old woman down. "That's not an option. It will still kill you. It only understands basic orders. It's programmed to take out anything in its path that resembles a human."

"Well, ain't this a pickle." She gave a half-smile and opened a wood cabinet. "There might be a way. Tunnels under-ground." She retrieved two large guns, a long, cylindrical object attached to the top of each.

"A scientist retro-fit these do-thang-a-ma-bobs on them for light. They'll shine bright enough for us to find our way."

My stomach churned the meat in anticipation.

"Don't know how much longer they'll work. One went out on me last night when I went to retrieve y'all."

"Those will never work against the heavy armor of an assassin," I warned.

"Call me ugly and paint me red, but one thing's for sure, we're outgunned. And my momma always said don't bring a carving knife to a shooting range. I'm packin', deary. In the good ol' days, I was a gun-totin' Republican."

I had no idea what she meant by being a Republican, but now wasn't the time to ask. No way would Emery be able to handle the sight of that creature.

I blocked Emery's view of the screen. We wouldn't stand a chance if she checked out right now.

"I'll be by your side the whole way. Don't worry. I'll protect you." I gave her a reassuring smile.

CHAPTER TWENTY-THREE

We raced through the corrugated underground pipeway.

Bang. The unmistakable sound of metal feet hitting the corrugated pipe reverberated through the tunnel. We all stopped abruptly, all standing absolutely still as the assassin's light illuminated the dark underground.

I held my breath.

"Much further?" Ryker asked.

Maggie shook her head. "No, come on."

We took two more turns and arrived at a ladder, which Maggie climbed nimbly.

Clank. The hatch swung open. Emery followed, hoisting herself up with two hands and one leg, while her metal one dangled in the air. I climbed the ladder, shielding my eyes, and nearly fell from the disorientation caused by the blinding light.

The assassin clanked closer. Ryker nudged my leg, urging me to move. Emery had already disappeared into the light. The smell of fresh air invited me up. Each step, my legs shook.

"Keep moving," Ryker commanded.

My body followed without protest, propelled by terror. I crawled out onto the road; broken rocks cut at my hands and knees. Ryker reached the top and smiled at me.

He slipped a few rungs down.

Maggie shined her light down past Ryker into the shaft.

The assassin had Ryker by the ankle. I choked out a cry. Maggie aimed her gun and shot twice.

Two more shots. And another.

"No! You can't have him." My heart and veins boiled in anger. I harvested the despair and focused on the assassin's metal tubing. Swirls vibrated my skull and my nails stung; the taste of iron and bronze invaded my tongue. Concentrating on the hoses and armor, I burrowed through a fissure in a tube. Visualizing each groove, I wiggled down into the deep, dark crevices. I caught a glimpse of his swollen face, one eye, no teeth.

Hatred ebbed from his soul into mine. I grew stronger, draining him as I tunneled deep inside his armor.

Behind all that heavy outer skin and beyond the anger, he felt fear...pain...longing. He might be horribly disfigured, but he was still a person.

An eruption of hot lava exploded from inside, blowing his armor from his body. Once the tubing was gone, he couldn't breathe.

Then a surge of frigid air flooded up the tunnel into my face.

"Secure the hatch!" Ryker grabbed my forearm and pulled himself up.

Maggie rolled the cover over and I melted the sides to the ground, sealing it for good.

"It was…human." I heard my own hollow words. "I murdered—"

Ryker wrapped his arms around me. "You had no choice, Valencia."

Lips pressed to my temple, hands stroked my back, but my gut wrenched with the knowledge of the perverse act I committed using my gift. I just took a life as mercilessly as my mother would have.

"I'm like her," I choked out.

"Who?" Ryker asked.

My body shook with the memory of invading the metal merged with skin and bone. "My mother…the queen."

"The Queen?" Maggie shrieked. "She's your—"

"Not now," Ryker ordered.

"V-Valencia." Emery bent down by my side and stroked my face with her delicate hand. "You s-saved my brother, your m-mother would've d-destroyed a life without p-provocation. T-trust me when I s-say, you're n-nothing like her." Emery's words came so clear and calm, yet her pupils constricted and dilated so fast it appeared they were having a seizure.

Sounds of another approaching ship startled us. We all looked to the sky but couldn't see what approached on the other side of the ruins.

"We need to get moving," Maggie barked and walked away.

I pushed to my feet and followed Maggie, Emery and Ryker at my side, as we hurried through the crumbled structures and rocky terrain.

"Good news is the fuel is down there a ways." Maggie continued down a narrow alley.

"Bad news is we'll never make it back to the ship," Ryker added.

"We'll figure something out," I reassured him, yet my pulse beat faster than my feet hit the pavement.

"I've got another ship. Been working on it awhile. Need petrol, though." Maggie tilted her head toward a large hill at the edge of the city.

"If you had a ship, why didn't you leave?" I asked.

"It ain't exactly a ship. And I didn't know if I'd make it someplace safe on my own. I've never left Chicago before." Maggie glanced back at the hatch. "No time for a tea party. Get a move on. We need more firepower for the trip. Let's split up. You three head for the petrol. Three doors south, go through the hall and down the stairs. At the bottom of the stairs, you'll find another door. Inside that door, y'all find several containers of petrol. I'll meet you at the top of the stairs with some extra ammo and a few toys." Maggie flashed a devious smile and ducked between two buildings.

With no time to protest, we followed her directions and raced through the third door.

The inner door was locked. I wrapped my fingers around the knob and it clicked open. We all took cover below and discovered a room with petrol cans set on shelving.

Outside, something thundered and the building shook. Emery fell back against the wall. Shelves crashed to the floor.

"Pekolot. What was that?" Ryker lunged for the door and peered up the stairs. "Nothing's up there."

"I've got a bad feeling." I helped Emery stand again and propped her against the shelf that still stood.

I maneuvered around Ryker and stood on the first step, gagging at the smell of oil. I stumbled down into the storage room. "We better get out of here."

Ryker lowered his head and arched a brow. "What is it?"

"You'll think I'm insane."

Emery laughed, "No m-more than m-me."

"Do you think the assassin escaped from the hatch?" I asked.

"No way," Ryker insisted.

I looked away. "You're right." What the hell was wrong with me? The implant must have short-circuited or something. "There's more than one. There usually is. They travel in packs."

Ryker brushed hair from my eyes. "Then we should collect the petrol and get out of here, quick."

We each grabbed a full plastic container and ran for the stairs. It sloshed by my side as I stayed on Ryker's heels with Emery on mine.

Another loud bang shook the ground beneath us. Ryker ran to the corner and peered around. "Prokleta taa žena. She's gonna get herself killed."

"What?" I pushed past him. Ryker grabbed my arm and snatched me back behind the wall.

"Now you're going to get yourself killed!" Ryker's pupils narrowed. His thumb dug into my upper arm. His fingers pressed so hard I thought they'd meet his thumb through my flesh. I squirmed away from him.

An explosion sent us flying back into Emery. Rocks tumbled from the building. Sand plumed around us. Coughs echoed in the alley.

Another bolt of fire shot our way.

I grabbed Emery by her vest and Ryker by his collar. "Run!"

Ryker flipped back onto his feet and swiped Emery up in his arms as we rushed to the other side of the building. I remembered the petrol and ran back.

Ryker yelled, but I couldn't make out his words over the rapid blood pumping through my ears. Down the alley, I spied a wick sizzling into a glass bottle. The old woman stood a few hundred meters away, waving her arms. I slid and grabbed the bottle then tossed it back down the road. It rolled to a stop at two metal feet. I caught a glimpse of tubes and a bronze head before the world lit into a golden sphere. A great boom reverberated through the streets. Then something sucker punched me in the chest and propelled me several meters, slamming me against a hard surface.

Then a white blanket...intense ringing...no breath.

Only gasps. I couldn't hear. Tears stung my cheeks as I clutched my stomach and curled into myself.

The white faded and colors bled into the scene, yet I couldn't focus on anything. I looked left and right. Each time my eyes changed direction, the white light stayed in the way.

The ringing in my ears dulled enough to hear another bang. No, someone yelling, but I couldn't make out the words.

Sharp pain turned to dull pulses and welcomed breath flooded my lungs. Then more pain. I scrunched my eyes shut, trying to clear the white.

Hands. Large, strong hands cradled my face. I opened my eyes and a little more life conquered the white. The silver and black hair, bulging biceps, and the unmistakable ink of his Mualite family symbol confirmed it was Ryker.

Through chapped, burning lips, I tried to speak but couldn't find my voice. Muscular arms wrapped underneath mine and I stood on two shaking pins that were my legs. Unfortunately, my brain and body didn't work together yet.

They were numb, but I could shuffle forward as long as he held me upright.

Not able to see more than a quarter of the world around me, I trusted Ryker as he led the way.

The taste and smell of the assassin returned. We had to get out of here. We needed the— "Wait, the petrol."

The words echoed in my head but I wasn't sure anyone else could hear them. I shouted again, but fingers covered my mouth. And I knew what I sensed was true. An assassin stood close by, and as I feared, he wasn't the only one. Maggie had been throwing useless bombs at them. A technique that only agitated them more, it was as useless as swatting a bee buzzing around your head before it stings you.

CHAPTER TWENTY-FOUR

The cadence of the assassins' boots hitting the ground matched the pounding in my chest. Blood trickled down the corner of my mouth. Stings pricked at my cheeks and forehead. I didn't want to know what my face looked like with the scattered cuts and dirt.

"Valencia, can you see me?"

"Some."

"We need to get out of here. Can you walk?" Ryker spoke into my ear.

The outline of his head appeared in the corner of my vision when he leaned back into the white light. "Do the assassins target based on heat?"

"Yes, that's how they track," I answered.

"That's why Maggie's throwing the firebombs. With all the flames and explosions, they can't decipher people from fire. Brilliant."

I needed to help. "Point me to one, and I'll melt the armor." Maggie was something else. But she couldn't take them all on.

Ryker waved a hand in front of my face. It faded in and out

of my vision. "No way, you can't even see them, and there are too many."

The light faded a little more. Ryker crawled on hands and knees and wrapped his fingers around the handle of the petrol container.

Only one? I tried to scan the area, but couldn't locate any others. How far could we make it?

I scooted forward. Through my blotchy vision I managed to spot an assassin—kinda. I tried to concentrate and melt his boots so he couldn't walk, but I couldn't focus on him. It kicked a broken canister, sloshing gas all over the ground. By the look of it, there was about to be a much bigger explosion. The trail of liquid ran from one canister, under another, and all the way to where we crouched in the alleyway. It wouldn't take long before the gas heated and exploded from the surrounding fires.

Maggie stepped out. I recognized her from the gray hair and old worn shoes. She had a bag slung over her shoulder and a makeshift bomb in hand.

Ryker pulled me to stand and placed my hand on his shoulder. "I'll guide you." Then he took Emery in his right arm and dragged her a few meters away from the fire.

Flames ignited and singed my boots. A strong odor of burned leather surrounded us. I caught a glimpse of the other assassin before reaching the alley. The only hope was for the flames to distract it long enough to get away.

Boom! I ducked. Flames blasted overhead. The other canisters exploded.

I tripped and fell to my knees. Ryker slid Emery to the ground and took my hands in his. "You okay?"

"Yes." I squinted at him.

Another assassin stepped out, blocking our escape route. The pale green light from the heat sensor pointed down the street at us.

We only had two choices. To face the one a few meters in front of us or go back in the direction we came where the fire still burned. And who knew if those two assassins had survived the explosion.

Trapped.

The strong odor of petrol and debris burned my throat and lungs.

Ryker stood tall, chest out. Light blue, the color of ice, surged to his fingertips, but the assassin didn't look affected.

"Armor, can't penetrate," Ryker said with strained words. "Need to get to the ship, wherever that is."

A fourth assassin emerged at the other end of the street. Its tubes still glowed with orange flames. He raised his gun.

Emery tried to stand, but Ryker kept her pinned down.

The gun fired with such intensity that the walls shook and threatened to tumble over us. Metal smacking pavement echoed through the alley. With each step the assassin closed in on us.

Emery took off before we had a chance to stop her. Ryker and I bolted after her. The pounding behind us quickened. We dodged left and right to avoid the persistent gunfire.

We rounded another corner and found the main street. Another shot hit the building; brick and mortar rained around us. We somehow managed to dodge most of the falling rock.

Emery stumbled and fell to her knees. I tumbled over her.

Another gunshot. Ryker hit the ground by my side. Emery screamed.

I covered his body with mine and tugged at his shirt. "No! No!"

No blood soaked through. We looked at each other in bewilderment then back at the assassin that should have crushed us by now. All that remained was a lump of metal tangled in a heap on the ground.

Maggie stood behind it. Smoke still oozing from the barrel of her gun.

Ryker stood. "How'd you—I mean you were—"

"Ya wanna stand here chattin' about it or get the hell outta here?"

"I w-want t-to get out of here, p-please," Emery said.

Ryker chuckled.

I blew out a puff of steam. "I am so glad to see you."

"No time to be celebratin'." Maggie lifted her gun. "Ah, shoot. That dang pile of worthless scrap won't die."

Another shot rang in my ear.

"Make a run for it, kids." Maggie dropped the gun to her side and left it hanging from a strap while she readied another jar.

The third assassin marched down the main street. "Got to go."

"Hold up, you can't take off without this." Maggie picked up a petrol can, jogged over and handed a note and the canister to Ryker.

"You're coming with us." Ryker's eyes grew wide.

"Someone's got to stick around here and tame these animals." Maggie gave a reassuring smile. If I didn't know better, I'd swear Maggie was enjoying this fight.

"Take those codes. It's what the ENR needs."

I couldn't bear to watch another innocent die.

"No. You h-have to—" Emery pleaded.

"Child, I've been here a long time. I can handle a few freaks." She smiled. "They give new meaning to the word *redneck*." At Emery's puzzled look, she said, "Oh, never mind, old term from back home. Let's go. I'll show you where the machine is and keep'em off your backs."

She grabbed Emery's hand and tugged. As we dodged pieces of fallen buildings, Maggie talked between gasping breaths. "Listen here, children. I like you. I can tell she ain't like her momma." She nodded her head at me. "You've got a problem. I'm your contact. Actually, I was just the middleman. The one you was supposed to bring along to the ENR was a man who passed me those codes, but Harrison managed to escape and the queen is hunting for him. He was some big wig war hero, but don't think he's gonna be helping the rebellion anymore. Pretty sure the queen's hunters will catch up to him eventually."

"Harrison? That was my father's name."

"It was your Dad?"

"No, my dad died five years ago."

"Sorry to hear that. But I have to warn you, there's a bigger problem. I intercepted some chatter when the ENR thought I was dead. Yeah, I see the surprise in your eyes. And yep, I have a gift, too. I don't believe in all that Mualite versus Slag shit. Y'all need to know that the ENR thinks the princess is a plant. They plan on trading her for that fella that was captured."

They wanted me? A spy? Great, that was all I needed. Did anyone in this world not want me dead or married?

"W-what do w-we do?" Emery clung to me. "Can't t-turn Valencia over t-to rebellion."

"We can't stay here, either," I said.

"You've got to convince the rebellion that Valencia is worth more to them than turning her over to the council. That doing so would give the queen enough power to defeat the rebellion. She's not to be trusted and will wipe'em out once she gets Valencia. Not gettin' involved, though. Y'all pass the message on that the queen is working on a new hybrid ship that's supposed to be able to take out all of what remains of Europe, squashing all trade to those territories and crippling any further resistance."

"That's gonna take a miracle. I hear those rebels aren't too forgiving," Ryker said.

"Think about what Valencia can offer. Your uncle was bettin' on her value when he agreed to this."

"Uncle knew?"

"Yep, didn't have a choice. But he sent Harrison to tell me Valencia might be the key in this fight." Maggie flicked a lighter and lit another rag before tossing it down the alley and shoving us to the ground. It exploded and the ringing returned to my ears.

"Head south. Only building left standing. Full of windows. You'll find a locked door. Valencia will have to melt the door down. Now get. I'll be right behind you." Maggie paused and lit another rag.

Emery whimpered as the mechanized creature approached.

I could see the struggle in Ryker's eyes. Leaving a man behind wasn't his style. None of us wanted to, but she wasn't going to take no for an answer, and we had to take care of Emery.

"Don't worry. I'll be along. My momma didn't raise no fool."

"Thanks, for everything." Ryker grabbed Emery and me by the hand. We took off running, but to where? For a ship to take us to a place where I was considered an enemy?

An explosion shook the ground underfoot and I caught a glimpse of Maggie a moment before a flash of light and another explosion.

My eyes widened.

"No!" Emery shrieked. "M-Maggie."

Ryker wrapped his arms around Emery.

My breath caught in my lungs as I listened for her crazy rants, but nothing came. "She can't be gone."

"What ya standing 'round gawking at? Get!" Maggie ran through the smoke. "I'm staying here. This is my land, and I'm not leaving."

Ryker scooped Emery up in his arms and rushed up the hill behind me. My legs burned as I powered through the climb. Ryker's face was red with exertion and I hoped he'd make it with the extra weight.

I struggled with the full container, but I didn't stop. A strong wind lashed us at every step, as if carrying the curses of Mother.

Drained. I wanted to return to our little ship with Ryker close by my side, as if I needed his touch to recharge.

Finally, Emery's sobbing stopped. Once again, she checked out, tucking her fear and anguish deep into whatever dark crevice she could find. It was the way she survived. And part of me envied her.

Slowly, we traversed the rocky cliff to the top. Ryker knelt on the rocky edge and Emery pushed from his arms. I wasn't sure if it was a ridge or a flattened neighborhood. Not that it mattered. I glanced back at the city below. There was no sign of Maggie. Something deep inside warned me to keep moving. Too much evil still remained.

"Come on," Ryker said through gasps.

Ahead was a brick building without a pane of glass. Despite the sea of empty windows grinning at us, relief flooded me.

Then reality slapped me in the face. The fierce wind would make taking off impossible. Yet, we had to try, to prove Maggie's faith in us was worth her efforts.

Vines crept up through the cracks in the building, inched up the sides, and invaded its interior via the empty windows. Ryker shoved a metal door open. His legs buckled under the strain. Rushing forward, I helped him up and we shuffled inside, then shut the door.

I slid down the wall next to him. "It looks clear. Nothing's following us, as near as I can see."

Emery remained near an opening, looking down toward the city.

For the first time in hours, I inhaled deeply and pulled my water container from my belt. The cool liquid soothed my raw throat and I relaxed for a minute. I handed the bottle to Ryker and a shot of calm soothed my shaking hand.

He bolted upright and ran to another metal door on the other side of the large room. "Over there. This must be it."

I managed to stand on my weak legs and stagger forward. I signaled for Emery, and she reluctantly joined us. Following Ryker's gesture, I clutched the lock in my hand and melted it. Wheels squealed against the metal track as we opened the door.

There was no ship. Just an old-fashioned, beat-up cross

between an ancient vehicle called a car and a tank I'd seen in one of my history books.

"Što po ģavolite e toa nešto." Ryker slammed his fist against the metal trunk.

That thing was not getting us to the coast—not without more petrol, and not on time.

CHAPTER TWENTY-FIVE

I clutched the smooth black metal and peered through the tinted glass. Something white rested on the seat. I lifted the handle and pulled the door open, sending the white paper swaying in the air.

A musty leather scent lingered when I bent down and retrieved the thin sheet. It was covered in black writing and signed "Mags."

"I think Maggie left us instructions."

"Couldn't have. She's still behind us." Ryker opened another door and searched the vehicle.

"It reads, *If you're reading this, I hope you find your way to the coast, whoever you are. Received word you'd be coming, so I got Beast here ready for you. It's a classic Land Rover. I know you're thinking 'this thing can't fly, so how's it supposed to get us anywhere?' Trust me. She's got some fight in her. Besides, they'll be looking for you in the sky and most believe the land between here and the coast is toxic. Probably been tracking your ship since you left the Mining Territory. You'll find a map in the glove box—that's the compartment to the right of the steering wheel—and supplies in the back. It'll take almost two days to reach where you're going. Your trading ship left, but I sent word to the ENR. They will meet you on the shore. You're gassed up and ready to go. The gas in the back, plus what you brought, should be enough. Don't worry. I'll take care of whatever is following you. Mags."*

"Knew she was crazy, but this?" Ryker walked around the tall vehicle and kicked the oversized tires, then opened the back hatch. "There're other containers of gas back here." He rummaged through some things. "Tent, wood, food, and some other supplies."

A blast sounded outside, reminding us of the urgency to depart. Ryker picked up the other canister and slid it into the vehicle. "Let's get going. This'll have to do."

"B-but w-what about—"

Ryker shot a look of desperation at me. "Have to go."

"Emery, we can't stay. Don't worry, everything will be fine," I murmured.

Ryker helped Emery up into the back seat.

"B-but Mags…"

Ryker stroked her hair. "Don't worry. She's tough. We'll see her again."

I slid into the driver's seat and found a key already in the ignition.

Ryker stood at my side, brow knitted. "What're you doing?"

"Do you know how to drive?"

"No, do you?"

More blasts closed in. The steering wheel vibrations under my fingertips were identical to the ones during the Mining Territory bombing. My hands shook, and not just from the distant blasts showering us with brick dust, but from the memories of watching the Mualites hiding in the underground while their loved ones above were murdered. Once again, I swore that I wouldn't fail them.

My sorrow surfaced and I used the pain to melt the lock from the massive door in front of us. Warmth remained at my core from the energy and the knowledge that I had melted metal from a long distance. My powers were growing and stabilizing.

Would Father have been proud of me? Could he be alive?

I shook the wish from my head. Many people had the name Harrison. There was no way it was him. I saw him die.

"Get the door," I ordered before starting the car.

Ryker raced over and jumped up, grabbing the chain that ran from ceiling to floor. His legs swung while he rode the rust-covered metal back down.

Lowering my head, I peeked under the rising barrier to the outside world. I readied for an armed assassin with its guns pointed directly at us.

No gold-colored feet waited to stomp us from the world.

I shoved aside the gnawing feeling of a trap, shifted into drive, and slid my right foot onto the gas pedal. The engine roared and we bolted forward. I smashed my boot down on the brake and the tires squealed to a stop. Ryker jumped out of the way and waved me through before he yanked the door down.

He slid into the passenger's side. "Try to kill me next time."

I stifled a nervous giggle. "Sorry, it's a little different from the vehicles back home, but same layout. I didn't know it had that much power."

I gunned it and drove over several broken dark gray sheets

of stone and debris. The smell of trees and dirt filtered in through the vents and, for a moment, it took me back home on another joy-filled ride through the wilderness.

How I missed the innocence of my childhood.

Ryker pulled the geo-map from his vest and unfolded the map Maggie had given us to compare the terrain. "Keep heading east. Straight shot from here. Maggie marked a place to stop for the night. Looks like she's been planning this for a long time."

My chest tightened at the thought of leaving her behind. So many had been lost or left behind in the last several days.

My skin burned with terror of what waited for us. What would Mother do if she knew of my part in the rebellion? I knew exactly what she'd do. She would capture the three of us and torture Ryker and Emery until I broke and revealed everything.

My lips parted to confess my fears, then stopped. Ryker held tight to the handle by his right side and stared out the front. I glanced in the rearview mirror. Emery had curled into a tight ball with her eyes shut in the back seat.

I couldn't tell them. This was something I needed to keep to myself.

I was probably just being paranoid. Blame it on all those years Mother monitored every move I made while aboard the ship. However, at this moment, there was no way she could know what I was doing in the middle of nowhere.

"Watch out," Ryker yelled.

I slammed on the brakes and we slid to a halt. A pile of old rocks blocked our path. Too large to maneuver, and with a ditch on both sides, there was no way around.

I took several deep breaths, then got out of the car. Only one person could help us get through. I opened her door and held her hand. "Emery, hon? We need your help."

Emery smiled and jumped down from the car, tentatively scanning the world around us. "Need s-some heavy lifting? W-what's w-wrong, big brother? T-too heavy for you?"

"Watch the perimeter," Ryker ordered as he followed Emery, and I readied for whatever followed.

The wind blew a fierce warning for us not to linger. Howls echoed in the distance, and I wondered what kind of creatures we had to fear out in the wilderness. Certainly nothing worse than what we'd faced already.

After a moment, I heard stones break and slide. Emery worked quickly to clear our path. I liked the woods, but my powers were almost useless if there wasn't any metal around to pull energy from. And I couldn't pull it from the car or we'd be stranded.

It must be nice to pull energy from nature—a neverending supply at your disposal from which one could draw power. Not that it had done Emery any good on Mother's ship. It seemed each power had its own pros and cons, its own limitations.

"Let's go," Ryker shouted from behind.

He waved me into the driver's seat while he and Emery remained outside. I watched through the rearview mirror as Emery recreated the barrier. Smart thinking. Not surprising, considering how Ryker always had a strategy.

With us safely back in the car, I barreled on. For several hours, we went through the same scenario of Emery clearing the path or driving around things. The sky turned a deeper orange and I hoped we'd reach where Maggie had set up for us to sleep that night.

Of course in the morning, I'd have to face the Mualites. If I was right, we were driving to face hell on the horizon.

"What is it?" Ryker rested his hand on my lower thigh and I relaxed.

"Nothing."

"Tell me. We've been through too much to keep secrets now," Ryker pressed.

"I'm thinking about what's ahead, trying to prepare for what's to come."

Ryker touched the back of my neck. "Don't worry. I know what Maggie said, but I won't let the rebellion turn you over. Uncle wouldn't have sent us if he believed they'd harm you."

His hand slid over mine, pulled my white-knuckle grip loose of the steering wheel. He kissed and lightly massaged my fingers. "We'll be fine."

"It's not that."

"What?"

"We shouldn't have escaped."

Ryker's brow furrowed. "Why do you say that?"

"Unless..."

"Unless what?"

"Unless the assassins weren't sent to kill us, at least not immediately. My mother would have another plan." I swallowed hard. "This could all be a ruse to figure out where we're going."

"Can the assassins' ships fly over water?"

"I don't know. From what I understand, the storms are fierce on the ocean and no ship that size could make it far without additional resources. Only my mother's ship could make a trip like that...and the ocean runners."

"So, if we make it to the coast, we have a chance?"

"Yes. Maybe. Let's hope we have enough fuel to get there. But even then, the assassins will make their move before we can board the ocean vessel."

An icy current flowed through my body as I thought of all those people on the vessel unaware of what was coming. Would they stand a chance?

Ryker squeezed my hand. "Don't worry, we'll make it."

"N-no w-we w-won't." Emery shifted forward and grabbed the back of the seat. "N-not enough fuel."

I looked down and watched the red line dip and knew Emery spoke the truth. I pressed the brake, rolling us to a stop. We only had one can of fuel left, which wouldn't get us far. For all of Maggie's planning, it looked like we would be stranded in the middle of the wilderness.

Ryker opened his door and hopped from the vehicle. I followed him to the rear and watched him rummage through the supplies in the back. Sounds of animals in the distance unnerved me. I'd never liked the unknown.

I stood behind Ryker, watching the perimeter. He unlatched a small black case and I nearly yelled in relief at the sight of the weapons.

He took one of the pistols and shoved it in his belt and handed the other to me. "We should sleep in the vehicle. We'll be protected from the elements."

I scooped two shiny silver blankets and some food into my arms. "We'll need to keep the engine off all night to preserve petrol."

"W-what w-will we d-do tomorrow?"

"Don't worry, Emery. We'll figure somethin' out."

I shot Ryker a sideways glance and shuffled around the car to the driver's seat. He dumped the remaining fuel into the tank and joined us.

"Best to be fueled up, ready to go." The strong odor of petrol remained on his hands. Of course, I didn't smell like flowers either. What I wouldn't give for a real shower.

He slid the geo-map from the dash. "Starting with the full tank plus two canisters of petrol, we're—"

"Can only go th-three hundred and t-twenty-two more kilometers on w-what's left in the tank in combination and with w-what you put in." Emery leaned forward and took some bread from the small pile of food.

"How would you…Never mind." Ryker gave her a warm smile. "Always a math genius, weren't you?"

It looked like the emotional issues didn't impact her mental abilities.

Emery yawned and leaned back in the seat, rubbing her eyes.

"Get some rest. We'll all need it." Ryker's voice sounded brotherly.

I rose onto my knees and leaned back over the seat to cover Emery with one of the blankets.

"You always be watching out for my sister. Thank you."

We both sat quietly and ate, waiting for Emery to fall asleep so we could speak freely without upsetting her too much. Once the slow, deep breathing started, Ryker opened his mouth but closed it again.

There was so much to talk about, so many things still left unsaid between us.

He leaned into me and rested his forehead against mine. We both closed our eyes and enjoyed the moment.

Static shot between our lips, and I pressed mine to his. The tight knot between my shoulder blades released, allowing me to lean further in.

The world silenced. No gun blasts, firebombs, engines revving, or screams. Only his touch, kisses, and gift pulsing through my body.

I longed to return to the cool lake water and warm sun, to swim beside him and rest on the sandy beach in his arms.

He pulled back and held my hand against his cheek. "I've missed you. For the first time since the war, I'm full of hope. You've given me that." Ryker squeezed my hand tighter. "When this is over, will you stay with me? I mean, Emery and me?"

For a moment, my heart soared to the skies. He wanted me to stay with him, but then so many other emotions weighted me back to the ground. "If the European rebels don't turn me over to my mother—" I chuckled. "I...I would love to return to the Resort Territory."

"What of the rebellion? What of Emery? I thought you cared about her now?"

"I hoped you two would both go with me. We could live freely."

"Don't you think your mother will look there for you?"

"I...I haven't thought that far ahead."

"You would be safer with us, fighting. We can win this war. Then everyone can find their own Resort or Oasis to live freely. We've come too far. We can't turn our back on everyone."

"I wasn't born to fight like you. My mother would be the first to tell you that I'm not cut out to fight."

"You *can* when it's for the right reasons."

He took the food from me, moved it to the floor, and scooted closer, taking both my hands in his.

I pulled away. If my suspicions were true, I'd never be able to get close to anyone. Mother would torture and kill anyone I had a connection to. It took me a long time to see it, but she would stop at nothing. "I'm tired of war. First, people are tortured and I'm forced to watch."

"You had no choice."

My stomach rolled. "Then friends and family die. When is it enough? When do we cross the line and stop being human ourselves?"

He pulled my head to his chest and rocked me. "Shh, it isn't your fault. You're trying to do the best you can. You've been forced to choose to fight your own mother. I can't imagine how that feels. Don't have to decide anything now. Sometimes, you make stops on your way to where you want to go. Maybe the European Rebellion has a plan—"

"That's it."

"That's what?"

"Stop on the way. Get the map." I wiped tears from my cheeks and grabbed the small device. "Here." I pointed to a dot on the map east of us.

Ryker shrugged. "What about it?"

"That's where most of the council members and their families live. They commute to the queen's castle on the steam train. We can make it there. Then take the train to the coast. I'm sure we can figure out how to get to the meeting place from there." It was a long shot, but our only real option. "But there's one problem."

"What?" Ryker asked.

"The steam train won't just be full of council members, but also the queen's guards. And they'll be instructed to shoot us on sight."

CHAPTER TWENTY-SIX

We bounced over several rocks and I jerked at the seatbelt cutting into my neck. "It won't be that easy this time. The guards will know of our disguise from the Mining Territory."

"Not too far now. Will we make it?" Ryker dropped my hand and leaned over me, blocking my line of sight to the plumes of dark smoke that floated into the morning sky. "The fuel is half what we had anticipated."

His shoulder brushed against my arm. The same involuntary response stirred my blood alive. Who needed coffee when they had their own personal adrenaline rush at their side?

"I've n-never seen a t-train before." Emery shot forward and pushed Ryker out of the way, breaking our energy.

Ryker leaned back and raked his hand through his hair. His lip curled in the corner like it always did when he was thinking. "Neither have I. Gotta figure out a way to get on board without being detected. Any cargo going?"

"It's hard to say." I drove over a few broken tree branches and watched the stick drop to the red line on the fuel gauge.

Cracking the window, I wiped at the foggy windshield. Damp earth, a richer scent than at the Mining Territory, and industrial chemicals mixed together, filling the interior.

"Best we stop outside Slag Territory. Probably not many vehicles like this one there."

"You're right. No cars. Just horses, mules, and a few motorized scooters."

Emery knocked on her leg that had been beaten and rendered nearly useless. "W-we have to w-walk?"

"I'm afraid so. We'll help you, but it would be best to keep that leg covered. I think we could pass for humans and reach close to the train that way, but only council members and their families are allowed to board. We'll have to think of something once we're there."

Our vehicle rolled to a stop and we sat staring out the window at the line of buildings ahead. Smoke stacks soared higher than the tree line.

"That's Acadia West, part of the ruling territory. I've ridden on the train and walked around the station a few times but never ventured into the city. I wish I had paid more attention to the area, but the first time I traveled here was right after my father's death."

I sighed at the memory and Ryker stroked his thumb over my palm.

"S-so b-big." Emery sat back and pulled the small red ball from her pocket, rotating it in the palm of her hand.

"Don't worry, your brother will figure out a plan. He always does."

Ryker's eyebrow arched. "Might be best if we stick to the less populated areas, try to blend in."

I got out and pressed my hand to the vehicle. "Goodbye, Mags. Thanks for all you did."

Ryker rounded the vehicle and stood behind me for a moment, not saying a word. Then he moved my hair and kissed my neck. "Mags is strong. I'm sure she made it."

My soul greedily absorbed his touch and craved more. He stepped away and helped Emery from the back seat as I shoved water and the pistol into my belt.

Cautiously, we walked to the edge of town and entered a series of bombed concrete buildings. A cold feeling of loss crept up my legs. At the edge of the last building, I pinched my nose to block a putrid scent. Coughs drew my attention to the corner of a series of makeshift board, brick and sack-cloth homes. An old man clutched his chest and fell to his knees.

I rushed to help, but Ryker blocked me with his arm and led the way with a cautious step. The sounds of babies crying, coughs, and moans haunted my ears. I cupped my hand over my mouth and took a breath, but nothing kept the stench at bay.

Ryker rested his left hand on the pistol. "You okay, sir?"

I hooked my left arm in Emery's and held my pistol along my right side, not sure I'd know how to fire the thing.

The bony old man with rotted teeth welcomed us to his world. "Son, whatcha doin' out there?"

"Sir?" I asked. "Son?"

"My boy, I knew you'd be comin' home. They said you ain't made it, but I knew. Never stopped believin'."

The old man's clouded eyes showed a lifetime of loss and sorrow. I moved my hand away from my gun and helped the man up. Ryker stood, checking the perimeter.

"I don't think it's a trap," I reassured him. "You live near here?"

"Yes, not like the olden days back home, but we make do. You his bride?"

Leathery skin raked my cheek and I had to force myself not to pull away from the foreign sensation. I'd take the deep wrinkles and leathery skin over the feel of cold metal any day.

"Show us," Ryker ordered.

I glanced at Ryker, standing with feet shoulder-width apart. Always suspicious, ready to fight, even as the man's dear old wife had hobbled out from a corner. "Come. Let me help you inside."

"Sweet girl." He tapped my face with his gnarled fingers several times in a loving gesture. "Did well, my son."

Emery wobbled ahead next to Ryker.

The man squinted at Emery. "Who's she?"

"A friend."

"She hurt?"

"She'll be fine." I didn't know how cognizant the man was, but knew I shouldn't chance Emery no matter how frail the man appeared.

The man pointed a crooked finger at a small, open doorway. "Here, here, my dear."

"Uncle, where you been?" A young male voice greeted before I followed him in. The nephew stood hunched in half. He was tall and looked like he hadn't eaten in months. "Who're these—"

"We found your uncle lost and thought we'd help him home." I gave a warm smile.

"Thanks." The bright green eyes narrowed at me, and I knew he could be trouble.

"Uncle, rest here."

"You see my son? He's come home. We'll be fine now."

"Yes, yes, Uncle. I see him." He lowered his uncle to a mat on the dirt floor.

Emery half fell over next to him. "Can I s-sit w-with you?"

The old man smiled and nodded. A second later, Emery snuggled up next to him as if he were Ryker.

"She'll be fine." The young man waved us out the door.

"Listen, we don't—"

"Shh, not here."

We followed him back out the way we came. Ryker's hand remained on the gun at his side. No one spoke until we reached the edge of the ruins.

"My name's Penton."

Ryker didn't respond.

"Can't believe I'm meetin' someone from the rebellion." Penton's face lit up. "I mean, I knew you'd come someday, but I didn't—"

"We're not with the rebellion."

Penton shook his head. "You can trust me. Look." He lifted his torn sleeve and revealed an ink drawing of a slanted letter T.

"What does that prove?"

"I'm a sworn protector of the Triune. Been waitin' for my day of callin'. Now you're here."

Ryker's brow furrowed with confusion.

I examined the small letter on the back of his wrist. I'd seen it somewhere before, but where? "Triune? Calling?"

"You don't know? But you have to be...I thought..."

Ryker grabbed my upper arm, pressing his thumb deep. "We're part of the rebellion."

"We are." I yanked my arm away. "But I don't know of this symbol." Maybe I was naive, but I sensed we could trust Penton. He couldn't be more than fifteen, but his hands were dirty and blistered from years of hard labor.

Penton waved his hands as if doing magic. "The one hope to free us. Three that join to destroy all evil."

"Oh." I trusted him, but I knew better than to tell him that the Scavengers, a handful of the Wasteland residents, and a handful of Mualites had already ruled us the Triune. This kid would probably tell half the people in the city we were here to save them. That was the last thing we needed if we were to keep a low profile.

Ryker shuffled while scanning the area. "Listen, kid, we need to get to the steam train. Point us in the right direction, and we'll be out of your way. We don't want any trouble for you or your uncle."

"I'll do better. Take you there myself."

"No. It isn't safe," I said.

"I won't turn my back on the rebellion." His gaze narrowed on us, then softened. "When the Triune comes, I'll serve them with no fear for my own safety."

Great. The kid was willing to sacrifice himself, so I wasn't about to confirm we were the supposed Triune.

"I know a back way. Only a few will see you; most are too blind or old to care. Others don't want any trouble. They're lost and forgotten and would prefer to stay that way."

"Listen, take us to the station, but remain out of sight. Sounds like you will be needed someday."

I winked at Ryker. He'd fed Penton what he needed to hear. The boy had a skip in his step now. Turning, I followed him.

Darn fool kid. It had only been a few days since I'd turned sixteen. Yet, I'd aged a decade in that short time. Life no longer allowed the luxury of being a scared child.

We went back to the small, dirt-floored home. "Emery, we need to go."

Emery hugged the old man and whispered something in his ear. His face lit with happiness and I wondered what Emery had told him, but there was no time to ask. Penton had already taken off. He slid between two small homes and raced along a path until we reached a stone wall—a huge structure that once must have been taller than the waterfall at the Resort Territory. We shimmied along a narrow ledge over a trench that was filled with things I didn't care to investigate any closer. Emery's oversized metal foot didn't fit, so she used the heel to stay up, Ryker close by her side in case she fell.

We ducked under a wood plank and crawled on hands and knees until we reached a small opening at the other end. Emery's leg ground against the solid floor each time, having to drag it as it no longer bent at the knee.

Penton peeked out then stooped and motioned us to follow. Not one soul walked down the stone street. However, horses clopped and conversations sang from the other side of another wall.

Penton raced down the street with Ryker close at his heels. Lagging behind, I stayed by Emery's side. Each time I passed an opening in the wall that led to the busy inner street, I held my breath, waiting for someone to spot us.

Emery stopped and panted against the stone.

Penton and Ryker turned the corner out of sight. I peeled Emery from the wall. "Got to go, hon. Not much further," I whispered.

We rounded the turn and I collided with someone. I looked up, expecting to see Ryker, but instead saw a person of elite class, a relative of a council member.

I sucked in a quick breath at the realization Ryker had continued ahead. It would be another minute or so before he discovered we were left behind, cornered. By that time it would be too late. We'd be captured when the woman screamed and a dozen of the queen's guards surrounded us.

Wind whipped down the tunnel connecting the two streets. I moved my hand to the pistol strapped to my side and swallowed hard. The woman raised her hands and opened her mouth to scream.

Bleach and floral perfume drew me right back to the ship. I was once again a frail child, facing one of the queen's council.

CHAPTER TWENTY-SEVEN

The lady clutched my arm.

Ryker appeared behind her, his hands glacial.

"No," I screamed and shoved the woman to the wall and Emery to the ground.

"She's one of us." Penton stood between them like a human shield. Stupid kid was going to get himself killed before this was over.

"But she's a—"

She stood up, straightening the tight, bright blue corset around her plump frame. "Slag, yeah. And you're a parasite. Now that we understand each other…" She studied me for a moment. "Just because we both look the part doesn't mean we have to act like savages and pretentious jerks."

Silver eyes shining bright, her crossed arms shielding her plump body… Then I saw it. A small, black T painted on her wrist.

"How'd you know we were here?" Ryker asked, his tone accusatory.

"Let's step out of the walkway before you're noticed. Then

I'd be happy to answer any questions you have. Personally, I'd prefer not to be executed at sundown for harboring a criminal."

I helped Emery up.

My gaze narrowed. "Criminal?"

"Your boyfriend here is accused of kidnapping you, Princess."

My mind spun. "But—"

"Listen, we can chat about the fact that you've got the hots for Mr. Eye-candy over there later. Right now, we need to find a less congested place for small talk." The woman hobbled over to the entry and looked out, then back at us. "Where were you trying to go?"

"The train," Penton answered before we could stop him.

She was obviously part of the same group as Penton, but it was more difficult to trust her. Perhaps it was because of her council clothing and allegiance to the queen, as opposed to the worn clothing and dirt-stained face of a human.

"Take them to the servant entrance at the third house down from the Queen's Square. I'll make sure it's unlocked. Hide in the basement until I can get there." She whirled around in a long swirl of sapphire material and disappeared into the crowd at the end of the passageway.

Penton nodded down the street. "Follow me."

"Trusting the woman because she wrote a T on her arm? Not only does it sound a mite suspicious to me, it could be a trap," Ryker protested.

"She's one of us and taking a great risk," Penton snapped at him.

"W-where are w-we going?"

I smiled and took her by the arm. "To a friend's place."

Ryker's energy blasted through the alley. "Too trusting."

"Tone it down. You want to freeze the entire wall? Like that wouldn't draw any attention now, would it?" I snapped. "If she wanted to take us down all she had to do was scream, and fifty guards would've appeared with guns drawn."

Penton held up his freakishly long arm and we all stopped.

Ryker maneuvered around Emery and me to join Penton. "What is it?"

"Lots of servants. You guys are going to have to keep your heads down, and don't talk to anyone. Some of them would turn you over for a scrap of food."

I pulled Emery's skirt down over her leg and stood to her right side, keeping her near the wall.

We turned down a slim walkway. Buildings shot up on both sides. No breeze drifted down the passageway; the stench of body odor drove me to pull my collar over my nose and mouth.

A child sat in his own filth, small bugs flying around his head. His left eye sat lazy while the right shot around like a fly in its socket.

I lowered my chin to my chest and continued through the crowd, trying to breathe through my mouth. Never had I witnessed such poor conditions, not even in the Mining Territory.

Penton's head whipped right and left, then he climbed four gray steps to a bright green door. He twisted a brass doorknob and leaned inside.

I didn't know what waited for us on the other side of that door, but the dozen eyes glaring at us made me itch to be anywhere but where we stood.

A welcomed floral and cinnamon scent drew me further into the home.

"Come on." Penton urged us to another door that opened to a stairwell.

My boots sunk into a lush red carpet with each step. Ryker's eyes darted from a massive chandelier overhead to the plush carpet. He'd probably never seen such wealth. He nudged a marble pedestal sending a gold statue teetering. He grabbed it before it smashed to the ground.

Penton held a long finger to his lips.

"I simply must go," the woman's voice from earlier echoed through the enormous home. "It'll be the social event of the year."

Penton ushered us down the steep stairs to a dark cellar. A click sounded, and a bright sphere—different from the luminaries back home—cut on. Furniture, boxes, and paintings filled the room.

No metal. No Earth. No escape route. The perfect trap.

Ryker paced the small area around the discarded items. Such a waste, considering the people who starved all around us.

The door opened above, and Ryker took his fighting stance. Crisp air formed a cloud that danced from his lips with each breath.

"Calm yourself. The queen would've executed you and married me to the general by now if they were going to betray us," I said.

The stout woman from earlier reached the bottom step. Clutching her large chest that spilled from the top of the corset, she panted. "I see you've made it."

I brushed by Ryker and greeted the woman with a warm smile. "Thank you for assisting us."

"So, the rumors are true. You have hooked up with a boy and run away from home." She chuckled, her breasts bouncing so much that I feared they'd bust free if she didn't stop.

"Are you gonna help us?" Ryker asked.

"Ah, yes, you are the hot-blooded Mualite. Definitely live up to the rumors about your...masculinity."

I didn't like the way her eyes roamed down his body as if he was her next meal to devour.

"I'm Ralona, Senior Council Member and sympathizer to the less fortunate. I must say, Valencia, you are not looking your best." She chuckled. "Yet, the warm glow of love gives you a new beauty."

Ryker scrubbed his stubbled chin. "Why would you risk all this to help us?"

Her eyes grew dark and sorrowful. "I wasn't always one who cared." She clutched the banister and shifted under his stare.

"What made you join Triune?" I asked in a soothing tone.

Ralona shook her head. "For one reason—to take down that pig who calls himself the general. The entire council doesn't respect him. The rest of the reasons don't matter. Listen." The tone of her voice changed, and her chubby cheeks tensed. "I'll make sure my husband is upstairs with me. There are three trunks in the front foyer that are supposed to be filled with my clothes. Crawl inside and don't make a sound. Those trunks will be transferred to the steam train bound for Acadia East this evening. You'll hide in the storage area until the train reaches the platform, then sneak off. I've already disposed of some clothing. I'll claim it stolen when we arrive."

Ryker reluctantly stepped toward Ralona. "Is there anyone else in the house that we should be—"

"My husband. No one else here. Not anymore." Ralona gave a half smile. "I wish you luck once you get there. This'll be the last time we speak. Oh, and hon—" She smiled at me. "I would've chosen him, too." She winked, then hobbled up the stairs.

Penton grabbed the banister. "I have to go before I'm missed. My shift at the factory starts soon. I'll be here, waiting to serve the rebellion under the guidance of the Triune."

I followed him back up, hugging him at the top of the stairs. He blushed and held up his wrist as if to salute an unknown force.

"Th-The m-mark." Emery smiled. "B-Boaz."

"I knew I'd seen it somewhere."

"No need to check. I'm sure it was the wind," Ralona's voice echoed down from the second story.

We raced down the hall and found three trunks next to the front door. I glanced out the front window. Tons of people walked along clean streets with no worries. A world of the elite and divine.

Three loud raps at the door startled us. Heavy footsteps thumped overhead.

Ryker and I helped Emery into one of the boxes. Then we each crawled into our own trunk.

A doorknob clicked. "We are here to take the delivery for the train bound for Acadia East this evening."

I listened, curled on my side and twisted in an awkward position.

"Yes, yes, they are over there," Ralona trilled.

I braced myself for a bumpy ride and held my breath as footsteps neared.

"Would you like to be present when we search them?"

"Search?"

"Yes, the queen will be on board tonight's train, so we've been ordered to search all cargo."

CHAPTER TWENTY-EIGHT

The latch clicked. Leathery air weighted down my lungs. My heart pounded in anticipation of the inevitable.

"How dare you touch my things!"

"What's the trouble, soldier?" The unmistakable booming voice of the general drove me to the brink of losing control. My hands burned and I could smell a hint of melting metal. I sucked in what little air filtered through the small holes pierced on the sides of the trunk. He'd be merciless this time. My stomach clenched like a belly-up desert beetle left to die in the sun.

"General, thank goodness you have blessed me with your presence. These worthless peasants wish to inspect my delicates." A mass of shuffling feet indicated a mad dash away from the trunks, and I knew Ralona had swooned. She was good. No one would want to tell the queen they caused her closest council member to faint.

"Sir, I—"

"I will deal with this personally. Be off with you," the general commanded.

I released my fist. An ache remained from where my nails had dug into my palm.

"Please forgive the intrusion. We'll have your trunks transferred immediately. Why don't I personally escort you to the station?"

The general couldn't stand the council women. He always found their girth revolting, but he was wise in the ways of politics and had great ambitions. He had a singular mission in life—to become King. If I escaped the marriage, he would be forced to either overthrow the queen or marry her. It was only a matter of time. And I was betting on the coup.

Ralona called up the stairs for her husband.

"Men, transport these trunks to the station immediately," the general ordered.

There was stomping of several feet, then my box lifted into the air. It teetered and I nearly fell out.

"Be careful. I have a gift for the queen in there," Ralona screeched before her voice became faint in the distance.

I prayed I wouldn't be separated from Ryker and Emery on the journey to the station.

The vehicle jolted forward and began the journey to the train. I let out a sigh and my aching shoulders relaxed. Not that there was much room to stretch. How had Ryker ever fit in the trunk? I sighed, imagining the bad shape he'd be in if he had to stay in there the entire trip.

I couldn't wait to speak with Emery. My mind spun with memories of Boaz. Each time, all I saw were his rosy cheeks and large grin, never his wrist. All those years he was by my side, and I never saw the strange mark. I had to have noticed it at some point but couldn't place where. Yet Emery, who'd only seen him for a short time, remembered it.

I dug deeper into my memories, but his sleeves always covered his arms and he never stood still for long, always jumping in and out of vents. Of course, we'd spent time together in the engine room when Emery was hidden there.

The wheels squealed beneath me for a moment, and the vehicle jarred twice, then stopped. I swallowed the little remaining moisture in my mouth and hoped there wouldn't be a search prior to loading.

Sweat poured down my temple into my eye. With my arms trapped, all I could do was blink. Finally, I gave in and closed both. The trunk rose suddenly in the air, causing my head to bang against the bottom. My knees ached from remaining in the same position.

At last, they shoved the trunk in and swung the door shut with a bang. Did I dare open and peek out? I had to know if Ryker and Emery made it.

Before I could move, a commotion erupted outside the door and I strained to hear. Were we discovered? If so, I needed to get out and help. I reached for the small button to the latch but the train lurched and I missed. We were moving. I waited for any sounds to indicate the others were near.

There was nothing.

I pressed the small brass circle and the latch popped open. Lifting the top slightly, I peered out. A rush of stale air greeted me. No sign of a guard, only several boxes and trunks. I pushed harder but something held the top down. With only enough room to fit a hand through the opening, there was no way I could escape. I shoved hard but met with more resistance.

"Emery? Ryker? Are you there?"

No answer. My arm shook under the weight of the lid until my elbow gave way and the lid slammed shut.

I scratched for the latch in the darkness but couldn't find it again. Hot air lingered. The weight of what held the trunk closed was nothing compared to my panic and the immense pressure pushing on my chest. I struggled to breathe. My nails scratched against the leather surface. No air. No one to help.

I opened my mouth to scream, but my throat closed. It was as if I'd been sent into the hole for reconditioning all over again.

Logically, I knew I wouldn't suffocate in the closed trunk. Yet, my mind couldn't grasp the knowledge. My thoughts swirled, unable to settle.

I thrust the lid with all my strength. Again, it stopped at the same position. I couldn't melt leather and whatever kept me caged wouldn't budge. Footsteps neared, and I held my breath. A muffled whistle blew in the distance.

Two raps but no words.

It wasn't Ryker. He would have lifted the lid and pulled me out. The only possibility was a guard or train worker. I could take one down.

Trunks and containers banged outside my small, poorly-ventilated world. Then the distinctive sound of a strap sliding.

The lid swung open and a flood of light blinded me. I blinked, then saw his skinny little face. "Penton. What are you doing here?" My heart soared at the sight of his freckled, dirty cheeks. "How'd you get on the train?"

Penton offered his hand and I unfolded my body with caution. With each move, my joints grinded. "Ralona thought you'd need some help. She signaled me to board. Good thing I came. You were belted in."

"Thanks. Where are Emery and Ryker? Are they okay?"

"Don't know. Haven't found them yet."

I looked back and forth, jumped out of the trunk, tumbling over into another one, then tried the locks on a few others.

Penton searched the last one. "They aren't here, but don't worry. I know they boarded without incident."

"There's no way Ryker can stay in his trunk much longer. I barely fit. We need to find him."

"Don't worry. We will. Come." Penton took me by the elbow and led the way to a silver door. We ducked below a square window, and he popped his head up and back down. "Looks clear."

I opened the door and grabbed the railing. The platform underfoot convulsed and I struggled to remain standing. Penton opened the next car door, and we found another cargo hold.

Wow, the elite sure loved their clothing. We spent an hour searching and knocking on trunks as the train sped to Acadia East.

"What are we going to do if we can't find them before we stop?"

"We'll find them," Penton assured me.

We searched several more cars until we reached the passenger cars and turned around. Hours passed, and no sign of either of them.

I rubbed my elbow at the memory of being locked inside that trunk. "Ryker is going to be in rough shape when we find him."

We reached the car I'd been in and made our way to the other end. Exiting out to the platform, Penton grasped the handle to the next car. Three guards stood only paces away.

"Wait." I pointed through the glass window, then yanked his arm from the handle.

"We've reached the end. There's no way we can get through that car," Penton said.

"Guess we'll have to wait until we stop, then scramble through. There shouldn't be more than a couple more cargo cars."

Through the window, a gold emblem on the side of one of the trunks on a wooden shelf caught my attention. I squinted to make out the writing. It was the emblem of the elite with the queen's seal. That was the cargo car we were all supposed to be in.

I clutched the door handle so tight it bent. A guard leaned against the trunk, smoking a pipe. It was the largest of the three trunks. Ryker's.

"Valencia, no." Penton shoved me from the door and we backed into the car we'd just left. "Listen, I'll help, but don't be stupid."

His face scrunched and he tapped his upper lip with his pointer finger. "Okay, I've got a plan. You'll go out to the platform. There's a ladder on the side of the car. Grab on and stay hidden."

"What are you planning?"

"Don't worry. I've been a snake in the sewers of Acadia West most my life. I can slither into some hidin' spot on the train. Trust me. It's what I'm best at."

"But—"

"Do you want to get Ryker and Emery out of there or not?"

"Yes, but—"

Penton wrapped his charcoaled fingers around my raised hand and I knew where he had stowed away on the train. If the site of black dust wasn't a big enough giveaway, the strong chemical odor confirmed my suspicions.

My chest ached for him, but there were no other options. "Please, promise me you'll escape. You understand what they'll do if they find you." I pleaded with my eyes for him to heed my warning. Flashes of mangled bits of a boy on the tracks during my last steam train ride made my mind scream not to let him go.

"I promise. Now go. We can't be too far from Acadia East."

I squeezed his hands, wanting to tell him how much I appreciated his sacrifice, how I was in awe of his bravery. But I couldn't find words that didn't sound condescending. Instead, I let go and checked the guards' positions through the window. They remained sitting on the trunks smoking and carrying on. If the queen caught them, they'd be thrown in the brig or tossed from the train like stowaways.

I swallowed hard and yanked the door open, ducked down, and crawled to the edge of the car. The wind hit with the force of a sandstorm. I clung to the railing and stretched out to the ladder. The rush of air knocked me back.

With one last shove, I wrapped my fingers around the rungs and propped my foot up on the railing. My heart beat faster than the rhythmic cadence of the metal wheels against the track.

I bent my knees and jumped for the ladder. Only one foot caught. The other dangled in the air. I yelped before I could stifle it. But no one could hear me over the thundering wind and rattle of the tracks. The ground sped by with fierce speed as I fought to stay on board. Finally, I managed to find my footing.

I heard faint shouts over the neck-breaking air rushing by

my ears. There wouldn't be much time. I needed to get into that car and retrieve Emery and Ryker before they returned.

With a deep breath, I let go of the ladder and reached for the railing. The train jerked right and my fingers grasped the rail, but my feet remained on the rungs. I hung between the two, unable to recover in either direction.

The train snaked left. The cars bent right and I threw myself over the railing before the cars had a chance to change direction again.

My limbs shook so hard I thought my tremors were the shimmy of the platform until I tried to stand and my legs were like gelatinous blobs.

Forced to move quickly, I crawled back to the door and pulled myself up by the handle. I looked through both windows. No sign of any guards in either direction. Penton had kept his word, but for how long?

I managed to stand with my arm bracing my body by hanging onto the door handle. My weight pushed the handle down, and the door swung open. I fell through and landed with a thud on the floor.

"Ryker. Emery. Where are you?"

Two swift knocks came from the trunk I'd suspected was Ryker's home the last three to four hours. The sound of his acknowledgment shot enough adrenaline through my body to help me stand and shuffle to it. Unhinging the buckle, I tugged the security strap free, then lifted the lid.

Ryker squinted up at me, and I leaned in to help him up. The sight of his large eyes and touch of his strong hand warmed my insides.

"Ah," he cried out.

I stroked his cheek, and he leaned into my hand. "Sorry, I

tried to get to you but there were guards, and we couldn't find you. We need to hurry before they return."

He lifted his head a little further while I tried to unfold his body. Every time I touched him, he cried out.

Grimacing, I finally admitted he wasn't moving fast enough. We still needed to find Emery. I pressed my lips to his and relished his salty taste. One day I'd finish that kiss, but for now, I needed him out of that trunk. "Ryker, drain some energy from me."

His eyes blazed. "Never."

"Only a small amount. Enough to get you out of this box before the guards return and we're discovered."

"Never ask such a thing again. I refuse to take life from you."

I leaned in closer. "Be reasonable."

He took my lips hungrily. My head swirled and I couldn't think of any words to argue with him. "No, stop. Not fair."

"You t-two always going t-to be doing th-that?" Emery's voice sent a wave of joy through me. I spun around to find her sitting on a trunk with a big grin."

The train screeched to a stop and I fell. Scrambling back to my feet, I yanked Ryker halfway up. Not sure where I found the strength, but if we were at Acadia East, we needed to move quickly.

Emery started humming and moaning behind me, and the tingling of warning moved across my skin. "What is it?"

Emery lifted a finger to the window. The hats of guards bounced up and down. They were headed back. No doubt to the front passenger cars to escort the queen to her palace.

Ryker managed to get to his knees.

I ran to the door and melted the handle. Nerves interfered

with my concentration, and I melted some of the door. Our only hope was that the general didn't see my signature work. If he did, he'd know we were here. I crawled back to Ryker. "Emery, you want to play a game?"

Her eyes lit up. "Game?"

"Yep, we're going to play hide and seek. You need to help hide Ryker so no one can find him."

"I love hide and seek." She jumped down and I wrapped my arm around Ryker's waist to help him from the trunk. Emery took the other side. Struggling under his weight, we shuffled quickly to the other door while I held my breath and prayed we'd make it out before the guards caught us. Pounding sounded behind. We dived onto the platform and darted over the side. I clutched Ryker's vest and rolled him under the car, then shimmied in beside him. Emery squeezed in at our feet. We remained hidden, listening to the passengers disembark.

We'd made it to Acadia East. I never dreamed we would make it across the desert, let alone all the way to the rebellion, but we had. I smiled at Ryker as he stretched and moved his body around.

Now, we had to make it to the ocean south of the city. Once there, we'd board the ship and for the first time in a week, we could fall into each other's arms and sleep for days.

He rolled over and stroked my face. "I know the rebellion will want your help. Mualites never sacrifice people. They aren't murderers. We'll have a chance to be together, really together, soon." He smiled, and his dimples sent tingles of hope through me.

The train whistle blew.

"I can walk now. We better find a way to reach the rebellion before dark, because I plan on spending the entire night with you."

My body warmed with nerves and excitement.

We shimmied out from under the train and looked around. The sun sat low in the orange sky, signaling another day behind schedule. "What if the rebellion's already left?" I didn't want to think about it, but we were late.

"We have no choice but to try. The communication codes are too important. Hopefully, they'll still be there."

My stomach churned. I was about to turn myself over to the rebellion so they could trade me to the queen. So much for days of slumber in Ryker's arms. Yet, if anyone could convince the rebels to keep me safe, it would be Ryker. Also, Fallon never would have sent me to them just to be turned over to Mother.

We raced to the station platform. Emery's leg caught on the tracks and Ryker lifted her up and ran to the shadows.

"Psst. Over here." Penton's familiar voice drew my attention. He waved us down to the end of the building. "You need a lift? Hear you've got somewhere to be."

I chuckled inside, not having the strength to laugh aloud. "Yeah, sounds good."

Penton waved his arms and a horse and carriage came around. We climbed in and the driver snapped the reigns, sending us backward. "I'm so glad you're okay, Penton. I thought for sure you'd been captured."

He snickered. "Can't catch a snake that easily."

"You shouldn't be here."

I bit back a smile at the worry in Ryker's voice. Every time Ryker worried for someone, he barked at them for doing exactly what he would have done.

"You wouldn't have made it to the ocean without my help," Penton retorted.

Ryker nodded. "And you," he turned to me and I braced myself for his reprimand that so often came.

"I'm so glad you're safe." He cupped my face in his hands. "No matter what, you're gonna stay with me. You're also not gonna run away the minute we reach the rebellion. Promise you they ain't gonna turn you over to the general. Won't let them."

My stomach knotted. "You can't guarantee that. But know this, I'd rather die on the run than marry the general or be converted."

"Promise, that'll never happen."

The carriage jolted left and right. We were off the main road and headed for the ocean.

My mind turned back to the people we'd left behind. I couldn't let them down. "Emery, are you sure about Boaz?"

"Yes. He t-told me not to t-tell you he was part of th-the rebellion. Th-thought it was t-too dangerous for you."

I twisted my hands in my lap. My heart ached at the thought. After all we'd been through, he didn't tell me he was part of a rebellion. "He didn't trust me?"

"Wanted t-to protect you."

The carriage bounced about, then stuttered to a halt.

Penton opened the door and jumped down. "We've got to walk from here. It's on the other side of the hill. Carriages can't make it over the rocks."

We climbed down and thanked the driver, but he didn't stay long enough to chat. Obviously, someone had paid him handsomely, but his job was over and he didn't want to be a part of our lives a moment longer.

Ryker held my hand while I laced my fingers through Emery's small ones. With each step, my legs burned.

We managed to stumble to the top. I'd never been this exhausted. All I longed for was to reach the ship and collapse into Ryker's arms.

And here was the rebel ship waiting for us.

Only we weren't the first to find it. The large ship lay in smoldering pieces along the beach.

I fell to my knees. The European Mualite Rebellion had been destroyed, and with it, all our hope.

Emery covered her ears and cried out, falling into the sand by my side. I cradled and rocked her.

"B-but w-we—" Emery's body convulsed in my arms. The weight of her small frame was nothing compared to the gravity of the situation pulling me down.

Penton stared at the carnage with a distant gaze. "It can't be. I was meant to deliver the Triune."

I clung to Emery. "There have to be survivors." I pushed Emery into Penton's arms and tumbled down the hill toward the wreckage. "Anyone out there?"

Emery's pleas to come back choked me with the knowledge that no one could survive the devastation sprawled in front of us.

Ryker stumbled down the hill after me. He landed at the bottom on his backside in the soft sand and ran to my side.

Lifting pieces of metal, I searched under them for life.

Ryker tugged my shoulder. "Valencia, stop. Your hands will burn."

They were blistered from the melting hunks of ship I'd combed under, but unlike a few days ago, I didn't feel a thing.

"Stop." He pulled me close and locked me into a hug, tight

to his chest, restraining me. His heart pounded against me, matching the thunderous beat of my grief.

"We have to find survivors. There has to be someone to tell us what happened or what we can do." My own voice sounded foreign to me.

He squeezed me tighter. "No one's here. No one could've survived this."

I clutched his arm, trying to cling to something on earth that still existed.

He led me to the edge of the surf and sank into the damp sand, holding my hand in the frigid water. I only knew it was cold because of Ryker's teeth chattering.

The surf beat against our skin, sending small debris onto the beach around us.

"They died waiting for us. If we'd made it here sooner—"

"Don't think like that. We did everything we could." His words sounded empty, hollow with his own grief.

"They died because...because of us. Their bodies..." I stopped shaking and jumped to my feet, sliding from his grip. "Ryker."

"What?" He pushed to his feet and tried to hold me, but I pushed from his arms. Scorching metal and chemical fumes carried on the ocean breeze, but no smell of flesh or blood, no bones.

"No bodies." I pulled a few more pieces of ship from the ground. My damp hands sizzled. This time the heat burned my hands and I dropped the shrapnel and cried out.

Ryker raced to my side and blew a small amount of energy over my hands. Only enough to fade some blisters.

He froze and scanned the beach. "No bodies," he hissed. He

dropped my hands and kicked a few more shards of the ship around. "You're right. No charred skeletons. Nothing."

A zing of hope raced through my body. Renewed energy drove me forward. We both searched through more wreckage. "Nothing," I agreed.

I pointed to a long piece of the bulkhead. "ENR. It was definitely their ship. Did they escape?"

"Escape…or captured." He pivoted and I glanced behind me to see Penton waving his arms madly.

Engines roared.

Sand spun up around us.

Ship.

Queen's ship.

Trap.

CHAPTER TWENTY-NINE

Assassins marched into view. Stopping in a line on the ridge, they captured Emery and Penton in their grasp.

Surrounded on all sides except for the ocean.

The queen's ship landed. Ryker laced his fingers through mine and stood tall. "It won't end here. I won't let them take you."

I stopped trembling and stepped in front of him. My hands glowed bright red. Wind spun Ryker's hair. It reflected off the debris and resembled a silver halo. The landing gear sunk into the sand and the engines rumbled, shaking the ground beneath us.

I directed my energy at the three metal supports and they bubbled before the ship sunk an inch further into the ground.

The bay door slid open and I redirected my attention before I could completely melt the supports.

Ryker stood by my side, icy energy sliding down his veins in bluish-white streaks. "Monster or savior, I'll take them all down. Damn the consequences." Ryker said.

This had to be a replay of Emery's rescue. Pain showed in the deep lines above his furrowed eyebrows.

The gangway smashed to the ground. Sand bellowed up in a plume of tan mist.

I went to work, cylinders sizzling in the bay. I remained controlled despite the fear bubbling up inside. I'd be facing Mother. The one person who made me feel less important than a sand flea in her presence.

Methodically, I concentrated on what would cause the most damage to the ship before we were shot.

At the first sign of a Slag appearing on the gangway, Ryker's hands lifted, his fingers arched toward the enemy.

Flaming red hair dancing in the bay of the ship taunted me. My blood froze, despite the heat of my gift. Every ounce of hatred centered on that figure.

Cackles echoed from inside the ship.

She laughed? Of course she laughed. This was all a game to her. She'd controlled me at every turn. No more.

A body rolled down the bay door and bounced onto the sand. "Boaz?"

His small frame was wrapped in ropes and three Slags followed with guns pointed at us. I quickly melted the barrels. Ryker sucked the life from them.

The queen continued to laugh. An electronic pulse shot from my brain through my arms and legs. I screamed and fell to the ground. Blood trickled from my ear, dyeing the golden sand a dark ember. Ryker collapsed at my side and scooped me into his arms. "What is it? What's wrong?" He pressed his hand to my temple and stopped the bleeding from my ear. "Can't find the damage."

"You can't help her, you useless parasite." The queen sauntered down the gangway. "So, you thought you were some sort of hero? Thought you'd finish what your parents started in the revolution?"

Her laughter rubbed every last one of my nerves raw. Ryker shot up to face her while I still clutched my head as the pain faded, but guns pointed from all directions.

"I'd check the ridgeline before you try anything."

Emery dangled in the air over the beach, held by an assassin. Penton struggled to free her, but another assassin tossed him down the hill. His body bounced and rolled.

Ryker spun back around. "Let her go."

Mother lifted a bronze plate on her arm and pushed a button. Another zap shot through my body. I concentrated on overcoming the knife through my brain so I could focus.

Mother marched to my side. "You're in no position to make demands."

I rocked back and forth on my knees, pressing my palms to my temples. "Make it stop."

Mother bent down. "My dear, sweet daughter. You don't think I ever trusted you, do you? Too weak-minded. Look. You even fell into the arms of the boy whose parents murdered your father."

She pressed the button again. My head stung as if thousands of sermechtapede pincers nipped at my brain. I fell over to a fetal position and panted. Ryker crawled toward me but guns snapped to attention and Mother backhanded him with her Slag fist, sending him flying sideways.

"I think you've done enough damage, parasite."

I moaned and managed to sit up to my knees. "You lie."

"Do I?" Mother ran her metal claw down my face. I cringed away from her.

"You installed a tamer in me?"

"The day you arrived. I didn't know if you were part of the plot to assassinate my beloved husband."

Hurt filled my chest at the accusations. "Never."

"You are the lover of the boy whose family did the job. I guess I had justification for my actions."

I blinked but no tears streaked down my face. I looked up at him, then narrowed my eyes. "His family did what?"

"Murdered your father."

He shook his head. "No, it can't be true. My parents were good people."

Mother lied. She always bent the truth to get what she wanted. It didn't matter. This was my chance to make a difference. I had to save Emery, Ryker and Penton. I'd give Mother what she wanted.

I struggled to my feet and lifted my chin. "Leave them here to waste away. They'll never make it back through the city."

Ryker clutched his chest. "It's not true. It's a trick. Don't believe her."

His words ripped a fissure through the center of my soul, but I couldn't let Mother see the pain. I stood firm. "Please forgive my disloyalty, Mother. I now see the error of my ways. I will do whatever you please. I'll marry the general and help rid the earth of any further betrayal."

The thought of him touching me tested my resolve, but sacrificing myself to save Ryker and Emery was a small price to pay compared to so many others I'd met the last few days.

A hum sounded, then Ryker flew off his feet. He lay on the ground, not moving.

"No!" I screamed.

"Don't worry, dear. You will suffer a worse fate as servant

to the general. The deal was for you to remain pure until you married him; now you're worth nothing to me. At least you look the part now." Her lips curled in disapproval.

"I didn't—" My words stopped.

"It's over, parasite. Die knowing the girl you loved will be used and abused for the rest of her days. You failed. I won."

Mother grabbed my hair and dragged me up the gangway. I fought, kicking and scratching at Mother's metal hand.

Mother paused at the top and cocked her head to direct the assassins and guards along the beach and ridgeline. "Kill them all."

I jerked my arm, but I couldn't pry loose of Mother's metal grip. "No! Do whatever you want to me, but let them go."

"You stupid—" A steel grip crushed my arm, bones cracked before she flung me down the gangway. "—pathetic—" A foot to my ribs. "—parasite."

Another kick to my abdomen and I face-planted onto the beach. I sucked in coarse sand. Gritty particles invaded my nose and eyes. I swiped at them with my good arm in vain.

Ryker crawled over and hooked his fingers into mine.

Mother's words stung almost as much as her brutality. But I knew one thing—I couldn't live as a servant to the general.

I rolled onto my back and forced my eyes open to see mother's lineless face. "You lie."

Another whack across my cheek. Sounds of bones cracking tested my resolve, but I reminded myself of what was yet to come if I lived.

"Stop!" Ryker yelled.

Mother ignored him. "That parasite betrayed you—"

"You said his family murdered my father, but that isn't his fault."

Mother cackled. The low-pitched yet loud sound carried over the ocean. "You stupid, girl. His people negotiated safe passage for those two parasites in exchange for your father."

My head whirled. "Father?" The visions...dreams. "I knew it. My father is alive."

Mother squatted by my side, her snarl only inches from my face. "He betrayed us, Valencia. The man you clung to all these years. Even after all my reconditioning, you attached yourself to a traitor."

A faint voice whispered in my ear. *I love you, Princess.* The image of a man above me, brushing my hair from my face. His bright smile melted my heart. "You knew all this time he was alive and never told me?"

"Told you? I tried to alter your disturbed, childish image of a perfect man that never existed." Mother rose, arms crossed over her chest. "Harrison came between us, forced my hand. I'm all you've got; you don't see your father here to save you. He's never cared about you. He's weak and stays in hiding."

I followed Mother's glance to the wreckage.

"She thought you were on board the ship," Ryker accused. He knelt by my side, his hands no longer clutching his injury, but pressed to mine. My heart warmed at the sound of his protective voice and healing hands.

"Her death would have been a casualty of circumstances. It would have been a grave loss."

My stomach clenched not only from where Mother kicked me, but from the bruise her words left on my heart.

She stepped closer, the orange moon reflecting off her leg. "I hoped you weren't, though."

"Really?" The words escaped my mouth before I could stop them.

"Yes, dear." Mother bent down to face me. "I still have a use for you. Council wants an heir."

My pulse thundered and I grabbed Mother's leg, but before I had a chance to melt anything, she shook me off and a skull-splitting pain ripped through the center of my scalp.

Ryker lifted his hands.Icy blue fingers pointed at the woman who gave birth to me but never loved me. "Stop."

"I'd think twice."

Ryker followed the queen's glance to the ridge. Emery had four assassins with guns pointed at her.

"Who means more to you, your sister or your whore?"

Ryker's jaw twitched. I knew more than anything, he wanted to kill the queen. He'd get one shot. It wouldn't be enough before they all fell to the ground dead. "You're a monster," I shouted.

A spasm ripped through my stomach muscles from my effort, and I tucked into a fetal position. I'd never said those heartfelt words out loud. Heck, I had tried never to say it. But now, the words soothed my aching soul, allowing me to ignore the pain of my body.

"Maybe you're not so spineless after all. Maybe there is some shred of me in you—"

"I'm nothing like you," I managed between stuttered breaths. "I wouldn't murder all those people then cast their bodies into the sea."

The queen's head shot up. "What did you say?" She didn't wait for an answer; instead, she made it a few paces on the beach before she remembered the sand. Shaking off the particulates that would cause her distress later, she wobbled back over to the gangway.

She lifted her gun and pointed it at Ryker. "This time I'll make sure to blow your brains from your head."

I uncurled my body and shielded him. But he resisted, still blocking me from the queen. I focused on the barrel of the gun, hoping to melt it before she fired off a shot.

"Go ahead, but I think we both know what happened with the bodies," he said in a light, happy tone.

Mother pivoted and followed his finger to the hillside. A large black mast rose into the sky. "Scavengers. Fools. They are no match for us." Mother shoved Ryker away and grabbed me by the hair. Sand spun up in an instant sandstorm that made the one in the Mining Territory look pathetic. Yet, it wasn't a storm. A wall of solid tan rose between me and Mother. Ryker yanked me from her clutches.

"Get us in the air." Mother's commands filtered through the sand.

I hoped the Scavengers would be a match for her ship and assassins.

"I'll take care of them," the general said.

I turned to Ryker. "Run."

Engines roared.

Sand dropped to the ground in a waterfall of disappointment. I glanced back and saw the assassins dragging Penton and Emery out of sight.

Before I could focus on the bulkhead, an electrical impulse shot through my body. Acid invaded my mouth and my eyes rolled back in my head. It was more intense, merciless, as if someone cranked the power up to fry my brain.

The general bludgeoned Ryker's skull with the hilt of a gun. Ryker cried out and clutched his head. Another thrust and the gun rammed into his ribcage.

The scavenger ship engaged the queen. Supernova-colored bullets flew overhead. Shining blue pellets exploded against them, sending a glitter of hot rain down. Crystals sizzled on my ripped, dirty pants. Smell of burnt hair made the finality of the situation clear.

I pushed to my feet and forced my gaze from Ryker, bleeding on the ground, curled on the sand, and focused on the general. "No one's going to follow a hideous monster like you. The council thinks you should be chained like an animal. You're my mother's pet."

"I'm better than you, a lowly Cursed."

My stomach flipped, and I forced down the bile rising in my throat. Images of him touching me tried to invade my mind. But I refused to let them cripple me with fear.

An explosion drew our attention. The side of the scavenger ship was engulfed in flames. My heart fell faster than one of the cannons from the side of the ship as it smashed to the ground.

Mother's ship circled like a sea snake ready to strike. I swore I could make out Josheb standing at the front of the ship, but it couldn't be him.

The dent in the general's chin deepened with his crooked smile. "That didn't last long. Your pathetic excuse for a rescue is doomed."

"You underestimate us." Fury roared to the surface without a second of concentration.

The bronze chest plate oozed down onto his one good hand. He yelped like a dog kicked in the gut. "You stupid wench."

The battle detonated around us, matching the one in my head. Booms and pops exploded in my brain. With every nerve shot, searing pain blinded me until they all melded into one gigantic sphere of excruciating energy. It pulsed against the inside of my skull. Pushing and shoving to break free.

I fell to my knees in a puddle of mush. No muscles worked in my body. It was as if the nerves had frozen and wouldn't send messages.

His voice echoed next to my ear. Too close.

"I won't kill you...yet."

The rock of energy melted. Hot lava bubbled between my temples. I sucked in a ragged breath.

He pulled me up by my hair. "I'll let you watch your friends die first."

Emery and Penton stood on the ridge, the assassins pointing their guns at them. The general sauntered to Ryker, dragging me by his side. He pointed the gun at Ryker's temple.

Yanking me into his left arm, he pushed my chin toward the sky. His foul breath overpowered the other smells of destruction. "Look. Up there."

Mother's ship looped in the sky. The dark orange metal dove. Two loud blasts echoed across the ocean and the scavenger ship plummeted from the air.

It crossed overhead and crashed into the sandy beach. Sliding to a halt, it rested powerless against the oncoming attack. Bullets ripped through the hull of the ship. Faint screams carried on the wind over the sound of rapid gunfire. Through it all, the general forced me to watch our only hope being annihilated.

CHAPTER THIRTY

"Yes, but are you a match for the ENR?" Ryker nodded behind us.

A massive, gray ship emerged from the dark blue water. Waves cascaded over the large wings. My heart soared at the sight of the European Mualite Rebellion.

Ryker yanked me from the general's clutches while the abusive Slag stood dumbfounded at the approaching vessel.

Ryker cradled me against his chest, his healing energy pressing into my broken arm and cracked cheek. The pain dulling with each surge until it faded away.

"I love you. Never forget that." Ryker released me onto the sand and rammed his shoulder into the general's side. The general teetered as his false knee, now locked from all the sand, didn't bend. Ryker took advantage and threw sand in his face. The mechanical eye stuttered.

I rolled to my feet.

Ryker lit up like a silver moon and wrapped his arms around the general. A shot fired and Ryker fell to the ground.

The general would just zap me if I neared them. I had to be

smarter. *Think.* A buzz like an irritating sand flea echoed in my head. I targeted the unknown fissures of my brain. It had to be metal. And if it was, I could find and melt it.

Of course, there was a possibility I'd melt half my brain in the process. If I knew exactly where it was, it wouldn't be so complicated.

Ryker rolled onto his side; his eyes morphed into the color of coal.

I closed my eyes and concentrated on the faint hum, maneuvering through blood vessels and veins leading deep into my brain. No, not there, the back. It was near the implant. The one they told me could never be removed.

I pushed the fear from my mind. The engines rumbled overhead. The ship gained altitude. The roar drowned the only hint I had of the device.

Meaty hands grabbed my arms. No more time. I unleashed the sting from my core and directed the impulse up my brainstem and stopped a few millimeters above the existing implant.

Energy pulsed against the back of my head twice. A zing of energy drilled down my spine until it reached my toes. The snap of electricity traveled back up and exploded in a mass of fire.

Everything went dark and my legs buckled under me. The ground met my knees with harsh resistance.

Then the world surged back in. Darkness retreated to the corners where it had formed. I pushed to my feet. The general's arm rose, his lips curved into a smile. He cranked the tamer to overload and pointed at me. "I'll make you a submissive vegetable yet."

My heart thrashed against my chest as I braced myself.

He hit the button.

I clenched my fists tight. Nothing happened.

It worked.

"My turn." I commanded my power with precision I'd never possessed. A steady stream of blood-orange rays seared his Slag leg to a pool of bronze liquid. Ryker shot a stream of energy, and the general collapsed to the ground.

All-out hell reigned over the beach. Ryker slumped, lifeless, in the middle of it all. I dove to his side.

His dark eyes reflected the battle overhead. "Ryker."

"Leave me," he managed.

"I won't. Take some of my energy."

"Won't risk you."

I knew he'd never agree, unless… "If you don't, we both die here."

"Go."

"Hurry, before we're shredded by stray bullets." I remained by his side.

Ryker's face twisted with grief.

A blue light whizzed by my head and I pressed my cheek to his chest, burying my head into his vest. More than bullets threatened us. An entire arsenal of lasers and old-fashioned guns roared.

He stroked my matted hair. A cool chill tickled my brain, then flowed into my chest. A cautious pull tugged at my core.

A light scraping took threads of energy one microfiber at a time from my essence of life. Not even enough to cause me to sneeze. I had to distract him enough to take what he needed, and quick, before his caution got us both killed.

I lifted my head and pressed my body to his. He stiffened under me, but I crushed my lips to his and kissed him with all

OF BLOOD AND CROWNS

the restrained desire I'd contained since we met. My body burned with want, my power surged the way it had the first time we'd kissed. The world silenced around us. The war drifted into the distance in a blur of reality.

His taste filled my mouth and I opened my heart and soul.

A rush of energy burned my lips, but I refused to release him. Not this time. My skin burned cool and surged with electricity. Each wave extracted a little more of my energy.

A bolt shot from my center and I flew from his arms, landing on the rough sand of the beach.

A large hand grasped my leg and I kicked and twisted to free myself.

"Valencia, it's me. Josheb."

I opened my eyes to the dark-haired man. Ryker stood at his side, panting.

"Go!" Josheb ordered us both. I scurried to my feet, but my legs wobbled under me. We ran, bent low for cover behind the downed scavenger ship. Bodies lay in awkward poses along the water's edge. My stomach twisted and threatened to spill its meager contents, but I suppressed my fear and redirected my attention to the battle at hand.

Josheb squatted at my side. "Glad we made it."

I stole a quick glance his way. "How did you?"

Josheb nodded at Ryker to my other side. "Think he had somethin' to do with it."

My heart warmed at the thought of both of them making it through this.

The gray ship with the ENR emblem proudly displayed on the hull flew overhead in pursuit of the queen. Scavengers climbed to better vantage points on the side of the overturned ship and clung to anything they could to brace themselves.

A missile shot from the tube of the queen's ship and hit the beach near our cover. I focused on the tube and tried to melt it before another missile launched, but it dipped low and I couldn't get a lock on it without a visual. I ran for the other end of the ship with Ryker and Josheb close at my heels, ignoring the throbbing pain in my head.

"Don't go out there," Ryker yelled from behind.

Something exploded, and I caught a glimpse of one of the scavengers blown from the ship. I risked a quick glance and saw the center portion engulfed in flames. My legs burned and threatened to give way, but I continued my sprint. I slid around the corner and landed, knees in the sand.

Several assassins had descended on the beach and were approaching for ground combat.

With the ENR in pursuit of the queen's ship, the scavengers wouldn't stand a chance against the heavily armed assassins converging on them. Their makeshift ammo would never penetrate their armor. They needed the ENR to focus on the ground assault or none of them would survive.

Ryker pointed down the beach. Emery sat at Boaz's side. My heart grew warm at the sight of them. Until I realized one of the assassins caught sight of them, too. Penton rolled down the hillside and raced toward the beach, but he'd never make it.

"Go!" I urged Ryker. "I'll be fine. Save her."

Josheb stood over me, gun raised. "I'll provide cover."

Ryker took off, spinning sand up in his wake. Josheb and Ryker would have to save them. I needed to end this, or they would all die before this was over.

I crouched and crawled to the edge of the ship. Another missile launched from the queen's ship, and I spotted the exit tube. Before I could melt it, the assassins opened fire, sending me back for cover.

Josheb shot in front of me, returning fire. I made it to my knees again and found the tube. I narrowed my focus on the small exit hole. The surface bubbled and merged together, sealing the opening.

I held my breath and waited to see if my seal would hold or if another blast would be the final blow.

A red light flashed. I ducked and rolled.

Fire erupted from Josheb's chest and he flew backward, slamming against a dead body behind him. I turned to help, but something snagged my ankle.

An assassin.

I turned my energy on him and melted his helmet. He grabbed his head and thrashed until he fell silent.

Several other assassins dragged kicking and screaming scavengers. A blast from Mother's ship sent a missile through what remained of the scavenger ship.

I couldn't catch my breath. Did Mother know the other missile tube was compromised?

I focused on the left tube, but the ship pulled up as the ENR nearly rammed it.

The assassins threw scavengers into a pile, their sweaty bodies sliding down one another into the sand.

Shots rang out from my left. An assassin executed a dozen people. I closed my eyes and envisioned a ball of fire melting all the assassins at once.

"Get down!" Hoping the others heeded my warning, heat raced to my temples and I pulled my arms around my chest, concentrating on building the energy quick while focusing it into one blast.

My hot energy compressed into a tight ball until I couldn't contain it. Spurts of fire shot from their armor in an eruption, melting each of the assassins into a pile of bubbling bronze liquid over lumps of human bones.

I shifted my concentration to the other circle of people.

With little time, I focused on the closest solid metal I could find to pull energy from before the assassins could react.

Mother's ship banked left, and the tail of the ship spun around. I pulled energy quickly, but before I could finish, an explosion sent shrapnel flying all over the beach. People I had just saved from the assassins now howled and fell to the ground. I clenched my fists by my side. The screams of my fallen comrades ripped my heart to pieces.

Mother's ship sustained heavy damage from the missile tube, but at what cost?

I sat on the ground near a ring of assassins with guns ready to execute several allies. Digging deep inside, I utilized the power from the queen's ship metal and melted the other set of assassins.

Plumes of smoke rose from Mother's ship, but it still fired lasers at the ENR ship, which sustained its own damage.

Emery, Ryker, and Penton reached my side. Emery took each of my hands and closed her eyes. Ryker dropped to his knees by my side.

Penton squatted beside us. "The Triune will win the battle."

Ryker glared at Emery. "Don't go thinking about being a hero."

"I w-won't. Need t-to connect w-with V-Valencia. Focus on th-the engines, V-Valencia. Ryker, get th-the people on th-

the bridge. I'll stir up a s-storm. F-feel my energy and f-follow."

Another ship approached from the distance. Slag reinforcements. My heart fell at the sight.

Penton held a gun in his hand and shot at a new row of assassins approaching. "Hurry."

I cast out the feeling of doom. We had to take down Mother's ship or all was lost.

A soothing, almost sticky sense covered my skin. I flinched at the invasion of someone other than Ryker's energy entering me. Emery smiled.

I focused on the ship and altering the engines. A cool surge, followed by a sharp blast entered my consciousness.

Wind blew like a great storm. Sand lashed at my skin. My mind sizzled with the surge of power from Emery and Ryker.

I penetrated the main bay door and melted anything I could in short bursts of energy. Then I saw it, the reactor. If it blew, the ship would go down.

I looked to Ryker and he nodded. We merged our powers as we did when Ryker was nearly executed back in Oasis. I concentrated on the reactor. My skin burned. I knew if it weren't for Ryker keeping me cool and both of them keeping me energized, I'd be a pile of goo on the beach by now.

Finally, after several attempts, an explosion rocked Mother's ship. Releasing my hold, I fell back on my heels, and watched my mother's ship nose dive. Flames licked at the hull as it spiraled toward Earth.

I glanced back at the other arriving ship stalled in the distance. A small craft shot from the side of the queen's ship.

She'd escaped.

There was no time to focus. Mother's ship descended, aiming straight for us.

Penton lifted Emery and ran for cover.

Ryker clutched me to his side and sprinted for the hill. A loud crash shook the ground underfoot. Sand pummeled our backs.

We crawled over the edge of the scavenger ship, the only part that remained intact. Bits of debris flew past us and we huddled behind our makeshift shelter.

A series of rapid-fire bursts, then silence—except for the roar of a nearby engine.

When we believed it was safe, we emerged and surveyed the battle scene. The aftermath nearly knocked me down. My heart twisted with grief, and I clung to Ryker.

The small ship that had been deployed before the crash docked with the ship in the distance before it turned and sped away. The battle was over. We had won, but the war would continue.

Emery pointed and tried to run, but her knee locked tight from the sand and she fell. Penton smiled. "I'll get him."

Boaz struggled against his ropes near the hillside. Someone had pulled him to safety but hadn't untied him.

The ENR ship landed on the beach and medics dispersed. A tall, strong man descended to greet us. "You must be Princess Valencia." His words were refined with a hint of an accent. He offered a hand.

"Valencia, please."

He smiled and gestured us onto the ship. "Of course."

Ryker halted. "I should help—"

"We have healers. Many of our fighters are gifted. Although, we are all equal in the ENR. If you still wish to help,

I bid you do so onboard once we have cleared the beach. Several of the queen's ships are on their way to this sector, so we must depart immediately."

A woman with crazy brown hair, goggles, and oversized boots stood at the gangway. "Gordon, we need to be goin'. Haven't ye had ye bit of fun?"

Gordon waved the girl to action. "Assist the healers and get everyone on board."

"Keep ye knickers on. I'm a goin'." She mock-curtsied and clopped down the gangway.

"She's my second in command. A fierce fighter, but a bit wild at times."

"Thanks for the assistance." Ryker squeezed my hand and watched Penton lift Emery to his chest and march onboard. The boy seemed to have taken a liking to Emery. By the look on Ryker's face, he planned to have a long talk with him later.

"We received a message from Mags. She directed us here and told me to let you know she's not too old to sling a bomb and rope a hog. Not sure what that means."

I chuckled at her colorful euphemism.

"What was with the ship being destroyed on the beach before we arrived?" Ryker asked.

Gordon sighed. "That was Harrison's deal. Smart man; it did the trick to distract the queen for a bit."

"Harrison?" My breath hitched. "Is he old enough to be my father? Mualite? Fought in the Great War?"

Gordon cocked an eyebrow. "Yes."

Ryker squeezed me tight. "Your father is alive."

Before I had a chance to ask any more questions, he ushered me toward the ship. The wailing of the injured caught my attention, and I stopped in my tracks. "Wait,

Josheb. He was wounded." I pulled from Ryker's grasp and started to run down the beach.

Two guards stepped in front of me. "Please, Prin...I mean, Valencia. My men will bring all bodies aboard. You may look for him there."

Ryker wrapped his arms around me and walked up the gangway, pressing me to his side.

CHAPTER THIRTY-ONE

I'd escaped one ship only to board another at the end of my journey, but exhaustion won and I followed Gordon's second in command through a winding corridor. "Me name's Mart."

One of the guards escorting us smirked. "Ya mean Martistenia Moroana."

"I meant, Mart. That's me name. Shut it, Scab." Mart shoved her sawed-off, two-winding-barreled weapon into a slot on the wall.

Ryker paused in the doorway. "Got some major firepower."

Mart stopped abruptly and scanned us with a look of contempt. "Keep movin'. Gordon'll want a debriefin'. Lost some good soldiers rescuin' ya. Best be worth it."

Her words grated on my last remaining nerve. I shot a narrowed glare at her. "We have wounded, too. None of us asked for this."

Mart turned from me in her oversized black boots with metal buckles and stomped out the door on the other side of the room.

Ryker squeezed my hand, but his eyes remained on the

weapons until we'd cleared the room, following Mart. "We need rest, food, and water." He tucked me under his arm and held me up. My legs wobbled beneath me. Obviously, his healing had helped him recover.

I nudged my elbow into his ribs and lifted my head to speak softly in his ear. "We need to check on Josheb first. And I want to talk to Gordon about my father."

"No need. Healers are workin' on him." Mart about-faced and stared me down. "Yes, appears the little princess needs her beautify sleep. Follow me."

I opened my mouth to protest, but Ryker shook his head. "Not now. Save your energy."

The corridor went on forever. Well, my legs ached as if it did. Finally, we met Gordon in an anterior hall.

"Would you like to eat and shower, then rest?"

Boom.

The ship rocked to the left, and Ryker slid into my side. He snatched me before I fell. "You all right?"

Gordon and Mart remained upright, steady on their feet.

"Fine. What was that?"

Gordon lowered a bronze tube from above and pressed his mouth to it. "Crash dive, level off one-hundred meters." His face remained stoic. "No need to concern yourselves. The queen only has spotter ships dropping depth charges. We're just getting out of range. Those don't have sonar. We crippled her main ship. Please, allow me to show you to the mess hall, then you can shower and rest."

He tipped his head, offering his hand to me. "Ryker, Scab will show you to your quarters. Valencia, I'll take you to the room you'll share with Emery. We separate the men and the women's quarters on the ship. I'm sure you understand."

Ryker squeezed my hand tighter. Even through my delirium from lack of sleep and food, I knew we couldn't risk alienating these people at the moment. Something deep inside still didn't click, but it was probably from being on the run so much. "It's okay. I'll go check on Emery and meet you at the mess hall after I clean up. I won't be long, promise. Please, go check on Penton for me. I'd like to know more about my father, too."

He whispered in my ear, "I'll feel better when we're all together again. Scream if you need me."

"I promise." With a forced smile, I sauntered past Mart's glare and took Gordon's arm.

We reached a fork in the corridors. Scab took Ryker right, while Gordon guided me left.

Mart remained at my heels.

"Is it true that Harrison is alive? Where is he?" I couldn't hold my tongue any longer.

Gordon nodded to a soldier that passed. "I assume he escaped the ship since it was his plan. I've only met him once. The last several years, he's been imprisoned by the queen. Beyond that, don't know much. There are a few back home that knew him. They could tell you more."

I sighed with disappointment, but at least there was hope when we arrived in Europe that I could learn more. It still seemed so impossible. I'd seen him die. Maybe it wasn't really him.

I'd drive myself insane if I kept trying to figure it out now, so I shut it into one of the little compartments in my mind to think about after a good night's sleep.

Running my fingers through my knotted silver ends, I lowered my gaze to my disheveled vest, torn pants, and mucked-up boots.

Gordon cast a sideways glance my way. "No need to worry, we have new clothes waiting in your quarters."

"Thanks," I mumbled.

A tremor startled me, but I refused to react. No need to add fuel to Mart's snarky little scared princess remarks.

"Here, Emery will be here momentarily. She's being checked by our healers. Please, make yourself at home. When you are ready, a guard will escort you to the mess hall."

Without another word, Gordon disappeared with Mart by his side. I nodded to the nameless face guarding my door, then entered the small room with two beds. The quicker I cleaned up, the faster I'd be back with Ryker.

The metal walls sucked me back to a few days ago when I was destined to be a princess. Stripping my clothes off, I stepped into the small shower stall. Hot water streamed over my tight shoulders.

Water, real water, not just sulfuric-smelling steam, cascaded over my sore muscles.

Despite the weird vibe, rude second in command, and depth charges nearly sinking the ship, I tried to embrace my new residence. At least here, no one was trying to kill me.

My eyes grew heavy, so I turned off the water that had already begun to cool and wrapped a soft cloth around my body. The bed called for me, but I knew if I even sat, I wouldn't be able to rise for days.

While drying my hair with the towel, I discovered a dress hanging from a hook by the bed. "Dress? Really?" Lace collar and flowing skirt to add salt to the wound. "Ugh."

Pulling it over my head, I slid my feet into a pair of short boots and stumbled into the hall. The guard snapped to attention and directed me to board a lift. It soared up a few flights, leaving my empty stomach below.

The doors swished open and the guard lifted his hands. "Through there, ma'am."

"Thank you." I exited the lift and found Emery, Penton, Boaz and Ryker already seated at a long silver table. Ryker stood. His clean-shaven face and green shirt made his eyes shine bright.

Boaz stood up on a chair, and I hugged him. "Good see, Princess."

"Good to see you, too, my friend."

Emery bounced on her toes. "W-we made it."

Penton smiled, his shoulders back with pride. He'd done it. In his mind, he'd assisted the Triune.

At this point, I didn't know or care what I believed. The aroma of delicious food drew my attention.

Ryker directed me to a bench at his side, and two young women dished out and placed plates full of food in front of us. My mouth instantly watered at the smell of fresh baked bread and peppery meat.

We all sat and devoured our food with only the sound of water swishing through overhead pipes and distant creaking lulling us. As if the food weighted my eyelids, they began to sag. Ryker kissed my forehead, slipped his arms under my knees, and nestled me up against his chest.

"No, I can walk. Don't give Mart the Miserable any ammo." My words came out slurred.

"Shh, rest. We have time now. Plenty of time."

CHAPTER THIRTY-TWO

I stood by Josheb's bedside. He'd remained in a drug-induced coma as the healers worked on him.

For two days, we'd been evading Mother's scouts. Gordon had refused to return to land until he was sure we weren't being tracked.

Time stood still as I waited for more information on my father. The only thing that kept me sane was my friends.

After reporting for hours to the scientists and senior officers on the ship about Slag technology, and sleeping for fourteen hours straight, I longed to find Ryker. It had been days since we'd spent any time together. There was always some reason to keep us apart. Part of me felt empty without him.

Gordon had been kind to us, but it was obvious his second in command, Mart, wasn't so trusting. Still, I was grateful of no talk about a trade. It was obvious by how the battle went down they'd chosen my side. But it still was nerve-racking to be questioned so much.

Yet, in moments of quiet, I relaxed. The ship rocked in a steady, soothing beat under the ocean. It was different than any of my mother's ships. I was shocked they possessed the technology to create such a large ship that could operate on land, sea, and in the air.

The guard had become more lax about escorting me around the ship, and after following several wrong passageways, I now stood outside P25, the room I'd been informed was Ryker's new private quarters.

I took a deep breath. The stale odor of the ship entered my lungs.

I paused by his door. Even after all we'd been through, my heart still fluttered at the thought of seeing him.

"I've been looking for you."

Ryker stood directly behind me. Goosebumps erupted all over my skin. I swallowed hard and inhaled. A familiar earthy scent mixed with fresh soap invited me to lean back. I fought the urge.

He pushed a clear plate and the door slid open. One hand slipped into mine and he led me into his room before the door slid shut.

We were finally alone.

He winked. "Like my upgraded quarters? You can visit me now."

My pulse quickened. My breath hitched. He dropped my hand and walked over to the glass. "Never thought I'd be aboard an ENR ship, let alone one beneath the ocean." He shifted back and forth between feet and looked at the floor.

What was bothering him?

"Sit?" He directed me to a chair and sat across from me on the bed. "I don't know if you believe this, but I didn't know about your father, my uncle, Boaz, none of it. I'd never keep something like that from you." He took my hand in his. "I can't imagine how you must feel discovering your father is alive."

"I'm shocked, but also a little disappointed." I fought the grief that threatened. "Why did he let my mother take me? Where is he?"

Ryker ran his thumb along my palm and my emotions steadied. "I promise you, I'll help find out where he is and why he isn't here with you."

He cleared his throat and drew back away from me. "Know we've grown close, quickly. And there's a war going on and all, but, well…" He stood and paced the room, running his hand through his hair before he sat back down. "Valencia, you twist me up inside. I've never wanted someone so bad in my life. But if you don't feel the same, tell me." He choked on the last words and looked at the floor.

His gaze locked with mine and my insides turned to mush. I knew one thing with absolute certainty. He'd never lie or keep the truth from me. I trusted him and Emery completely. "I feel the same way."

His lips curved into a teeth-baring grin. He shot up and hauled me into him. Strong arms wrapped around me, pulling me against him as his lips claimed mine.

To be continued…

Check out book II, Of Blood and Betrayal, to continue your journey.

ABOUT THE AUTHOR

Come fly away with Raven More

Although, Raven has enjoyed a successful career as a hybrid author—USA Today bestseller in multiple genres—a great love of all things "not of this world" is Raven's true passion. The one mission of this new secret identity is to create an escape for all those who need one.

If you enjoy epic tales with profound characters and twisty plots then welcome to the imagination of Raven More.